The Vampire's
Mail Order Bride
Nocturne Falls, Book One

Kristen Painter

THE VAMPIRE'S MAIL ORDER BRIDE
Nocturne Falls, Book One

Copyright © 2015 Kristen Painter

This book is a work of fiction. The characters, events, and places portrayed in this book are products of the author's imagination and are either fictitious or are used fictitiously. Any similarity to real person, living or dead, is purely coincidental and not intended by the author.

ISBN: 978-1-941695-07-4

Published in the United States of America.

After seeing her maybe-mobster boss murder a guy, Delaney James assumes a new identity and pretends to be a mail order bride. She finds her groom-to-be living in a town that celebrates Halloween every day. Weird. But not as weird as what she doesn't know. Her groom-to-be is a 400-year-old vampire.

Hugh Ellingham has only agreed to the arranged set up to make his overbearing grandmother happy. In thirty days, whatever bridezilla shows up at his door will be escorted right back out. His past means love is no longer an option. Not if the woman's going to have a future. Except he never counted on Delaney and falling in love for real.

Too bad both of them are keeping some mighty big secrets…

Welcome to Nocturne Falls, the town where Halloween is celebrated 365 days a year. The tourists think it's all a show: the vampires, the werewolves, the witches, the occasional gargoyle flying through the sky. But the supernaturals populating the town know better.

Living in Nocturne Falls means being yourself. Fangs, fur, and all.

For Gladys Gonzales Atwell and Leslie Wolf Barnes
– you two are always there when I need you. Thank you.

Strawberry was a possibility. Maybe raspberry. Although pomegranate had potential. Or did it? Pomegranate might be a little tapped out. Best to stick to a classic. So raspberry truffle filling. With a dark chocolate shell, because dark chocolate was everything.

And what on top? What went with raspberry? Something borderline savory. Something a little unexpected. Delaney James stopped dead on the sidewalk. A thyme sugar sprinkle? That could work.

Her phone chimed with an incoming text, but she ignored it to nod her head in happiness over what might be her best new truffle idea yet. She was kind of a whiz with candy, cakes and confections, but chocolate was a special passion. Someday, she'd be the Mrs. Fields of confections. She could see the boxes now. Mrs. James, best sweets in the world.

Well, it wouldn't say *Mrs.* James, would it? Because she wasn't married, which was fine with her. And if she ever did find a superhero worthy of making her a Mrs., he'd have to be something special.

The name on her shop certainly wasn't going to be Mrs. Betts, because Russell was a jerk. Definitely not superhero material. Hell, he wasn't even qualified to be a sidekick. She should have known. A man without a sweet tooth was not to be trusted. She snorted softly. He'd be so sorry he'd cheated on her when she ruled the confectionary world.

Right now, however, she was a server and part-time pastry chef at Rastinelli's Trattoria. Actually, she'd filled in for the pastry chef only once, but it was a start.

Rastinelli's was also known as Brooklyn's most potentially mobbed-up Italian eatery. She didn't think it was really mobbed up. Well, *maybe* it might be a tiny bit. The crucifix next to the pictures of Al Pacino and Marlon Brando was a little on the nose.

Either way, the rumor brought people in by the truckloads and the tips were good, so whenever a customer asked about the possible mob connection, she just shook her head no while giving them a sly wink.

The thought of tips brought her to a stop again. Crap. She's left her apron on the counter, and not only did it need to be washed, but her tip money was in it. She had no choice but to go back. It would add an extra fifteen minutes to her walk home, and Captain Underpants, her enormous black and white Maine Coon, would yowl his displeasure when Delaney got home. Captain Underpants did not like to wait for his dinner. She had originally named the cat Princess Buttercream, but as it turned out, Princess Buttercream was a boy. Delaney was a whiz with candy, lousy at guessing cat gender.

She headed back to the restaurant, wishing there were more hours in the day. It had been dark for two hours already, but her last deuce had lingered like they thought there was a prize for being the final ones out of the joint.

Even Mr. Rastinelli had given them the stink eye. He always treated his customers like gold, but on Thursdays he hosted a private, after-hours poker game in the restaurant's private dining room. Another fifteen minutes and the Sandersons would have had to buy into the game or leave their tiramisu behind. (The tiramisu was good, but nothing like the tiramisu she made. It's how she'd won Russell over, despite his lack of a sweet tooth. In retrospect, it had been a complete waste of perfectly good mascarpone.)

The restaurant was just ahead. Knowing that Mr. Rastinelli would be occupied with his poker game, she went around to the alley and crossed her fingers that the back door would still be open. It was. *Sweet.*

She slipped in as quietly as she could. Her apron was right where she'd left it—on the counter next to the walk-in. She'd set it there when she was talking to Jose, one of the line cooks. She'd gotten wrapped up in a conversation about Mexican versus Madagascar vanilla while waiting for her table to check out.

Raised voices carried in from the private dining room, which had a side entrance to the kitchen. Mr. Rastinelli and his friends, no doubt. But the voices didn't sound friendly. She snuck closer to the kitchen door to listen. It was wrong to be nosy, but everyone had faults.

There was shouting this time. Mr. Rastinelli was accusing someone of cheating. Her brows shot up. That wasn't good. She nudged the swinging door open a crack, but that didn't help. She grabbed her phone, brought up the camera and stuck the phone far enough through the crack so the lens caught it all.

She stared at the screen.

Holy fudgeballs. Anthony Rastinelli was holding a gun. *That* looked mobby.

She tried to breathe. This was Brooklyn. Lots of people had guns, right? Sure, but it was still scary. She should go. But her feet wouldn't move.

There were only two other poker players. A guy

she didn't recognize and Little Tony, Mr. Rastinelli's son. The table in the middle held plenty of money—more than she'd ever seen in one place—but no cards or poker chips. Nothing to indicate there had actually been a game.

Some twisted sixth sense made her tap the record button.

The other man stood, hands out, face worried but earnest. "Anthony, this is ridiculous. I'm not holding anything back." He gestured toward the money. "I swear on my mother's grave, that's everything I collected this week."

Mr. Rastinelli pointed at the stacks of cash with his gun. "It's two G's short."

Little Tony sniffed and jerked his shoulders. "Maybe more."

Little Tony was one of her least favorite people due to his general smarminess and his excessive use of hair gel and cologne.

The other guy's face collapsed a little, and he wrung his hands. "I would never skim, boss. I would never do anything to go against you."

Boss? Skim? Sweet crispy crackers, that sounded *very* mobby.

Mr. Rastinelli's expression remained steely. "Benny, Benny. If you would never go against me, why did Lefty and Little Tony tell me they saw you talking to Dominic Ardito?"

Benny took a step back, his eyes wild and

searching, but Mr. Rastinelli was blocking the only exit, unless Benny went for the kitchen door. "I never talked to the man."

Anger bent Mr. Rastinelli's mouth. "You telling me my *son* lied to me?"

Little Tony made a fish face. "You know I would never lie to you, Pop."

Mr. Rastinelli glared at him. "Shut up when I'm doing business already." Then he turned to Benny. "Well?"

"No…I mean…" Panic curdled the other man's voice. He shot a look at Little Tony, but that putz sure wasn't going to help him. Benny tried Mr. Rastinelli again. "I'll make it up to you. The money plus whatever else you want me to do."

She bit her lip. She needed to leave. Whatever was going on, it was *not* her business.

Mr. Rastinelli shook his head slowly. "You stole my money. You lied to me."

Little Tony scratched his neck. "Don't forget he besmirched my name, Pop."

Huh, how about that? Little Tony not only knew a big word, but had used it correctly.

Mr. Rastinelli cut his eyes at Little Tony. "You talk too much." He lifted his gun in Benny's direction. "I need people I can trust in my organization. You're not one of those, Benny. Not anymore."

He pulled the trigger.

The pop of the gun covered her gasp as she jerked back, almost dropping her phone. Holy mackerel, Mr. Rastinelli had just shot Benny! And she'd recorded it.

Swallowing hard, she backed up. Benny was moaning. So, not dead. Yet. But *she* might be if she didn't get out of here before Mr. Rastinelli or Little Tony realized she'd seen the whole thing.

She grabbed her apron, reached for the back door and opened it as quietly and as carefully as she could. She had one foot outside when her cell phone chimed *loudly* with an incoming notification.

If she lived through this, she was deleting Facebook.

"Who's there?" Anthony Rastinelli shouted.

She jerked the door wide and took off. She was a baker, not a runner, but adrenaline fueled her feet. She raced down the dark alley and took the first right she came to, then another alley, then another turn. She zigged and zagged, doing her best to lose the tail she undoubtedly had.

There were more bars and restaurants ahead, but Mr. Rastinelli was well known in the community, and if he was really mobbed up, which seemed a sure thing considering, what would stop those owners from turning her over to him? He'd probably reward them! She avoided the bars and ducked down a small side street.

It was pretty dark, but one of the businesses

looked like it might still be open. The blinds on the front window were closed, but bright light shone through the slats. The word *Eternamate* was painted in neat script on the door. Whatever that meant. She grabbed the handle and pulled, praying someone was working late. Thankfully, it opened.

She ducked inside. It looked like a pretty typical office space, one front desk with several doors leading off to other offices. A little messy maybe, but she wasn't about to judge the stacks of boxes and towers of paperwork on every cabinet. Especially when she was being chased by a murderer and his son. Odd there wasn't a computer in sight. Whatever. She had bigger fish not to sleep with.

She leaned against the wall and took a few deep breaths, her heart slowing but nowhere near normal. She stuck her phone in her jacket pocket.

"I'll be right there," a female voice called out with a slight French accent.

Delaney opened her mouth, but nothing came out. Too much shock still coursed through her system. She needed to call the police. Then what? She became a witness for the prosecution? If it was anything like TV, they'd change her name, give her a new identify and hide her away in some gross motel until the trial. Then she'd have to sit in front of Anthony Rastinelli and tell the judge and jury what she'd seen while he was right there in the same courtroom.

She wasn't a coward, but…those witnesses in the movies seemed to end up dead about 99% of the time.

Germans eat twice as much chocolate as Americans. She rolled her eyes. *Shut up, brain. Now is not the time for useless facts about chocolate.* Everyone had their nervous tics, right?

An older, sophisticated woman with an armful of files walked out from one of the back rooms, exuding so much class that Delaney forgot everything that had just happened for a split second.

The woman smiled. "My apologies for the wait. We're a little understaffed at the moment."

Tall, with dark hair pulled into a twist, pin-straight bangs and narrow black-rimmed glasses, the woman wore a slim suit in midnight blue and a single strand of gunmetal pearls at her throat. A slick of burgundy lipstick, winged eyeliner and perfect brows completed the look. Those brows lifted slightly as she took Delaney in. "Ah. You're not here about—never mind, you're here for the secretarial position, aren't you? Very good. I'm Adelaide Poirot, and you are?"

Not French, that was for dang sure. Delaney had never felt more like a slob in her entire life. Fortunately, the office phone rang before she had time to respond.

Adelaide rolled her eyes good-naturedly, but

her smile thinned with frustration. "I'm afraid I must take that." She set the files on the front desk. "I'll be with you as soon as I can."

Delaney nodded.

Adelaide disappeared back into whatever dimension of perfection she'd come out of.

Delaney grabbed a brochure from the stack on the filing cabinet next to her.

Eternamate. Specializing in unique and exceptional arrangements.

Arrangements? There wasn't a flower in the joint. She opened the brochure.

While Eternamate caters to the particular gentleman, we pride ourselves on providing only the most capable and understanding partners in our arranged matches.

Oh. *Those* kinds of arrangements.

*Many of our couples even fall in love…*blah, blah, blah.

Delaney put the brochure back. She needed to call the cops, not find a man. Benny might be dead. She had to tell the police what she'd seen. It was the right thing to do.

Even if she ended up dead too.

Her stomach knotted. She pulled her phone out and stared at the dark screen. How was she going to testify when she couldn't even find the courage to dial?

Okay, calm down. Anthony Rastinelli didn't even know she'd been there. How could he? She'd call in the shooting anonymously, then send the video in from some random library computer that couldn't be traced back to her, and that would be that. She tapped the screen to bring it to life.

Two text messages waiting. She brought them up and almost peed. The first one, the one she'd ignored on the walk home, was from Anthony Rastinelli. But wait…that was well before the shooting. The second one was from her phone company, no doubt telling her the bill was due.

She opened the first message.

D, you left your apron.

Her throat squeezed shut, making it impossible to breathe. When he saw that her apron was gone after he'd texted her about it, how would he *not* assume she was the one who'd been there? He'd know without a doubt she'd been present for the shooting.

Twenty-seven was too damn young to die. She closed her eyes and tipped her head against the wall. *Think.* There had to be a way out of this.

Adelaide's phone conversation carried from the back office. "I have the files together and the women have their matches, but I haven't sent any of them the travel information yet."

Travel information? Delaney opened her eyes and straightened. Her gaze went right to the files. Were those the files the woman was talking about? She glanced toward the back. She could hear

Adelaide, but not see her, which meant Adelaide couldn't see Delaney either.

Delaney stuck her phone back into her pocket, snatched the first file off the top of the stack and flipped it open. No picture, just a name. Beatrice Mackenzie, age thirty-three, dog lover, so on and so forth. Delaney skimmed Beatrice's info until she came to a box near the bottom labeled Matched. In that box was scribbled a man's name and address. The guy Beatrice had been fixed up with was in Scotland, and she was supposed to meet him in two weeks. Good for her, not so much for Delaney.

She grabbed the next file. No picture in this one either. Maybe they didn't do pictures? At any rate, this woman, Annabelle Givens, age twenty-eight, had been matched with a guy in Nocturne Falls, Georgia.

Georgia was about thirteen hours away. Maybe more like fourteen with stops for gas and the added factor of traveling with Captain. A long drive however it worked out, but very doable. She could be there by tomorrow afternoon.

A tingle of something shot through Delaney's spine. Fear? Hope? Stupidity? Probably all three. There was no time to think about this. Anthony Rastinelli and his greasy son could be headed to her apartment at this very moment. Her breath stuck in her throat. Captain was there! If they hurt him, she would make sure they went to prison.

Then she would send them poisoned cakes.

She paused. Except they'd be going to her old address. She'd moved a month ago and had yet to give Rastinelli her new info. There was hope yet.

She looked at the info in the file again. Annabelle wasn't expected for another week. A phone call from Adelaide's new *assistant* and Annabelle would have to understand this match just wasn't going to happen.

Delaney would make that call on the way. Right now, she had to get Captain Underpants and herself packed for a trip.

She jammed the file under her arm and raced toward home.

"How are you, Grandmamma?" Hugh kissed his grandmother's barely wrinkled cheek, catching the fragrance of violet water even though it competed with the arrangement of fresh flowers that adorned the top of the piano. He braced himself for the worst. She wore violets only when she was in an obstinate mood.

Come to think of it, Elenora Ellingham wore violets often.

"Not well." She held a lacy handkerchief to her nose and looked toward the marble fireplace. She might have been turned in her sixties but she'd been a handsome woman even then. Becoming a vampire had only made her more beautiful.

He stifled a snort as he settled into the velvet Louis chair across from her. "I'm sorry to hear that. You're not thinking about facing the dawn, are you?"

She dropped her hand to her lap and glowered at him. "I like you least of my grandsons."

He nodded dutifully, suppressing the grin that would only get him into more trouble. "I know."

She shook her head at him. "You hardly visit me anymore."

"We went out to lunch two days ago, and three days before that we were all together for Sunday supper."

She took a deep breath and stared toward the window. The crescent moon was just visible in the night sky. "I've decided enough is enough."

"What is?" Oh, this had the makings of something epic. He waited to see what he'd done now.

"Of you being alone. Of you mourning Juliette and breaking hearts." She raised her brows. "It's been over three hundred years. Plenty of time for you to move on and give me some grandbabies."

His jaw fell open, but he was powerless to close it.

"Shut your mouth, Hugh. I can see your fangs." She frowned at him. "It's not like it's impossible for vampires to procreate. As long as both parties have been turned, they have as much chance of producing a child as a mortal couple. You know the rest, I assume, or would you like me to have that talk with you as well?"

"Have you gone mad, woman? No, I don't need

to hear the birds and the bees from you." He pressed his fingers to his brow in an attempt to stave off the headache that would be hitting him at any moment due to the influx of questions barraging his brain. He wasn't sure where to start, so he chose the topic of least resistance. "Why am I suddenly the one responsible for carrying on the Ellingham line?"

"Well, your brothers aren't going to do it, are they?"

"Sebastian...no, never mind." His eldest brother had also been married when they'd been turned, but unlike Juliette, Sebastian's wife had survived the transition. Their marriage had not. She'd decided she enjoyed the vampire life so much she'd rather try it unencumbered by a husband. The whole ordeal had soured Sebastian on women and wedded bliss.

Hugh understood. To an extent. Sebastian had taken it hard, where as if Juliette had simply left Hugh as opposed to dying, he could very well imagine he would have been remarried by now. "Sebastian may never get over Evangeline."

"I've come to accept that." She nodded. "Sebastian is broken. I don't believe there's a woman alive who could mend that man's heart."

"There's still Julian—"

"Oh, please." She waved her handkerchief at him. "Julian is a complete and utter charmer, but he's also a man whore. He's made a mockery of monogamy. It will take a woman of a very particular kind to set him on a loyal path, if such a creature exists, and I don't have the time or patience to wait."

He squinted at her. "You don't have the time? Grandmamma, we've been vampires for almost three hundred and fifty years, and there's no reason to think we won't be vampires for another three hundred and fifty. Time is not something we lack."

"You're an insolent child." She huffed. "It doesn't matter how long we've been alive or will be alive, I want grandbabies. I want to see my boys settled down and happy. Or at least one of them. You."

"I am happy." He wasn't jumping up and down with joy, but he was fine.

She gave him the stare that destroyed lesser men. "You rattle around all alone in that house of yours, working on your formulas, wallowing in your grief—"

"I do *not* wallow and I am *not* alone. I have Stanhill." His man-in-service was a faithful companion, his rook in vampire terms—a half-turned human who served a vampire's needs in exchange for immortality—but their association was a purposeful one and didn't disrupt Hugh's routine. He liked his life the way it was. All that uninterrupted time to spend in his lab.

17

And maybe a little wallowing. But it grew less with each passing year. At least, he liked to tell himself that.

Her brows shot up. "Stanhill is your rook, not a *wife*."

"No, he's not. Thankfully." Because that was something Hugh was never going to have again. He stood and tried to change the subject. "How about lunch tomorrow? We could go to—"

"Sit *down*."

Blasted woman. He sat. "No lunch tomorrow?"

"I've taken the liberty"—that didn't bode well—"of arranging for a suitable young woman to come visit you."

A frisson of anger worked up his spine. He loved his grandmother with all his heart, such as it was. She'd saved him and his brothers from certain death by turning them into vampires, so on some level he owed her his life. But this was a step too far. "What the hell does that mean?"

"Hugh! Language." She clucked her tongue at him. "Just that next week, there will be a woman arriving at your home, and you're to entertain her as a possible mate."

"Are you bloody kidding me? No. I won't. This is the twenty-first century. There is no duchy to protect, no titles to pass on, no need to produce an heir. You realize you are the dowager duchess in name *only*." Although in public, he and his brothers often called her Didi as a bit of a tease for that very reason. That, and she wasn't keen on them calling her Grandmamma in public.

"Just because we lost our land and titles doesn't mean we have to behave as though we've lost our manners and sense of civility."

This was an old argument and not one he wanted to unpack yet again. He let a moment of silence pass to clear the air. "People don't have arranged marriages anymore."

"Some do. The werewolves do."

"Only for their alphas and only to secure pack treaties. And I am *not* a werewolf." He stared right back at her. "I am never marrying again. I don't know why you can't understand that." Any woman who was going to be with him would have to become a vampire, and he was never going to risk the life of another woman that way again.

"If the transformation hadn't killed Juliette, the plague would have." His grandmother sighed. "Stop punishing yourself for her death."

He looked away, unable to make eye contact with her in that moment.

She continued, "Her death broke all our hearts, but that woman loved you and she loved life. She would not want you living this way."

The muscles in his jaw felt like they might pop if they tightened further.

"You will at least give this woman a chance."

He turned to look at her. "Or what?"

She returned his gaze, letting the moment lengthen almost to the point of discomfort. "Or I will revoke your amulet."

His hand went to the pendant and chain that hung from his neck. "You wouldn't."

She broke eye contact to stare at her handkerchief. "I would. I am very serious about this, Hugh."

"Apparently." The amulets were sacred. Necessary. They all wore them. The stone at the center held an ancient magic that protected vampires from the sun. Without it, he would never see daylight again. "Does Alice know about this?"

"I do." Alice Bishop walked into the room. The slight woman had aged a little more than his grandmother, but nothing that belied her almost three hundred years upon the earth. At best she looked to be in her late fifties. But then, keeping the years at bay was nothing for a witch powerful enough to create an amulet capable of shielding a vampire from the sun. She was also powerful enough that Didi had had no need to turn the woman into a rook to save her life.

Alice stopped at the back of his grandmother's chair. "Your grandmother only wants what's best for you, Hugh."

He had a thousand arguments to that, but held his tongue until he could find a calmer answer. "I appreciate that, but *I* know what's best for me."

Elenora sighed deeply. "I'm only asking that you give this a chance."

"Demanding would be a better description." The only chance he wanted was to leave. "How long?"

"One month."

He closed his eyes. One month was a torturous amount of time to spend with a marriage-minded woman in his home, but there were ways around that. He could lock himself in his laboratory, for example. He opened his eyes and nodded. "One month. And then this...game of yours is over."

She sighed in frustration. "As Alice said, I only have your best interests and your happiness at heart, my darling."

"I am happy."

"Yes, you positively glow with *joie de vivre*. Is that why you and Piper called it quits? Because you were happy?"

Alice smirked as she went to sit on the other side of the room.

Hugh sighed. "You know why we broke up."

"I do. For the same reason you broke up with Suzanna, Heather and Kim. They weren't the one or some such nonsense."

He lowered his lids in boredom. This was another old conversation he was tired of having. "Putting aside the fact that Juliette died during her transition, do you know why I haven't found another woman to spend my life with yet?"

His grandmother leaned in. "No, but I'd like to hear this."

"Because I have yet to meet a woman who's made me think about marriage or children the way Juliette did, one who's had that kind of chemistry with me. Do you think I should settle for less than what I had with Juliette?" And wasn't that what love was about? Feeling something so deeply you were willing to risk everything for it?

A little half smile lifted her mouth. "If you expect the same feelings from a different woman, no one's ever going to be the one, Hugh. You've got to give someone a chance."

"I give them plenty of chances."

"Yes, you're good at the relationship part. You can hang on to a woman for…how long did you and Veronica last?"

"Ten months."

Her eyes widened in surprise. "Impressive. More on her behalf than yours, but still you can hang on to them, can't you? You just can't close."

"Now you're deliberately trying to rile me up."

"I've hit a nerve because I'm right, aren't I?" She waggled a finger at him. "You can't commit."

"Won't and can't are two different things." He sighed. "And I'm upfront with all of them. I tell them I am never getting married again. And I won't, because none of them has been the right one." And none of them ever would be.

She nodded, clearly enjoying herself. "Well, then this woman I've arranged for should be perfect. She's been handpicked to meet every specification you could have."

"How would you know what those specifications are?"

She smirked. "I've known you your entire life. I changed your diapers more than three and a half centuries ago."

"No, you didn't. The nursemaid did that."

"Pfft. The point is, I know you, and I knew Juliette, and I know what you like in a woman."

She probably did. He frowned. "Does this woman know I'm a vampire?"

"Yes."

"That's a rather sensitive piece of information to share."

"Pish posh. The agency I used specializes in finding matches for all kinds of supernaturals. It's all on the up and up. Very confidential. They don't even use computers or share pictures of the prospective mates."

He'd had no idea such a place even existed. He crossed his arms. "Is she one of those romance-novel-reading, tween-movie-watching vampire lovers? Because if I have to share my home with one of those sorts for any length of—"

"No, she's not. She's a lovely young woman from upstate New York, but you should be very thankful for those romance-novel-reading, tween-movie-watching women. They've had a big hand in making our town a success."

"And Julian's love life, once he learned to spray himself with glitter."

She pinched her lips together. "That aside, their money is just as green as yours, so have some respect."

"I do respect them. And their business." He sighed. "Is *she* a vampire?"

"No, but she's willing to convert."

"You know how I feel about that." And he wondered whether this woman was really seeking a husband or the chance at immortality. Wouldn't be the first time he'd encountered such a person. Live as long as he had and nothing would surprise you. He decided right then that this woman wasn't going to get the big vampire show out of him. He was going to play it straight-up mortal. See how *that* appealed to her.

"I do, but let's cross that bridge when we come to it."

"So in a month, when she's not the right one either, what then? Will you leave me alone and let me live my life with no more threats to take away my amulet?"

She exhaled a long, exasperated sigh. "I suppose I'll have no choice."

"Good." He stood up, still angry, but at least this insanity had an expiration date. "Thirty days cannot pass soon enough."

Delaney woke with a start, the rumble from an eighteen-wheeler fading as the enormous vehicle passed her car on its way out of the rest stop. Captain Underpants was wound into a snug little ball on her stomach. Delaney yawned and pulled the lever to bring the seat back to an upright position, causing Captain to slide to her lap.

Sleep had started to get the better of her as she'd crossed into Georgia, and though she had only a little farther to go, she'd pulled over for a quick nap. "Move, Cappy. Mama's got to get us back on the road." She hefted the cat onto the passenger's seat.

She checked her phone, taking it off silent. She'd been asleep a little over an hour. During that hour, she'd gotten three messages.

All from Anthony Rastinelli.

D, call in when u can. I changed the schedule. Yeah, she bet he'd changed it.

D, need 2 hear from u asap. Of course he did. He wanted to know what she'd seen.

D, how'd you like 2 b new manager? Let's talk promotion!

"Hah! He really thinks that's going to work to keep me quiet? Like I don't know the only people who get promoted in that place are family." She looked at Captain Underpants, who was currently engaged in cat yoga on the seat beside her, licking his back leg. "You'd think a mobster could come up with something better than that."

She fired up the navigation on her phone, made sure her destination was still plugged in, then hit Start. Three hours and they'd be there.

She stared into the trees lining the berm on the rest stop's edge. The idea of pretending to be someone else and passing as some guy's perfect, arranged match was insane, but her desire not to end up as another victim of Anthony Rastinelli's was stronger.

On her drive out of New York last night, she'd stopped for gas and found what might have been the last working payphone in the tri-state area. She'd used it (and all of her spare change) to call the cops and report what she'd seen. She'd sent them the video she'd taken too, right after she'd emailed a copy to herself for safe keeping. But the cops' response had been a lot less interested than she'd expected.

Maybe that would change when they found Benny's body.

A cold realization swept her. What if they didn't find Benny's corpse? Wasn't the Mafia good at hiding bodies? What if they dumped him in the East River? Or maybe Rastinelli had a cop on the take? It might never be safe for her to go home.

She bit her lip and glanced in the rearview mirror to see the stuff she'd brought with her. Besides supplies for Captain (including the litter box on the floor in the backseat), she'd brought her laptop, a suitcase full of clothes and a weekend bag filled with her most prized candy-making supplies, her journal of ideas and her copy of *The Sweet Life*, the candy-making cookbook that she'd inherited from her grandmother. That book had changed her life.

If only her grandmother were still around. She'd have known what to do about this whole murder thing. Just like she'd known what to do when Delaney had essentially become parentless at fifteen.

With a bittersweet sigh, Delaney looked at her phone. One more thing to do before she got back on the road. She flipped open the file on Annabelle Givens, found her phone number and dialed.

Annabelle answered on the second ring. "Hello?" She sounded classy. Not at all like Delaney.

Delaney crossed her fingers and hoped for the best. "Annabelle Givens?"

"Speaking."

"This is Adelaide Poirot's assistant." Delaney poured on the professionalism, trying to channel her inner Adelaide minus the French accent. "I'm calling about the recent match Eternamate set up for you. Unfortunately, your match has decided he's not quite ready to commit so we're canceling that arrangement. I'm terribly sorry." She was also a horrible liar, but it was good practice.

"Oh." Annabelle sounded miserable. "He sounded so nice."

"I promise we'll be calling within the month with an even better match." Delaney's voice had reached a level of chipperness on par with a game show host.

"You will?"

"Absolutely."

"Okay. Thank you for letting me know."

"You're welcome. Have a great day." Delaney hung up and deflated. Being "on" for her job as a server was one thing. Pretending to be someone else was exhausting.

The next few weeks might kill her. If Rastinelli didn't do it first.

She cranked on the radio, pulled out of the rest stop and put her mind back on her driving. Captain

Underpants shifted to take advantage of a two-inch sliver of sun and fell asleep.

Three hours later, Delaney took the exit for Nocturne Falls. Nerves from being this close to her destination raised her heart rate and her temperature. She cracked the window to let in some fresh air as she passed a large pumpkin-shaped sign that read, *Welcome to Nocturne Falls – where every day is Halloween*.

Really?

The speed limit dropped to thirty-five, which was just as well because she couldn't help but slow down when she hit the main drag.

She'd never seen a town like this in her life.

The general color scheme of everything—signs, buildings, benches and a tourist trolley with the word *Summer Spooktacular* emblazoned on the side—seemed to be black and orange, with purple and green coming in a strong second. Hot pink and midnight blue weren't far behind in third.

Metal brackets in the shapes of cobwebs angled off the street lamps. Some of the buildings were deliberately slanted to look rickety. A large fountain with a man-sized gargoyle front and center decorated the beautifully landscaped park that made up the large main square. Through the trees, the gargoyle actually seemed to be moving. Animatronics maybe?

She shook her head in disbelief. This place was kitschy and crazy but in a very cool way.

The voice on her navigation app urged her to make the next left, but she kept driving just to check the place out. The businesses had names like Misty's Boo-tique, The Hair Scare (which didn't exactly instill confidence in the final product), The Ice Scream Shop and Hats In The Belfry. There was a bar called DOA, which apparently stood for Drinks On Arrival, a beer and hot dog joint named Franks-n-Steins and a diner dubbed Mummy's whose slogan was "Our food is to die for!"

"Are you kidding me?" But tourists mobbed the streets. It was May, months away from Halloween, but even so a few of the adults and almost all of the little kids wore costumes. There was something cheesy but charming about it. "Cappy, this place is like Willy Wonka does Halloween."

Captain sighed in perpetual feline boredom and shifted to cover his face with his paw.

"Thanks for chiming in." She made a U-turn at the next light just to shut her navigation up. She followed the prompts, winding through the back roads (who knew Georgia had hills? Mountains? Whatever.) until she came to a community called Ravenswood.

She turned into the development as another of the *Summer Spooktacular* trolleys was pulling out. Apparently, this was part of a tour.

After the town, nothing should surprise her, but the neighborhood looked like it had been designed by a Hollywood set maker. Most of the houses, all Gothic or Victorian, resembled the precursors to some really good haunted mansions.

The homes were intricate, immaculate and beautiful. Sculpted topiaries ala Edward Scissorhands dotted the manicured yards.

"This is like Stepford meets the Addams family. Who built this place? Tim Burton?" Cappy had no response. She followed Poe Avenue to Hitchcock Lane and made the turn.

A stand of tightly spiraled evergreens blocked her view for a second as she pulled into the long drive of 19 Hitchcock Lane. Then she saw the house. Estate. Mansion. Whatever. It was too big and too grand and too ivy-covered to be just a *house*. Everything about it, from the toffee-brown brick, vanilla-white columns and trimmings to the gorgeous arched windows and slate roof, was fairy tale perfection.

"Wow," she whispered.

Captain Underpants snored.

His lack of enthusiasm didn't ruin the moment. Then she realized that she hadn't showered in almost twenty-four hours, meaning she still smelled like garlic (one of the unfortunate side effects of working at Rastinelli's), and that the man who owned a house like this might not even let her bring her Captain inside. Well, it wasn't like she was actually here to marry him, was it? So who cared if he thought she was gross? But if he was some weird anti-cat guy, she'd make a big fuss and tell him the agency had promised pets were okay.

Although she would like to stay long enough for things in Brooklyn to cool off. If cooling off was actually a possibility.

She parked beneath one of the massive shade trees that bordered the property, then flipped down the mirror on the visor and took a look. "Yikes."

She finger-combed the waves around her face into submission, pinched her cheeks for color, wiped off some of yesterday's mascara that had melted under her eyes and sighed. It was what it was.

She looked at her still sleeping companion, who was clearly on the verge of caring. "If he won't let you in, we're bugging out. Promise." She kissed Captain on his silky head. "Be right back." No point in waking him if they weren't staying.

She got out of the car and trudged up to the house, straightening as she reminded herself she was Annabelle Givens, resident of upstate New York, not Delaney James, Brooklyn resident on the run from the mob.

As she walked up the steps to the impressive wraparound porch, the door opened and a man stepped out. "Hallo, miss. Can I help you?"

Okay, so Annabelle's perfect match was a little older than Delaney had imagined. He was silver fox handsome in the way of Mark Harmon or Pierce Brosnan, though, so it wasn't going to be a hardship to spend some time with him. Especially not with that swoony British accent.

"Hi." She waved nervously. "I'm, um, Annabelle Givens. Eternamate sent me." Out loud the words sounded so blatantly false she expected him to call her a liar-pants and shoo her from the property.

"Ah, yes, Miss Givens. We weren't expecting you until next week."

Okay, no liar-pants. "Next week? I'm so sorry, I'm horrible with dates. I must have misread the paperwork." She rummaged in her bag like she was looking for it, which she wasn't, hoping he'd stop her.

He did. "It's not a problem, miss. We are delighted to have you."

She raised her brows. "We?" What exactly had she gotten herself into?

"Master Ellingham and I, that is."

"You're not Master, I mean, Mr. Ellingham?"

He laughed. "No, miss. I'm Bartholomew Stanhill. I'm Master Ellingham's secretary." He held out his hand. "Call me Stanhill. Everyone does."

"Nice to meet you." She shook his hand, a mix of relief and disappointment coursing through her. Stanhill wasn't her match after all, which made sense considering the age difference, but he seemed like such a nice guy. Maybe his employer would be too. "Is Master Ellingham here?"

Stanhill smiled. "Yes, but he's a rather late sleeper, which is why I came out to meet you and help you with your bags."

A late sleeper? Must be nice to be that independently wealthy. She felt a pang of remorse at taking this guy away from the real Annabelle. "About the bags…I brought my cat with me. I hope that's not going to be an issue."

Stanhill merely nodded. "Not at all, miss. You can't be expected to leave your pet for the entire month you're here, can you? And after all, if things work out, your cat will be living here too. Might as well see how everyone gets on, eh?"

"Absolutely." They expected her to be here only a month? Maybe she wouldn't have to try quite so hard then.

He raised his brows. "Shall I get your bags, then, and leave you to the wee beastie?"

"He's not so wee, but yes, that sounds good."

"What's the large beastie's name?"

"Captain Un—I mean, just Captain." Annabelle Givens didn't seem like the sort of woman who'd name her pet after a series of children's books that generally encouraged bucking authority. Or celebrated underpants. But Cappy's black and white markings clearly made him look like he was wearing a pair of tighty whities, and so, after the Princess Buttercream fiasco, the name had stuck.

Stanhill peered into her car. "Well, I see what you mean about him not being wee. Gorgeous creature, though."

"Thanks." She opened the passenger door and scooped Cappy into her arms, nearly throwing her back out with the effort. "He's a Maine Coon. They can get to be twenty-five pounds."

Stanhill studied Captain. "And this one?"

Delaney's mouth twitched. "Twenty-six. And a half." She sighed. "He's a little spoiled, but we're working on it."

Stanhill chuckled. "Likes his kitchen scraps and such, does he?"

"Too much. Keep the bacon locked up." She nudged the door closed with her hip. "I'll come back for the litter box."

Stanhill grabbed her suitcase, weekender and laptop bag. "Very good. Follow me and I'll show you up to your room."

The house was as gorgeous inside as it was out, but Delaney tried to keep her oohing and aahing to a minimum so she wouldn't seem like she'd never been inside a nice house before. "Mr. Ellingham has a lovely place."

"Feel free to make yourself at home. The only room that's off limits is the basement." Stanhill nodded as he led the way up a flight of stairs and down a long, gracious hall. "And I'm sure he'd want you to call him Hugh, miss."

Knowing the basement was off limits made her want to immediately run down there and check it out, but that would have to be without Captain in her arms. Any further and she'd need a hand truck to get him the rest of the way. Fortunately, Stanhill set one of her bags down in front of a door, opened it and stood aside for her to enter.

There was no holding back a gasp this time. "Oh, this is beautiful." It was less a room and more a suite, complete with a sitting area with a fireplace, an enormous four-poster bed and an adjoining bathroom. The place was bigger than her entire third-floor walk-up. Actually, the bed might be bigger on its own. She bent her head to whisper in Cappy's ear, "If you destroy anything in this room, I will trade you for a dog."

Stanhill brought her bags in and set them at the foot of the bed.

"Thank you. I'm going to keep Captain confined to this room for a few days. It'll be easier for him to adjust to the new surroundings that way." And it would give her a reason to keep her door shut.

"Very good, miss. Would you like a tour of the home? Can I get you something to eat?"

She smiled wistfully. "It was a long drive, so if it's all right with you, after I get Captain set up, all I really want is a hot shower and a nap."

"Of course. Should I wake you for dinner?"

"Yes! In fact, I'll set my alarm. What time should I be down?"

"Six P.M. And if I can get you anything before then, just let me know."

"I'm good. Just need Cappy's bag of supplies and his box. Oh! Would I be able to use the Wi-Fi?"

"Certainly. Log on to Ellnet, then the password is twilight1665. I'll leave you to it then, miss."

Twilight, huh? Maybe Hugh Ellingham was a fan of the books. Then again, considering the town he lived in, it might also just be an attempt at humor. "Thanks again."

Stanhill gave a little nod and left.

She put Captain on the bed, then jogged back down to the car and grabbed the rest of his stuff. Stanhill hadn't hesitated to give her the Wi-Fi code or acted strangely around her at all. Except for the basement thing. If he suspected she was a phony, he'd hidden it well.

Now she just had to convince the man who actually owned this place. More than that—she had to make him believe she was his perfect match.

Being able to walk in daylight didn't mean it was Hugh's preference, nor did it change the fact that it was in a vampire's nature to favor the evening hours over those awash in sunlight. Unless there was pressing business to attend to, he compromised by rising late, when the sun was lower in the sky and the shadows longer.

He walked into the kitchen to find Stanhill sitting at the table polishing silver. "Are we having company that I forgot about?"

Stanhill snorted. "Indeed, Ellingham. Your *match* has arrived early."

"My what?" Then he swore softly. "She wasn't due until next week." He instantly retracted his fangs, his decision to appear as human as possible to deter his new guest's advances firmly in place.

"Or the dowager blurred the truth a little."

He scrubbed his hands over his face. "That's more likely. Where is the love sick woman?"

"Asleep in the ivory suite for the last five hours."

"Good. Maybe she'll stay there."

Stanhill set down a spoon and picked up a serving fork. "She doesn't seem particularly love sick."

Hugh poured a large black coffee and took it to the table. He sat across from Stanhill. "That's promising. What *does* she seem like?"

"Nice. Pretty, probably more so when she's not worn out from all that driving. Good natured. A light packer. For a woman coming for a month's visit with a man she hopes to marry, she only brought one large suitcase and one small one." Stanhill shrugged, then added, "And she's an animal lover."

"That's an odd quality to call out. What makes you think that?"

Stanhill's mouth bent oddly, and when he raised his gaze to Hugh's, his eyes held a curious spark. "She brought her cat."

"She did what?"

"Did you expect her to leave it alone for a month? Seems fairly harmless, though."

Hugh inhaled. "Bloody hell. I smell it already."

Stanhill frowned. "No, you don't." He picked up the bottle of silver polish. "This has ammonia in it. Calm down, your lordship."

"Don't call me that."

"Don't act like a spoiled peer that needs to be spoon fed. It's a cat, not a wrecking ball."

Hugh grimaced. "You like her."

Stanhill cut his eyes away from his work to give Hugh an incredulous look. "After centuries of no one but you for company, how could I not?" He smiled. "Besides, it'll be nice to have someone else to talk to. Especially of the female persuasion."

"You have Corette and I bloody doubt it," he snarled.

Stanhill went back to his work with a grunt. "Woke up in a mood, too, I see."

"You would have too if you were having a bridezilla thrust upon you."

At the soft clearing of a throat, he and Stanhill turned. A very pretty woman stood in the kitchen doorway. From the look in her big green eyes, she'd heard him loud and clear. His gut sank with that realization. Whether or not he wanted this, it wasn't her fault she was here.

She bent her head, and the soft chestnut waves framing her face closed around her pained expression like a curtain. "I didn't mean to eavesdrop. I was just…I'll be upstairs."

She turned and fled before Hugh could stop her.

"Now you've mucked it up," Stanhill said. "She leaves and the dowager is going to snatch that amulet from around your neck quicker than you can blink."

Hugh glared at him.

Stanhill put down a butter knife and shook his head. "Well?"

"Well what?"

"Go fix it, you dimwitted night crawler."

Hugh shoved his chair back and went after her. She'd beaten him to her room, and her door was closed. He knocked softly. "Miss Givens?"

After a few seconds, she answered, "Yes?"

"May I have a word with you?"

She opened the door. Indignation danced in her eyes. "You mean a word besides bridezilla?"

He took a deep breath. "My apologies. That was unwarranted."

"I'd say. You don't even know me."

He held his hands up. "You're absolutely right. Can we start over?"

"Maybe." She made no move to let him in, leaning against the door frame and crossing her arms under her breasts.

The move created a valley of cleavage that erased his thoughts for a moment. What had she said? Oh, yes. "Maybe?"

"First, tell me why you said I'd been thrust upon you. Didn't you want me to come?"

He raked a hand through his hair. The woman had guts, he'd give her that. She was also nothing like the women he usually dated. Not blonde. Not reed slim. Not coiffed to within an inch of her life.

"It's not so much I didn't want you to come as I only found out about you yesterday."

Confusion clouded her pretty green eyes. "Did you not know what Eternamate was when you signed up for it?"

"I didn't know Eternamate existed." He smiled as best he could given the circumstances. "And I didn't sign up for it. My grandmother arranged all this on my behalf." Didi might not be fond of being referred to as grandmother outside family settings, but seeing as how she was responsible for Annabelle being here in the first place, all bets were off.

Annabelle's eyes widened, then she snickered. "You poor thing." The joy left her face a second later. "I suppose you want me to go, then."

"No, actually. I don't." He wasn't about to explain that his grandmother had threatened to take the amulet that allowed him to daywalk, either. It was bad enough Annabelle knew he was a vampire. Those amulets were a family secret shared only by his brothers, his grandmother and Alice Bishop.

She made a face. "You don't have to pretend to be nice to me. If your grandmother set this up, why would you want me to stay?"

"For that very reason. She arranged this and I love her dearly, so for her sake, why not see what happens?" That was convincing, wasn't it?

Annabelle frowned. Perhaps not as convincing as he thought. "You're willing to let me stay because of your grandmother?"

He nodded. And hoped he looked sincere. It wasn't entirely a lie. He very much needed her to stay because of Didi. Preferring the darkness of night was one thing, being eternally confined to it was another.

Annabelle pushed the door open a little wider and walked back into the room. "For her sake, then."

With his relief, his smile became sincere. "Excellent."

A small cow walked toward him and meowed. "What on earth is—Stanhill mentioned you brought your cat. He failed to mention the creature is the size of an SUV."

She gave him the side eye. "His name is Captain. Don't worry about getting to know him, he doesn't like men."

Captain continued his stroll toward Hugh, then wound around his legs like a furry snake. "Yes, I can see how much he loathes me."

"Traitor," she hissed.

Hugh gave Captain a scratch on the head. The beast was surprisingly silky. "I'm forgiven then?"

She tossed a pink, stuffed mouse across the room and the animal gave chase, leaving Hugh's legs untangled. She tipped her head to one side as if considering her options. "For now."

She gave no quarter. He kind of liked that. For a woman who knew exactly what he was, she certainly wasn't intimidated. Maybe Didi knew what sort of woman worked for him after all. He grinned. "Good enough. I'll see you downstairs then."

She nodded. "Maybe you can give me a tour of the house then. Except for the basement, of course."

He blinked at her mention of his lab. Stanhill must have said something. He recovered quickly, and smiled. "My pleasure."

He headed back downstairs with the shocking realization that he actually meant what he'd said. Getting to know the curious Miss Givens might not be the worst thing that had ever happened to him.

Delaney shut the door, then leaned against it, closed her eyes and exhaled the nervousness she'd been tamping down since Hugh had knocked on her door. She was so thankful she'd showered and put on a little makeup before going downstairs. Looking presentable had given her the courage to act exactly the way she thought Annabelle would in this situation, although some of the hurt had been real.

What if Annabelle had found out this guy never

really wanted her? Kinda funny to think that here she, Delaney, had been so worried that he was going to send her away, when come to find out, he wasn't even responsible for bringing her here.

Which maybe explained why the man was kind of an ass. Built like a superhero, stupidly beautiful and, okay, willing to apologize, which was more than she could say for Russell, but still an ass. Speaking of, she hadn't gotten a good look at Hugh's backside, but it was probably just as gorgeous as the rest of him. Dark hair, stare-right-through-you ice blue eyes with the body of an Olympic swimmer and a dash of dangerous thrown in on top of his bone-melting English accent. She couldn't quite put her finger on it, but there was something about the guy…something dark and a little feral.

And undeniably sexy.

Her eyes widened. She'd just moved in with James Bond. That was about as close as anyone could hope to get to a real-life superhero.

It wouldn't be difficult spending time with a guy like that, but the best part was he *didn't* plan on marrying her.

The relief of that coupled with the idea that he wasn't being completely honest with her about *something*—maybe whatever was going on in the basement—made her feel slightly better for using his house as a hideout. Not that he owed her any kind of honesty. They'd known each other all of five minutes.

Still, it was a strange way for him to start a relationship with someone who could end up being his wife. If that was even what he was thinking. But he probably wasn't. He hadn't invited Annabelle Givens here, after all. If not for his desire to appease his grandmother, he might already have escorted her out the door. To avoid that happening before she was ready to leave, she needed to embrace her role as his prospective fiancée. The best course of action was to be sweet and nice and make him the focus of her attention. Basically, pretend he was a customer she was waiting on at the restaurant. She could do that. All. Day. Long.

Since she'd passed out as soon as she'd gotten into the room, she took a few minutes to fire up her laptop and log on. Captain was busy disemboweling his catnip mouse. She quickly scanned the New York news sites for mention of the shooting. Nothing. Frustrating. She was dying to know what was happening. Okay, bad choice of words.

She closed her laptop. She'd think about it later. Right now it was time to play the potential fiancée. She trotted downstairs, deliberately making her steps heard so there'd be no accidental eavesdropping again. Stanhill was alone in the kitchen, busy with dinner.

He smiled at her. "Master Ellingham is out on the back patio. Just through the foyer and out the French doors in the great room. You'll see him."

"Thank you." She followed his directions, taking her time as she wandered through the house. The decorating was heavily masculine, but reserved and classy. Kind of British hunting lodge meets the Deep South. Each room was more impressive than the next. If Hugh had done the decorating, it said a lot about him. Like maybe she'd misjudged his being an ass based on one comment. Which, considering he hadn't been the one behind bringing her here, was pretty excusable.

Sheers muted the view through the French doors. She opened them and took a breath. The garden beyond was charming. Very...English in that slightly constrained-but-overgrown-enough-to-look-lived-in sort of way. A few last rays of sun broke through the trees, giving everything a golden glow.

Except the man of the house.

Hugh stood in the shadows on the flagstone patio, a glass of red wine in his hand, looking very regal. And utterly handsome in black trousers and a crisp white shirt. If Delaney wasn't careful, she might get her heart broken. He turned, a subtle smile erasing his serious resting face. "Hello again."

"Hi." She moved closer but not enough to

invade his space. "This place...the house, the garden...it's incredible."

"Thank you. I've worked hard on it. My home is my sanctuary. But then I guess that's true for most people." He took a sip of his wine. "What's your house like?"

She froze. Did Annabelle live in a house? An apartment? She had no idea. *He's just a guest at the restaurant, keep him happy.* She laughed. "Nothing like this. Did you pick out everything yourself?"

He glanced toward the great room. "It's really more of a collection than a deliberate act of decorating."

If that was his idea of a collection, then her random assortment of candy molds was more like a flea market accident.

His gaze shifted to her in a very purposeful way. "I just like what I like."

The little hairs on the back of her neck lifted the way they did when someone flirted with her. Was that where they were now? Flirting? She looked toward the garden and bit her tongue before her nerves caused her to blurt out a random chocolate fact.

"I'm sorry," he said. "I'm a terrible host. I haven't offered you a glass of wine. Red all right? It's very good. Local, actually."

Anything but Chianti was fine with her. "Great." So long as she didn't drink too much and forget who she was pretending to be.

"I'll just be a moment." He slipped inside.

Before she went to sleep tonight, she was going to Google Annabelle Givens and study that woman until she knew everything about her. Maybe that would help with her nerves.

Hugh returned and handed her a glass, then raised his in a toast. "To new beginnings?"

So much for keeping a safe distance from him. He was so close she could smell his cologne. It was spicy and complex, like good dark chocolate. Her mouth watered. *Down, girl.* "New beginnings."

They clinked, then drank, and for a moment, she could picture herself in this place being the woman she was pretending to be. Sophisticated, cultured and assuredly beautiful Annabelle Givens. Annabelle had to be that kind of woman, or Adelaide Poirot never would have matched her with a man like Hugh.

The sun dropped a little farther, turning the sky the most vibrant shades of orange and pink. "It's really beautiful here. Lots of trees and nature."

Nothing like Brooklyn. She took another sip of her wine.

He gave her an odd look. "Doesn't upstate New York have a lot of trees and nature?"

She drank some more wine, buying herself a little time to cover her slip. "Oh, sure, but it just seems greener here. More quiet and peaceful too."

He laughed. "If you like quiet and peaceful, don't go into town."

"Gets rowdy, huh?"

"After dark, things really start up. Plus, this weekend is the Panic Parade." He sighed and shook his head like he thought the whole thing was a little nuts.

"The Panic Parade?"

"I believe it grew out of the traditional May Day celebration. Except May Day has been reinterpreted as a cry for help as opposed to a celebration of spring."

"I get it." She canted her head and laughed softly. "Although, I have to admit, the whole every day is Halloween thing threw me. What's up with that?" Ugh. Annabelle had probably never said *what's up with that* a day in her life.

His grin didn't fade. "It's how the town makes money."

"Halloween?"

"Tourists." He took a deep breath. "When my family bought this town—"

"You own this town?" Oh boy. She was in deep. No wonder he was filthy rich and didn't need to get out of bed until the day was nearly over. He owned everything! *All right, slow down on the wine.* And no wonder Annabelle had been so bummed her match had been canceled.

"We only own parts of it now." He made a small

face like it was nothing. "But when my family bought the town, it was floundering and on the verge of bankruptcy. The winery was closed, as were most of the other local businesses. The whole idea of every day is Halloween turned things around."

He raised one eyebrow. "It's America's third-favorite holiday, you know."

She almost laughed at how official sounding his voice was. He must tell people that a lot. "Halloween candy sales topped two billion dollars last year." Crap. The random candy fact had just slipped out. At least it was relevant.

He nodded. "The candy shop in town is one of the most popular stores, so that seems about right."

The news that Nocturne Falls already had a sweet shop inexplicably took her mood down a notch. "I love candy. It's kind of..." She'd been about to say, *It's kind of my dream job*, but that was Delaney's thing, not Annabelle's. "Everyone's favorite, I guess." Wow, she sucked at being someone else.

She changed the subject before he asked her more about sweets. "Is there really a falls, or is that just part of the name?"

"There's a waterfall. A few of them, but the largest is Nocturne Falls, the town's namesake. It's in the hills. Bit of a hike, but a popular destination."

"Why Nocturne?"

"When the moon is especially bright, when it's full mostly, you can see a moonbow in the mist."

Her brows lifted. "A moonbow? Is that like a nighttime rainbow?"

"That's exactly what it is." His eyes sparked with amusement. "There will be a full moon while you're here. We'll go see it."

"Awesome! I've never seen anything like that." This place was already getting better.

He sipped his wine, still studying her. "Would you like to take a walk through town after dinner?"

"Sure." Talking about the town would give her a topic that was less likely to cause her to blow her cover.

As if on cue, Stanhill opened one of the French doors. "Dinner is served."

Dinner, it turned out, was served in the formal dining room on fancy china with three sets of heavy silver utensils and lots of sparkly crystal stemware. If she got through the meal without breaking something, it would be a Halloween miracle. "Do you eat like this all the time?"

Hugh looked at her, clearly unsure how to answer.

She backtracked. "I mean, it's beautiful, but I feel a little underdressed for this much crystal and silver."

He nodded. "It's not often I have company. If you'd prefer something else—"

"No, it's really nice." And she just needed to shut up and play her part.

Stanhill brought out two covered plates. He smiled as he set hers in front of her and lifted the lid. Steak, whipped potatoes and roasted Brussels sprouts. Her stomach growled its approval, but the blood pooling on the china was a little off putting. She bit her lip.

"Something wrong, miss?" he asked as he delivered Hugh's plate.

"I hate to say anything—" She really did. "But I think my steak might be a little underdone for my taste." Pink was one thing, mooing when she cut into it was another.

"I'd be happy to put it back under the broiler for you." He took her plate and disappeared with it.

Which meant Hugh was now waiting for her food to return, even though he had a full plate in front of him. He poured more wine for them, seemingly unfazed by the waiting.

"Eat, please," she urged. "Your food will get cold otherwise."

"That wouldn't be very gentlemanly."

She shrugged. "You can open a door for me later."

He smiled. "You're different than what I'd thought you'd be. Not that I had any real idea having only just found out about you."

Music to her ears. "What did you think I was going to be like?"

He stared at his wine glass for a moment before answering. "If I'm honest, desperate. You don't strike me as desperate at all. And certainly not a woman whose only thoughts are finding a husband."

"So not a bridezilla?"

He laughed. "Not at all."

What he didn't know was that she really was desperate—desperate to stay alive. Desperate to get married? Not so much. "That wouldn't be a very healthy existence, would it?"

"No." He lifted his glass. "I like you, Annabelle Givens. After Didi told me what she'd done, I was furious."

"Didi is your grandmother?"

He nodded. "It's her nickname. Her real name is Elenora."

She lifted her glass to return his toast, and they both drank. The crystal was paper thin and glistened like a prism. She set it back down carefully. "I can understand being upset with someone else making life decisions for you. Why did she do it? Because she wants you to get married and have grandbabies?"

He nodded "Exactly."

"So why did you agree to it? You're a grown man. You could have said no."

His mouth thinned almost like he was embarrassed. He covered it by drinking his wine.

A second later, Delaney figured it out. He was a wealthy man who didn't seem to have an actual job and whose family had rebuilt the town of Nocturne Falls. The picture was as clear as the goblet she was drinking from. "She threatened to take away your inheritance, didn't she?"

Hugh choked on his wine. "Something like that."

"So what's the deal? You agreed to put up with me for a month and make a good show of it in exchange for what? Keeping your name in the will?" It was Anthony Rastinelli and Little Tony all over again, except Anthony had only ever threatened to take away Little Tony's Cadillac Escalade if he didn't "fall in line." She had a much better idea of what that line was now.

Hugh set the glass down and stared at her. "Are you psychic?"

She laughed. "No, I just work for a big family, and I know how those kinds of things play out sometimes." Then her humor faded. Once again, she'd said something that might not be true of Annabelle.

Fortunately, Stanhill returned with her food at that moment. She kind of wanted to kiss him for it. "Thank you!" The words came out with a little more enthusiasm than she'd intended.

His brows lifted slightly. "You must be hungry."

Sure, let's go with that. "Starved." The steak did smell incredible. She picked up her knife and fork and looked at Hugh. "Shall we?"

"Absolutely."

Around bites of food, she kept the conversation directed at him, asking him questions about the town, his family, the house—anything she could think of to keep herself out of trouble. She learned he had two brothers, a little more about the history of the town and that apparently he wasn't a lover of vegetables because, while he devoured his steak, the Brussels sprouts and potatoes remained largely untouched.

The meal flew by, and before she knew it, Stanhill was clearing their plates. "Dessert now or later?"

"None at all." Hugh set his napkin on the table. "We're going to go into town."

Stanhill nodded. "Would you like me to drive you?"

"Yes, but we can walk home." Hugh looked at her. "It's only a fifteen-minute walk. Is that all right with you?"

"Totally. I walk a lot at home so—" She shut up before she said too much again. Oversharing was now her thing apparently—and her potential downfall. "Walking would be great. I'll just run upstairs and grab a jacket." She stood.

Hugh got up at the same time she did, and she realized it was out of politeness, not because he was as eager to leave as she was. "I'll meet you in the foyer then."

"Great." She held her smile until she hit the stairs.

She was never going to manage pretending to be another woman for an entire month.

There were no true weekends in a resort town like Nocturne Falls. A Monday night could be just as busy as a Friday night. That was one of the reasons Hugh rarely went into town, unless Didi or one of his brothers requested he put in an appearance.

Being the Vampire On Duty was really Julian's job, but every once in a while, Hugh filled in as VOD. Sebastian never did. Sebastian rarely left his house. Hugh was okay with that. Sebastian did enough keeping the family's finances in order.

"What do you think?" Hugh asked Annabelle as they strolled Main Street along with the rest of the visitors.

Her gaze ricocheted from one thing to the next. "It's amazing."

It kind of was if he imagined it through her eyes. At night, the town was lit up like a jack-o-lantern.

All the buildings were outlined with fairy lights. Shifts of character performers, every one of them a genuine supernatural (although the tourists didn't know that), walked the streets taking pictures with tourists who wanted to show their friends on social media how they'd howled with the wolfman or the witch had almost turned them into a frog. And then, of course, there was the ever-present *threat* of being bitten by a vampire.

"Speak of the devil," Hugh muttered.

Julian was a block ahead of them, posing with a group of college girls. Hugh pointed to one of the touristy shops that sold souvenirs. "Let's go in here."

"Where?" She stopped in the middle of the sidewalk and looked at him.

Hugh pointed again, taking her elbow and trying to aim her toward the store.

Too late. Julian's voice rang out over the pseudo-scary soundtrack piped in through hidden speakers. "Well, well, well. Look who's decided to grace the streets of Nocturne Falls this evening." He parked himself in front of them, hands on his hips, *cape* billowing out behind him. To say that Julian embraced his role as VOD was a substantial understatement.

"Hello to you too." Hugh smiled tightly. "You look busy, so we won't keep you."

Annabelle stuck her hand out. "Hi, I'm

Annabelle. You must be a friend of Hugh's. Love the getup, by the way." She winked at him. "Very authentic."

Julian took her hand, turned it over and kissed it. "A friend? Sweetness, this bastion of boringness standing next to you is my brother."

"What?" She grinned and looked at Hugh. "This is Julian, the man whore?"

Julian dropped her hand and his grin.

Hugh's smile was instantaneous. He might have fallen a little in love with her right then and there. "Yes, this is my brother." He put his arm around Annabelle as he turned to Julian. "And this vision of loveliness is Annabelle Givens, whom you will not try to sleep with. Understood?"

Julian clutched at his chest as though he'd been mortally wounded. "I would never try to move in on your territory." He wiggled his brows at Annabelle. "Unless you'd welcome such an invasion."

She grimaced.

Hugh sighed deeply. "She's not my *territory*. She's my guest, and as such, you will treat her with respect."

Annabelle reached up to where Hugh's hand rested on her shoulder and interlaced her fingers with his. The unexpected contact sent a little jolt of heat through him.

"Of course, brother dear." Julian gave him a

mock salute, then looked at Annabelle. "See," he whispered loudly. "Bor-ing."

Annabelle gave Julian an appraising glance. "Boring is in the eye of the beholder."

"Don't you have tourists to bite?" Hugh asked.

"As a matter of fact, I do." Julian flashed his fangs in a wide grin and a silvery glint seemed to light his eyes then he swerved around them and took off down the street only to be stopped again by another gaggle of female tourists.

Annabelle watched him go. "Boy, he sure takes that vampire thing seriously."

"Well…yes." Hugh wasn't sure what to say. Did she not realize his entire family was vampires? Maybe she thought just he was. She had yet to mention it, which seemed odd.

"He really sells it." She shook her head. "I know he's your brother, but he comes on a little strong."

"Sorry about that," Hugh said.

She shrugged but didn't let go of his hand. "He's your brother, not your son. It's not like you're responsible for how he turned out."

Hugh smiled. "You want to see the candy store?"

Her eyes lit up, rewarding him. "I'd love to."

"C'mon." They started walking again. They passed a witch in a pointy hat and purple robes. Every time she swept her wand through the air, sparks followed it. Tourists were getting pictures with her as she cackled. Hugh didn't know the woman. Must be one of Julian's new hires.

Annabelle laughed and she shook her head as she stared back at the witch. "This place is crazy."

Up ahead, Sheriff Merrow leaned against his patrol car, parked in one of the emergency lanes. Hugh gave Merrow a nod as they strolled past. "Sheriff."

The werewolf-turned-officer of the law nodded back. "Ellingham. Ma'am."

Annabelle gave him a little wave as they continued past.

Not until they walked into the candy store, Keller's Sweets-n-Treats, did Hugh drop his arm from her shoulder. The place was full of customers filling bags with their favorite sweets, but despite his disdain for public displays of affection, he wouldn't have minded holding on to her a little longer. "What do you think?"

Instead of happy, she looked disappointed. "It's nice."

"You don't like it."

"It's...not what I expected."

Vicky Keller, the owner, came up to them. "Hello, *Hugh*."

"Vicky."

She tugged her sweater together like she was covering up a national treasure. "Word around town is you and Piper Hodge broke up."

Old news, but apparently still worth mentioning. Or maybe Piper had put a notice in the *Tombstone*. He refrained from rolling his eyes. "Yes, we did."

She glanced at Annabelle then back at him. "I see you've moved on."

The Kellers were the one hold-out family who'd refused to sell to Didi. As a result, there had been bad blood between the families. Vicky had no personal stake since it was her great-great-grandparents who'd refused to sell, but she acted like the Ellinghams had run over her dog. "Annabelle, this is Victoria Keller, owner of this establishment."

Annabelle nodded at her. "Hi."

Vicky stared back. "Heard you say you don't like my shop."

"No, I think it's lovely." Annabelle smiled. "And so well stocked. Most of this candy is impossible to get anywhere but online."

Vicky softened a little. "That's why we carry it." She looked at Hugh. "Because tradition means something to us."

"Tradition is great," Annabelle interjected. "But shaking things up is fun too."

Vicky's exterior returned to its normal brittle shell. "I suppose you're one of those who likes salt on their chocolate."

"I do." She reached into a nearby bin and pulled

out a handful of wax paper wrapped pastel discs. "But I also love Necco wafers. They're one of the oldest American candies, you know."

"Yeah." Vicky smirked. "I know. You actually going to buy those or are you just touching them for fun?"

Hugh was on the verge of snarling at Vicky. "We'll take the whole bin."

The woman's smile didn't reach her eyes. "Isn't that generous of you." She snapped her fingers. "Mary, ring up this bin of Neccos for Mr. Ellington."

"Ellingham," he corrected, knowing the second that the word was out of his mouth that he'd given her exactly what she wanted. Recognition.

With an evil little smirk, she spun on her heel and walked away.

Mary Keller, Vicky's daughter, ran up to help them. She smiled at Hugh and blushed a little. "Hi, Mr. Ellingham. I'll take care of that right now for you." She scooped up the candies and headed off to the counter.

Annabelle shot him a questioning look that included crazy eyes.

He snorted and nodded. "Yep."

As soon as they were back outside, he lifted the bag of candies. "You really like these things, huh?"

"Ugh, no, I hate them. They're chalky, flavorless discs of...chalk. I just didn't want that woman to win the argument. Don't worry, I'll pay you back."

A burst of laughter tore out of Hugh. When he caught his breath, he just shook his head. "You're a madwoman. I can't adequately express how entertaining you are." He hefted the bag. "Best money I ever spent, so don't even think about paying me back, but what are you going to do with all of these dreadful things?"

She held out her hand for the bag. "Every day is Halloween, right?"

"Right." He gave her the bag.

Two little girls dressed as whatever Disney princesses were currently the rage came toward them, their parents in tow. Annabelle crouched down. "Are you Elsa and Anna?"

Shyly, but smiling, they nodded. "We are."

"Your dresses are beautiful," Annabelle cooed. "Do you have treat bags?" They did. Every child in Nocturne Falls did. They held them up. Annabelle added a generous handful of Neccos to each one. "Happy Halloween," she said.

Then she linked her arm through Hugh's. "I'll have these gone before we hit the end of the street."

Delaney was shocked by how much the owner of the candy store's treatment of Hugh had bothered her, but handing out the candy and seeing the kids' faces light up was fun. Getting rid of the candy and being able to hold on to Hugh without being interrupted was even better. His hand was tucked in his pocket and her arm was laced through his. The connection was surprisingly easy and oddly comforting. Whether or not he felt the same, she couldn't tell, but he'd made no move to change it. Either way, she felt safe with him around. Not that she was in any danger here.

"Piper was your ex, I take it?"

He nodded. "Yes." Then he changed the subject. "You're really good with children. Actually, you're good with people in general."

"Thanks. I like people." Him included, which was almost worrying her. "Speaking of, why doesn't Vicky like you?"

"Long story."

"I have twenty-nine days left. If you can't tell it in that amount of time, I don't want to hear it."

He smiled. "Perhaps it's not that long. Her family refused to sell when my family was buying up the town. She's still bitter even though it was ages ago and she wasn't even born yet."

"She resents your money and your influence, despite the fact that without your family's intervention, she wouldn't have a business to run."

"Pretty much."

Delaney sighed. "People like that wear me out."

"You never did get your dessert, you know." He

glanced down at her. "Would you like something sweet?"

"Always."

"What would you like?"

She almost said a kiss. Where that had come from, she had no idea. Her pulse jumped at the freshness of her own thoughts. "Chocolate is always good. Unless you're in the mood for something different?"

The wicked glinted in his eyes lasted for half a second, then he looked down the street. "There's a great little coffee shop just down the way. They have biscuits, er, cookies and little cakes and such, too."

"Homemade?"

"Homemade."

"Let's go."

Two blocks down, they turned onto Black Cat Boulevard and found the coffee shop on the side street.

"The Hallowed Bean?" She laughed. "You guys really take this Halloween thing seriously, don't you?"

He shrugged as he opened the door for her. "As they say at the chamber of commerce meetings, Ween sells."

"Please tell me they don't really say that."

"Sadly, they do."

She stepped inside, the delicious smell of roasting

coffee and fresh-baked goods welcoming her with open arms. "I already love this place."

He nodded at the one open table. "Why don't you grab that spot, and I'll take care of ordering. What would you like?"

She thought for a moment. "Surprise me." He ought to know what the best stuff was, right?

"Oh, good. No pressure." He got in line.

"You asked." She wound through the other tables to snag the one in the corner. It was a prime spot, well suited for people watching. One very handsome person in particular.

Hugh.

Talking to him and being around him was getting easier by the second. She might not be his intended match, but she couldn't imagine why any woman wouldn't enjoy his company.

That proved itself out when he got up to the cashier. She greeted him with a big smile and small talk before taking his order. He was obviously well known. Kind of like Nocturne Falls royalty, she imagined. When the woman handed his change back, her hand lingered on his a second longer than necessary.

So maybe not royalty so much as the most eligible bachelor. That raised a lot of questions. Like why he wasn't already married.

He approached the table with a small tray, setting it down between them before taking his seat. "Let's see if I got this right." He picked the short cup off the tray and put it in front of her. "Drinking chocolate. Very strong, very rich."

She waggled her head and did her best imitation of Mae West. "That's how I like my men."

The side of his mouth quirked up in a smile. "I hope you feel the same way about your brownies." He slid the only plate on the tray off to her side. "Espresso cherry brownie. This combo is known as death by chocolate."

"Seems appropriate. What did you get?"

"Black coffee. Simple and uncomplicated. Which is in no way an indication of what I look for in a woman."

She laughed. "Point taken."

He glanced at her cup and raised his brows. "So? How'd I do with my choices?"

She bit into the brownie. The top was slightly crisp but then instantly gave way to a fudgy interior redolent of coffee and chocolate. Her tongue found a piece of cherry, and the fruity tang cut through the richness in the most perfect way. She tried not to moan. "Exceptionally well. That was easily the best thing I've put in my mouth in a long time."

The muscles in his jaw twitched, and she realized he was fighting hard not to say something about her inadvertent innuendo. He sipped his coffee instead.

She laughed and tried the drink he'd brought her. It was like bathing her mouth in liquid chocolate. There was no holding back the moan this time. "Oh, that is…wow, yeah, good. Please tell me we can come here again."

His gaze fixed on her mouth for a long second. Then he shifted in his seat and answered. "Whenever you want. Although with the Panic Parade this weekend, it's going to be mobbed."

The word made her blink twice. She shook her head to clear Rastinelli's image. "Are we, uh, going to that?"

"The parade?" He seemed taken aback by her question. "I wasn't planning on it. Do you want to go?"

"Sure. Sounds interesting at the very least. I'm here, right? Might as well see what this place is all about." She canted her head. "You don't come to town much, do you?"

"No."

"Why not?"

"It's just…not my thing."

"I don't know why. Except for Icky Vicky, the townspeople seem to love you." She took another bite of the brownie, hoping he'd share something to dispel some of the mystery surrounding him.

"I'm just more of a private person."

Hello, open door. "Is that why your grandmother thinks you need help finding a woman?"

"It isn't so much that she thinks I need help finding a woman as it is she thinks I need help learning to commit."

"And an arranged match was going to do that how?"

He growled softly in frustration. "She believes if I meet the perfect woman, I won't find a reason to break things off."

"Oh, I get it. You're a love 'em and leave 'em type."

"No," he said sharply. "*That* is Julian. I have been in plenty of meaningful, long-term relationships—"

"You just can't put a ring on it."

He frowned. "Something like that." He sat back, twisting slightly so he could cross one long leg over the other. He planted his hand on his ankle and studied her. "Why did *you* need a matchmaker?"

"I…" *Think, Delaney. You're not you, you're Annabelle.* "I just got out of a relationship."

"Not rich or strong enough?" He smiled.

"Not faithful enough." She rolled the edge of her paper napkin under her fingertips. "Money and physical attributes I can take or leave. After all, they're both attributes that can come and go depending on the circumstances. But I will not abide a cheating man."

"Is that why your last relationship didn't work?"

She nodded, thoughts of Russell ruining the taste in her mouth. "He forgot his phone at my place." She held her hands up. "I didn't snoop on purpose. It chimed, I looked and the rest is history. He knew when he came to pick it up he'd been found out." She forced herself to smile. She was sitting across from an exceptionally handsome man, eating the most amazing brownie she'd ever had. Now was not the time to mope about Russell. "How about you? Why'd your last relationship fizzle?"

"The same reason they all did." He stared at his coffee. "She wasn't the right one."

"How long did it last?"

"Five months. I've had longer. Ten months. But she wasn't the right one either."

She nodded. "Five months or ten months, either one is long enough to know. Clean break?"

"Not exactly. She thought I was proposing. I wasn't."

"Yikes." Delaney's brows shot up. "Is this Piper we're talking about? The woman Vicky mentioned?"

He nodded. "Her family owns the local newspaper."

"I think I know why you don't like coming into town."

He snorted softly. "My relationships don't often end that badly, but..." He shook his head.

"You probably want to go home, huh?"

He hesitated, and a slow smile curved his mouth. "I'm actually having a pretty good time."

"Me, too." She took another bite of the brownie. Hugh was a nice guy. She'd judged him based on his initial reaction to her, but that had been all wrong. He was a guy reluctant to make a commitment for whatever reason, and that was okay with her. After her mother died, her father had remarried so fast she'd doubted the institution of marriage herself for a while. Whatever Hugh's reason for staying single, it would certainly make things easier. "Why don't we make a deal?"

Curiosity sparked in his eyes. "What kind of deal?"

"You're not looking to get married, but you have to make a good show of things for your grandmother, so let's just agree to have fun for the next twenty-nine days, no strings attached."

"No strings attached. I can do that. Except…" He squinted. "Didn't you come here trying to find a husband?"

She couldn't very well say no to that. Instead, she shrugged. "Sure, but I'm also not going to freak out if that doesn't happen. You might not even be my type." He was so her type. She just hadn't known it until now. She drank the last of her chocolate. Darn, that had gone way too fast.

"And if you fall in love with me? What then?"

"Conceited much?" She laughed. "I could ask you the same question." She gave him her sexiest look.

He laughed. *Ouch*. Not the response she'd been going for. Then he pointed to the corner of his mouth. "You have a little chocolate right here."

Oh. She licked at it. "Gone?"

His gaze seemed to be stuck to the spot her tongue had just been. He closed his mouth and swallowed, his Adam's apple bobbing. "We should go."

"Why? What's wrong?"

He stood and looked toward the street. "Nothing."

Delaney got to her feet and followed him out. Clearly, she wasn't the only one bad at lying.

Annabelle was saying all the right things. Whether or not that was on purpose, Hugh couldn't find it in him to care. Maybe she was a witch. Maybe she'd put some kind of spell on him. When her tongue had darted out to lick away the smudge of chocolate, he'd had the most overwhelming desire to kiss her.

Worse than that, his stomach had done something…odd. Something that felt very much like *chemistry*.

The minute he stepped outside the Hallowed Bean, he took a deep breath.

"I don't believe you." She was too close. He could still smell her perfume and the chocolate she'd been drinking.

"What are you talking about?" He couldn't think with her this close. Well, he could, but those thoughts were only going to get him into more trouble.

"You said nothing was wrong. If that's true, why did you get up and leave like that?"

Did she know how gorgeously pink her lips were? How the sight of her tongue had sent a shiver down his spine? "I needed" — *you* — "air."

Her eyes narrowed. "Are you claustrophobic or something? Is that why you don't want to go to the parade? Look, it's not a big deal. I can—"

He threaded his hands into her chestnut waves and kissed her. She gasped into his mouth, opening her lips so that his tongue could dart across hers. She tasted like she smelled, sweet and chocolaty. He was doomed.

That didn't stop him from kissing her some more.

He drove his hands deeper into the silk of her hair, holding her close, savoring her warmth. His body responded the way it normally did when he kissed a beautiful, available woman, except there was more to it than the usual reaction. Something stirred within him, something deeper than just the tightening of his body and the burn of desire.

He broke the kiss and stared at her. "Witch," he whispered.

Her breath was coming in deep gulps, the rise and fall of her chest distracting him. She blew out a small breath. "What was that?"

"I had to see…" He shook his head. There were no clear thoughts in it. Just feelings and emotions stripped down to the raw essence of what they were. Need. Want. Desire.

"You had to see what?"

He couldn't explain what he'd done. What was going on in his head. Not now. Not after *that*. "We should go." He turned.

And almost ran into Piper.

She glowered at him and Annabelle. "Hello, *Hugh*." Her brows shot up as she gave Annabelle the once over. "New girlfriend already? Guess that shouldn't surprise me."

"Hello, Piper."

Annabelle inhaled, a small sound, but one that cut through him.

Piper crossed her arms. "Aren't you going to introduce me? Or would you rather pretend I don't exist?"

With a sigh, Hugh put his hand on the small of Annabelle's back. Next to Annabelle's lush curves, Piper's thinness made her seem brittle. "Annabelle Givens, this is Piper Hodge. My ex-girlfriend."

"Hello, *Annabelle Givens*." Piper smirked. It was an ugly look. "There are a lot of us ex-girlfriends in town. Trust me."

He'd had enough. And part of him actually cared what sort of impression Annabelle might be forming. "If you'll excuse us, we're on our way home."

"Home?" Piper practically screeched the word,

which had definitely been a poor choice. With a righteous glare, she leaned toward Annabelle. "I didn't let him take me home until the fourth date."

Annabelle didn't budge. "You have no idea how many dates we've been on."

Piper wasn't so easily put off. "You know, he's a serial dater. A real piece of work. Not like his brother, mind you. At least with Julian, you know what you're getting. A fun night, nothing more. But this one leads you on."

She was really working up steam now. "Makes you think things are going somewhere, then buh-bye. All done. It's not me, it's you."

Annabelle tapped a finger on her lip. "I think you mean it's not you, it's me."

Piper scowled. "That's what I said."

Annabelle cocked her brows and looked down her nose at Piper. "No. You didn't."

Hugh stepped between Annabelle and Piper and got a big whiff of chardonnay. "You're making a scene."

"I'm not making a scene," Piper snapped back, her diamond stud earrings flashing. "I'm just telling my *replacement* what to expect."

She looked around Hugh at Annabelle. "If you think he's going to marry you, he's not. Ever. If you don't believe me, ask half a dozen other girls in this town."

Annabelle put her hand on Hugh's arm and

eased him back a step. "You've got me confused with one of those women who needs a ring on her finger to feel complete. I don't put those kinds of expectations on men. And I'd say I'm sorry things didn't work out between you and Hugh, but based on your current amount of crazy, I'd say he dodged a bullet."

Piper's jaw dropped.

Annabelle gave her a nod. "You have a good night now." Then she started walking.

He didn't need any coaxing to join her. He waited until they were out of Piper's earshot before speaking. "That was bloody brilliant."

She pulled him into an alley and turned to him. "I'm glad you enjoyed that, but you don't get to kiss me and just walk away. Not after we had the whole no strings attached talk."

He faced her, aware of the tourists milling by and peering down the alley at them. The small crowd that had followed them. "You're right. But I'd rather not explain here." He pointed to the street behind him. "Let's keep walking."

Thankfully, that seemed to be all right with her because she fell into step with him as he left the alley. She didn't link her arm through his as she had on Main Street, but he was okay with that. Touching her at this point might take him down a more dangerous path.

As they left the crowds behind, they walked

without speaking, without looking at each other. It gave him time to cool off and find the words to explain himself. "I apologize if I startled you or if my advance was unwelcome. I was feeling...very affected by you, and the urge to kiss you became overwhelming. I gave into it."

She was silent for a few seconds longer than he would have liked. Long enough for him to think his kiss hadn't been welcome. "You're a strange man. Not strange, exactly. Curious."

He'd been called worse. "Why so?"

She cut her eyes at him. "We'd just made a pact about no strings, and then you freak out and kiss me. You don't think that's curious? Not to mention the whole encounter with your ex, who is, wow, *very* pretty. That was fun. And yes, I know you had no control over that."

"I did not *freak* out." Three-hundred-and-seventy-seven-year-old vampires did not freak out. "I just felt like I was feeling something and wanted to be sure."

Amusement danced in her eyes. This was not supposed to be funny. "You felt like you were feeling something? Oh, men slay me." She stopped walking. "And?"

He came to a halt beside her. "And what?"

"Did you feel what you were feeling?"

He frowned. "Now you're mocking me."

"Not mocking. Just trying to be *sure*." She

crossed her arms. "Or maybe you need to kiss me again?"

The idea stirred his blood and raised heat in his belly. Perhaps because it was a brilliant idea. He clamped his jaw shut. Not brilliant. Awful. "No, I don't need to kiss you again."

Her brows lifted and her mouth pursed. "Okay, good to know." She started walking again, leaving him to catch up. "I guess we should get home then."

Delaney yawned and blinked at the bright light coming through the bedroom windows. Sleep had taken forever to come last night. After feeding Cappy, she'd lain in the big four-poster bed, her body on fire and her head a jumble of thoughts involving Hugh, his ex, and the kiss. Well, mostly Hugh. And the kiss. The only thing that was clear this morning was that the trip into town with Hugh last night had taken a very unforeseen turn.

She fluffed her pillow. Captain Underpants was firmly ensconced on the other one, having declared that side of the bed his. She rolled over to scratch his head. "A man kissed your mother last night and you don't even care, do you?"

Not even a yawn.

"Philistine."

She rolled back over and listed the things she knew for certain about her current situation:

Hugh was a horrible liar.

But an excellent kisser.

She would be willing to kiss him again.

She was in big trouble.

How was she going to last another twenty-eight days? She sat up abruptly. She'd been so distracted by Hugh's mouth she'd gone to bed without checking the news at home *or* Googling the real Annabelle Givens. She grabbed her laptop off the floor beside the bed and fired it up, checking the same local news sites as the day before. Nothing about the shooting or about a missing man or anything.

Her phone vibrated. She set the laptop aside and picked up her phone off the nightstand. Two waiting texts.

First one was from Samantha, a friend and fellow server at Rastinelli's. *Where u at? Boss is going to call the cops if u don't show. Says he's worried about u.*

Anthony Rastinelli was going to call the cops on *her*? She doubted that.

The second text was from Russell. She rolled her eyes before she even read it. *Hey babe. Thinking about u. Missing u. Call me.*

That was also not going to happen.

She was about to toss the phone on the bed

when she checked the time. Almost one in the afternoon. Working the dinner shift had made her more of a night owl, but she hadn't slept that late in a while. She started to get out of bed when someone knocked on the bedroom door.

"Miss?"

Stanhill. "Just a sec." She hustled into her shorty robe and opened the door. "Hi."

He nodded. "Good afternoon. I hope you slept well."

"I did, thanks." No need to tell him she hadn't really, thanks to his employer playing tonsil hockey with her on the street last night.

"Good. Lady Ellingham has requested you join her for tea."

"Lady Ellingham?"

"Master Ellingham's grandmother." He smiled awkwardly. "They come from a titled line…"

"Sure, that would be fine. What time is tea?" Might as well meet the woman responsible for this whole thing.

"Four o'clock."

"That's plenty of time to get ready, but I'm not sure I can wait that long to eat."

"I'd be happy to make you whatever you'd like."

"Oh, I didn't mean you should make me something." The idea of that seemed odd. She was the one who waited on people, not the other way around. "I can find my way around a kitchen. I'll just get ready then come down and make myself some eggs. If that's okay with you."

He nodded. "Whatever makes you happy, miss."

If only everyone was as agreeable as Stanhill. She shut the door, then jumped into the shower. Half an hour later, she walked into the kitchen, her hair still damp but her makeup done. The space was magazine-worthy. Miles of granite countertops, stainless steel appliances and windows that filled the work space with natural light. Oh, the sweets she could cook up in here...

Stanhill sat at the table, reading a local paper. He looked over the top of it. "There you are, and don't you look lovely?"

She glanced down at her lavender sundress and little white cardigan. "Thanks, I wasn't sure what to wear for tea." Fortunately, she'd packed a few cotton dresses. They didn't take up much space, and this was the South, after all. "You're sure you don't mind me rummaging around in your kitchen?"

"Not at all." He put the paper down to bend his head toward a door near the far wall. "Just stay out of there."

"Basement, right?" She curled her fingers against her palms. There was no way she could pretend to accidentally open that door now.

"Right-o. Shall I show you where things are?"

"All I need is a pan, some eggs and the butter. I'm sure I can figure it out. Oh, and coffee. Lots of coffee."

Hugh wandered in. "I could use some of that myself."

It was unfair that a man could look that sexy while half asleep and unshaven. Her fingers itched to touch the stubble darkening his face. At least he was wearing a robe. Although, besides his pajama pants, there didn't seem to be anything else on under it. Except for a thick silver chain with a quarter-sized disc hanging off it. The stone in the center was carved with some kind of design. The deep vee of naked chest beneath the chain was far more interesting, however. She forced herself to turn, open the fridge and search for the eggs and butter. "Morning."

He sat and grunted a reply, further solidifying his position as a night owl. "You look nice. Did I miss something or do you always dress up for breakfast?"

"Tea with your grandmother." The fridge was well stocked with high-end edibles. She grabbed the eggs (organic, brown, cage-free) and the butter (European, from pastured cows) and went to the stove.

He grunted louder this time. "Bloody hell. I don't remember anything about that. I better go shower."

"Sit down," Stanhill said. "You weren't invited."

"Good," Hugh answered.

Smiling, Stanhill handed her a small frying pan. "Can I fix you a cup of coffee?"

"Yes," Hugh said.

Stanhill looked at him. "I was talking to Miss Givens."

Hugh frowned.

She chewed her lip to keep from laughing. "I can get my own coffee, thank you."

"Nonsense." Stanhill poured two cups but handed the first one to her. "Cream and sugar?"

"That would be perfect, thanks."

He got her the cream (also organic) and sugar (unbleached), then gave Hugh his coffee before returning to the paper.

Hugh took his coffee without a word. He stared over the rim of the cup at her. "Be careful of Didi. She's wily."

Stanhill noisily turned the page.

The butter was just about melted. She cast a glance at Hugh. "And you're not?"

"Not compared to her." Hugh put his cup down. "You have no idea what she's like."

Delaney cracked two eggs into the pan, tossed the shells into the disposal, then leaned her hip against the stove (stainless steel, six burner, restaurant quality). "So tell me."

Stanhill's paper rustled some more.

Hugh took a long pause before answering her. "She can manipulate you into allowing things you wouldn't normally allow."

She crossed her arms. "Like letting a strange woman into your house."

"Exactly."

Her gaze narrowed. "Or letting a strange man kiss you? Sorry, letting a *curious* man kiss you?"

Stanhill's paper went very still.

Hugh leaned back a little, the light in his eyes smoldering with something dark and wicked. His jaw worked, but for several seconds, he said nothing. "Yes. Like that."

She smiled, somehow holding on to her calm exterior, even though she kind of wanted to jump him. "Thanks for the warning. I'll let you know how things go when I get back."

"I'll be waiting. In fact, why don't we go into town for dinner tonight?" Hugh stood and shot Stanhill a look. "Then we can give Stanhill the night off."

Stanhill said nothing.

She nodded. "Sure, that would be nice."

"I'll make the arrangements. I'm sure I can find a spot you'll like." Hugh picked up his coffee, gave her a look that finished melting her insides, and left.

Stanhill drove her to Lady Ellingham's estate. She did a quick Google search on Annabelle, but came up empty. Which sucked but also meant Delaney could say whatever she wanted. Sort of. She put her phone away and watched the scenery.

A house loomed ahead. "Is that the estate?"

"Yes," Stanhill answered.

The house made Hugh's place look like a travel trailer. A really nice travel trailer, but still. Her estate sat across from the winery and looked down over the rolling vineyards. More acreage sprawled out around the property, making it both grand and secluded.

She stared out the car window. "This place is gorgeous. Wow, these people have money." She cringed and looked at Stanhill through the rearview mirror. "Sorry, I really didn't mean that the way it sounded."

He laughed and gave her a wink. "Not to worry, love. They do have money. Not like you were telling tales, eh?"

She sighed. "This is going to be more fancy china and multiple forks, isn't it?"

"I'm afraid so."

She glanced at him. "Is she going to grill me? Should I expect the Spanish Inquisition?"

He shrugged. "She hired you. Shouldn't be too bad."

That failed to instill any confidence in Delaney.

He parked and came around to open her door. When she got out, he handed her a little card. "I've written my mobile on there. Call when you're ready to come home, all right?"

She nodded. "Thanks."

He tipped his head toward the house. "Off you go."

With a nervous smile, she headed to the door and knocked. Stanhill went back to the car, but didn't pull away. A prim woman with kind eyes answered and let her in. "You must be Annabelle."

Delaney nodded. "Yes."

"I'm Alice Bishop, Elenora's assistant. She's in the solarium. I'll show you in."

Delaney followed Alice as Stanhill finally drove away. A broad, winding staircase led off the foyer. The rest of the house was like a European museum, all creamy marble, soaring ceilings and statuary. Their footsteps echoed through the vast space, but the solarium was much cozier. Bright and cheery and filled with plants, except for the back corner, which was shaded by potted palms. Elenora sat at a wrought iron and marble table beneath them.

She stood as Delaney entered. "Hello, there."

"Hello." Delaney squelched the urge to curtsey. For the grandmother of three adult men, she barely looked a day over sixty-five. She must have had work done. Good work. Not the kind that made a woman look like she had a chip clip holding everything together on the back of her neck. "Thank you for inviting me. Your home is incredible."

"Thank you, dear. Please, join me." Elenora pointed to the chair across from her.

Delaney took the seat and tried not to fidget, but she felt as out of place as a meatball in a box of truffles. The table was already set with delicate china cups and plates and scroll-handled silverware.

Alice returned with a tea trolley. An *actual* tea trolley. She poured tea for both of them, then added creamer, sugar and a three-tiered platter of finger sandwiches and petit fours to the table. There were two sets of silver tongs.

"Help yourself, dear." Elenora used her tongs to select a few items and put them on a small plate. "How are things going with Hugh?"

Right to it then. "Good. I'd say good." Delaney picked up her tongs and studied the tiers. The petit fours were gorgeous, all iced like tiny cakes. And the little sandwiches had no crusts, their sides pressed into herbs to give them borders of green.

"Do you have any romantic feelings for him yet?"

Delaney clanked the tongs loudly against the platter. Was that the British way of asking if she'd had sex with him yet? She took a breath and said a mental prayer that she wouldn't break anything. "It's...sort of soon for that, don't you think? I've only been there a day."

"Can you tell if he has any for you?"

He'd kissed her. But sharing that felt like betraying a trust. That kiss had been a moment of intimacy between her and Hugh. Not something his grandmother needed to know about. "I know he likes me. We get along very well. As for romantic feelings..." She smiled as she put a triangle of cream cheese and salmon bordered in dill on her plate. "I think it's going to take a little more time."

Elenora's cool demeanor was a little hard to read. "What do you want out of life, Annabelle?"

What did Annabelle want out of life? Delaney wished Google had been able to help her. "A loving husband, a good marriage, children." All answers Delaney imagined Annabelle would give. Then she gave one of her own, because pretending to be Annabelle was exhausting. "I'd love to have my own shop, too."

Elenora perked up a bit. "What kind of shop?"

Delaney grinned. There was no way to be unhappy talking about candy. "A sweet shop."

"Nocturne Falls already has one of those." Elenora's nostrils flared in annoyance. "Those Kellers are so...unpleasant."

"That's not a sweet shop. That's a candy store."

Her brow furrowed. "What's the difference?"

"I'm talking about a place where everything is made right there. Nothing prepackaged, nothing out of a factory. All of it handmade in small batches. All of it fresh and interesting and local. Premium sweets."

Elenora's interest seemed piqued. "This is something you could do?"

"I could. I can. I do it now in my own kitchen."

Elenora went silent for a few seconds, then her shrewd gaze tapered. "I thought you'd be blonde. I know *Eternamate* has a policy about matching people based on characteristics, but I told Ms. Poirot my grandson likes blondes. His last three girlfriends were all fair-haired beauties."

"Yes, I met Piper."

"Did you?" Elenora paused, somehow straightening further. "Do say. How did that go?"

"About as well as could be expected. She didn't take the break up well, did she?"

"No." Elenora tapped one slender finger on her chin. "Back to the blonde issue. How would you feel about becoming one?"

"I'm sorry, what?" Delaney wasn't sure she'd heard correctly.

"My girl in town is very good. I'm sure she could fit you in if I called—"

"No. Thank you." So much for the connection Delaney thought she'd been making. A tiny bit of anger stiffened her spine. "I'm *not* changing my hair color for a man." She leaned in. "And since those last three girlfriends couldn't get Hugh to commit, maybe blondes really aren't his thing."

Elenora's mouth opened, and for a moment, Delaney thought she'd just blown it. Then Elenora laughed. "You've got ambition *and* guts, child. I'll give you that." She added sugar to her tea. "Hugh could use a little of that in his life. Someone to stir things up. Get him out of that lab."

"Lab?" Delaney ate her little sandwich. The eggs she had for breakfast hadn't really been enough.

"I'm sure he hasn't shown it to you. It's in his basement."

"No, he hasn't." What on earth did he do down there that was off limits? Curiosity burned in her like a batch of hot sugar. "What kind of lab is it?"

The older woman barked out a very unladylike laugh. "You think he shares that with me?" She reached for another petit four, and a bracelet slipped from the wrist of her lace jacket. A large, familiar pendant dangled from it.

Delaney stared at it. "That's a pretty little charm. Is it a family thing? Looks like the same one Hugh wears on a chain."

"You could say it's a family crest of sorts." A sly look crept into Elenora's eyes. "You've seen my grandson without his shirt."

"No. I saw him in his robe in the kitchen this afternoon and noticed it."

She nodded like she didn't quite believe Delaney's explanation. "It's our family emblem." She put her hand on her lap below the table, hiding the charm from further scrutiny. "As I'm sure you can understand, it's very important to me that Hugh be happy. I believe you can bring him that happiness. I want you to do whatever it takes to make him fall in love with you."

"I'm not sure I know what you mean." If the woman was hinting that Delaney sleep with him, well, that was kind of an icky thing for a grandmother to suggest.

"I'm not sure I do either. And if I knew what it was going to take, I'd tell you." She sat back and sighed. "What I do know is men are simple creatures. They like to be complimented. To feel powerful. And, especially important, to feel useful."

Delaney nodded. "I appreciate your advice. I will do my best." Not really. But what else was she going to say? *Hey, I'm just hiding out from the mob, so don't get your hopes up.* "Thirty days isn't a long time."

Elenora nodded thoughtfully. "Then perhaps more incentive is needed. Get him to propose and set a date for the wedding before that time is up and you'll have your sweet shop. I'll finance everything you need from the building to the supplies, right down to the pretty little boxes with your name on them, if that's what you want."

Boxes with her name on them. Delaney's heart stuttered at the offer. But it meant manipulating

Hugh into marrying her. She forced herself to smile, even though the thought of using another person that way made her a little ill. "That's a very generous offer, Mrs. Ellingham."

"So you'll think about it?"

"Yes." It was probably all she'd think about. Her dream was being dangled in front of her like a sugar-crusted carrot.

"Excellent. Let's finish our tea, shall we?"

Hugh shook his head. "She can't stay here."

"Ready to give up the daylight hours, are you?" Stanhill took a seat on one of the lab's metal stools.

"No." Hugh paced in front of his work table, the lunch Stanhill had brought down completely ignored. "But that woman is…bothering me."

"You mean the way she forced you to kiss her."

"She didn't make me—" Hugh frowned. "That was merely an experiment to see if there was *anything* there."

Stanhill's small grin was infuriating. "I'd ask what the conclusion was, but I can see that for myself."

"It was nothing. It meant nothing." It had meant too much.

"You're a horrifically bad liar, you know that?"

Hugh slumped against the counter. "I can't think, I can't work…it's awful."

"Is it really all that bad? Maybe she's the one. Why is that such a ghastly thing?"

Hugh glared at him. "You know why."

"And you know from the research you've done that Juliette's failure to survive the transformation was a rare occurrence."

Hugh spat out the next thing he could think of. "Women are fickle."

"That's Sebastian's story, not yours."

"Then what if I'm the one who changes my mind?"

"Like Julian? You're much more mature when it comes to relationships than your brother. Stop making excuses." Stanhill shook his head. "You enjoy spending time with her?"

"Yes," he groused. Stanhill's questions had a pretty clear path.

"And you get along well?"

"Yes." They did. He'd yet to find an irritating thing about her, although it was early days yet.

"Then have a go at it. See what happens. It may come to nothing."

"And it may lead to...something." And the possibility of that something was unsettling. Hugh started pacing again. "She came here to get married, don't forget that."

"But she didn't exactly arrive with a wedding dress packed, did she?" Stanhill sighed. "Didi is a rotten piece of work for setting this whole thing up.

I know she means well, but—"

"And that's another thing." Hugh spun around. "Who knows what that woman is putting into Annabelle's head at this very moment?" Why couldn't his grandmother just stay out of his life? Of course, then he'd never have met Annabelle. But oh, he'd pay for it the rest of his life if things went the way Didi wanted. Which they would *not*.

Stanhill shrugged one shoulder. "Undoubtedly she's singing your praises and urging the woman to make an honest man of you, but Annabelle strikes me as a woman with her own mind. Don't you think?"

Hugh raked a hand through his hair. Stanhill had finally said something that made sense. "She does."

"Then set aside the concerns about her surviving the transition to vampire and tell me why do you think this—she—is bothering you so much?"

Hugh looked at the far wall of equipment. "Can you see yourself sharing your life with a woman after all these years alone?" Even as he spoke the words, he knew that wasn't the real reason commitment eluded him. Yes, he enjoyed his time alone and loathed any thought of giving it up, but that was only a small part of what worried him. There was no putting aside the fact that Annabelle would have to face death if she wanted to spend the rest of her life with him. It was too much to ask.

Too much to risk. Losing another woman he loved that way would end him. He could feel it.

"I wouldn't call life with you solitary confinement, but I ken what you're saying. There'd be some adjustments to make for sure. But love—"

"Love. Bah. Look at my brothers then tell me that really exists."

"Look at your parents and your grandparents and tell me it doesn't. Look at your life with Juliette."

"That's dirty pool."

Stanhill brushed a bit of lint from his trousers. "Get out of your own way. She's only here for a month—"

"Twenty-eight more days."

"Not that you're counting." Stanhill's phone chimed. He straightened as he pulled it from his pocket. "Just give the whole thing a chance. At the very least, you'll make your grandmother happy and keep her from pulling a stunt like this again." He glanced at the phone and made an odd face. "I have to go."

"Annabelle?"

"So it seems." He headed for the steps.

"I might go see Sebastian."

"You do that," Stanhill called back. "Maybe you should feed too. You sound like you could use a topping off."

"I fed yesterday, for your information." But

Stanhill had already shut the cellar door.

Hugh gripped the edge of the worktable and studied the notes before him, but it was impossible to make sense of them with the memory of last night still stuck in his head. And trying to erase it to clear the way for anything scientific was equally pointless. All his brain wanted to do was replay that kiss. Taste again the sweet softness of her mouth. Feel the tentative, searching way she'd kissed him back. The silkiness of her hair as it slid between his fingers. The press of her body against—

"Bloody hell!"

Enough. He knew one surefire way to change his thinking. He stormed up the stairs, grabbed his keys and headed for his eldest brother's home. There was no question Sebastian would be there. Sebastian was *always* home.

Sure enough, when Hugh rang the bell, Sebastian's man ushered him into the study. Sebastian sat at his desk, ledgers spread out before him. Sebastian kept the books for the family business and preferred to do things the old-fashioned way, with pencil and paper, before entering it all into the computer. He looked up. "Hugh. What brings you by?"

Hugh took a seat in one of the high-backed leather chairs fronting Sebastian's desk. "I need advice."

"Always happy to help. What can I do for you?"

Hugh frowned, trying to find exactly the right words. "I need to know how you got over Evangeline."

Sebastian's smile flat-lined and angry embers lit his gaze. "I've asked you and Julian not to speak her name in my house."

Hugh nodded. "I know, and I wouldn't, but getting over her, how you did it, is something I need to understand how to do too."

"Then that's going to be a problem."

"Why's that?"

Sebastian pulled out a bottle of whiskey and two glasses. "Because I never have gotten over her." He poured a dram into both glasses, then pushed one toward Hugh. "You may not want this, but I do."

Hugh stared at him. "Are you telling me you're still in love with her?"

Sebastian drained his glass, refilled it, then turned his chair toward the windows. "You think I'd be this miserable if I wasn't?" He drained the second glass. "Why are you asking me about her anyway? You've never been heartsick over one of your entanglements before."

"It's not that exactly. It's..." Hugh gave him the quick and dirty version of Annabelle coming to stay with him.

Sebastian shook his head. "Didi is out of control. If I were you, I'd give her the damn amulet and be done with it."

"Yes, but you rarely leave the house anyway."

"We're vampires. It's unnatural for us to be outside when the sun's up."

Hugh laughed. "We're vampires. Being vampires is unnatural."

Sebastian topped off his whiskey. "Speaking of, how's the formula coming?"

"I thought I'd had a breakthrough, but the last batch only held out for five minutes." A little of his blood mixed with the formula, then set beneath UV lamps. Same test. Same miserable results.

"And then?" Sebastian quirked a brow in interest.

"Up in flames."

Sebastian made a face. "Damn shame."

"I am getting closer, though. The one before that only went thirty seconds."

Sebastian straightened the pencil on his desk so it was perfectly parallel to the ledger page. "We need that formula. I love Didi, but she uses those amulets against us too often. And I'd like to travel."

"Leave your house? I'm aghast." Hugh smirked. "Where do you want to go?"

"Europe. Asia. Anywhere that isn't part of Didi's domain."

"You want to look for Evangeline."

Sebastian changed the subject. "About this woman...do you have feelings for her?"

"It's too soon to call whatever's happening feelings, but she definitely affects me."

"That's too bad. Sounds like it might be too late for you to stop the natural order of things then."

"Natural order?"

"You fall in love, she breaks your heart, you suffer." His brother capped the whiskey bottle. "But if you're not going to give Didi the amulet back, you've got no choice but to go along with it and at least make a decent show of things."

Hugh stood. "That's what I was afraid you'd say. Bloody lot of good you are."

"Just don't marry her." Sebastian turned back toward the windows. "That's when the hell really begins."

Delaney didn't wait for Stanhill to open her door. She jumped into the car as soon as he came to a stop.

He twisted to face her. Something unspoken clouded his gaze. "How did it go?"

She stared at the enormous manor house she'd just left. "It was…interesting." She met his eyes. "Mrs. Ellingham is a woman with a very clear idea of how things should go, isn't she?"

He nodded. "Yes. And it's almost always in her direction."

Delaney laughed softly. "I'm glad it's over." She looked closer at him. "Is everything okay?"

He hesitated. "Why do you ask?"

"You seem not quite yourself."

"Everything's fine. Let's go home, shall we?" He turned around and threw the car into drive without waiting for her answer.

He was quiet the rest of the way home, so she used the time to check news on her phone. Still no mention of a body, but there were more texts from Russell and Samantha, both asking where she was and if she was okay.

Delaney deleted both messages.

When they got back to the house, Stanhill unlocked the side door that went through a mudroom and into the kitchen. He waited for her to enter then shut and locked the door behind her.

Weird, but not that weird. "Is Hugh home?"

"No, he's at his brother's." Stanhill leaned against the granite counter top. "We need to talk."

She'd been headed upstairs, but his words stopped her. "We do?"

He nodded, pulled out his phone and turned it around so she could see the screen. "Who's D. James?"

His caller ID had shown her real name when she'd called to be picked up. Fear dried out her mouth and turned her tongue to dust. "I can explain…" She could. If she didn't lie. And she was so tired of lying.

"I'm waiting." The slightly scary gleam in his eyes strengthened her resolve

She pulled out a chair and sat at the kitchen table. Just in case her nerves caused her knees to buckle. "I'm D. James. Delaney, actually."

She took a deep breath, but already the act of coming clean was easing her mind. Whatever the consequences, she'd face them. She explained everything—about the shooting, about stealing the file, about hiding out from her mobbed-up boss.

Stanhill's face remained virtually unchanged through her story. He was clearly angry. And protective of Hugh. When she was finished, he nodded. Then, after what felt like an hour but was probably four or five seconds, he said, "I see."

The two words sounded like a death sentence. She stood, unable to make eye contact. "I'll go pack my things."

"Why?"

She looked at him. "Aren't you going to tell me to leave?"

He shook his head slowly. "No." He came over and sat at the table. "What you did, you did out of self-preservation, yes?"

"Yes."

"Can't fault that."

She sat back down. "You can't?"

"Your boss sounds like a dangerous man."

"I had no idea until I saw him with that gun."

"And you're not here to hurt Hugh in any way, are you?"

Her brows pulled together. "Not at all. I swear it."

"What else do you know about him?"

Was this a test? "He's wealthy. Guarded. And a little secretive. But I guess a lot of wealthy people are like that."

Something worked through Stanhill's brain. She could see it in his eyes. "Then I see no reason why you can't stay."

Her mouth came open a bit. "Really?"

Stanhill nodded. "Between us, for all Hugh's blathering about this arrangement, I think he quite enjoys your company."

"I'm not sure he'll still feel that way after he finds out I've been lying to him." She traced the grain of the wood table. "I'll tell him tonight at dinner. At least we'll be in public. That should keep the scene-making to a minimum."

"Why don't you hold off on filling him in?"

She stared at Stanhill. "Do you think that's the best idea?" She wasn't sure what surprised her more—Stanhill's willingness to collude with her or his desire to keep his employer in the dark.

"I know Hugh very well. If he's not in the right mood for this kind of news, it could go badly. And you don't want to ruin your dinner. Or mine. I've got a date tonight myself." Stanhill patted her hand. "When he's in a good mood, we'll tell him together."

She couldn't argue that Stanhill knew Hugh better than she did. And she liked that he didn't want to keep the news from Hugh indefinitely. "Why are you doing this for me?"

He smiled. "I like you. You're in a spot of trouble that's not of your own doing, and you make Hugh happy. I'd surmise he makes you happy as well, yes?"

She relaxed. "He's not bad company. Not at all."

"I'd hate to see either of you miss out on a chance for something more all because of a little misunderstanding."

Lying about who she was seemed like more than a little misunderstanding. "I should go get dressed for dinner." She stood but didn't leave the kitchen. "You know I'm not here looking for a husband in any way, shape, or form."

"I know." He got to his feet. "Funny what you find when you least expect it."

Hugh shut the door behind him harder than necessary as he entered the house. His conversation with Sebastian had done nothing to better his mood or help him make a decision. So far he had Stanhill for and Sebastian against. Talking to Julian and his grandmother would only add another check in each column. The decision about pursuing Annabelle was firmly in his court.

Maybe he was worrying about nothing. Maybe they'd have a dreadful evening and that would be that. Or maybe his grandmother had filled Annabelle's head with the kinds of promises and ideas that changed a woman's mind and turned her into a marriage-hungry maniac. Hugh leaned against the door and closed his eyes.

All he wanted to do was kiss Annabelle some more. But he also didn't want to lead her on. Did that make him just like Julian? He groaned.

"Something wrong?"

Hugh opened his eyes. Stanhill stood at the entrance of the foyer. Hugh frowned. "I don't know. What happened with Annabelle and Didi?"

Stanhill shrugged. "Not much of anything that I'm aware of."

"Where is she?"

"At her own estate, I'd imagine."

Hugh growled softly. The twinkle in Stanhill's eyes said the man knew exactly what Hugh had meant. "Annabelle, not my grandmother."

"Take your mood out on someone else. I'm your rook, not your servant." Stanhill frowned at him.

"A decision I regret daily." He could give as good as he got. "Did she come home from Didi's talking marriage?"

"No. More about how your grandmother seemed like a woman who enjoyed getting her way."

"That's an accurate assessment." Maybe Annabelle had kept her head about her. "Where did you say she is?"

"I didn't, but she's upstairs. Getting ready for the dinner you promised her."

Hugh ground his back teeth for a second. "Blast it. I completely forgot about making reservations." With the Panic Parade this weekend, the town was crowded. And it was Friday night. The restaurants, at least the good ones, might be tricky to get into.

"Any chance you made some for me?"

"No. And I'm off to the movies with Corette." He waggled his brows. "Now there's a fine woman."

"She's got three girls. That's a lot of responsibility."

Stanhill rolled his eyes. "Her daughters are twenty-eight, twenty-nine and thirty. It's not like Corette's trying to find them a new daddy."

"She's also a witch. Literally. They all are. That doesn't bother you?" He wasn't especially fond of witches. Not with the way Alice Bishop plotted so willingly with Didi and her schemes.

"I'm not the one beholden to a witch's magic to keep me from crisping up in the sun's light, so no, it doesn't bother me. Corette is a fine, upstanding citizen. And an amply endowed one at that."

"I don't need details."

Stanhill's brow furrowed. "Have you and Annabelle had any discussion about who you really are?"

"You mean that I'm a vampire? No."

Stanhill nodded. "I'd suggest you keep it that way. For now."

"Why?" He'd actually been waiting for Annabelle to broach the subject just to see how eager she was about the whole thing.

Stanhill waved his hand as he walked away. "I don't really have time to explain, I've got woo to pitch."

Hugh stifled a growl. Love ruined everything. He pulled out his cell phone and started dialing restaurants as he walked upstairs to his room. By the time he'd shut the door, his first two choices were out unless they wanted to eat either five minutes from now or three hours. Sometimes, being an Ellingham didn't make that much of a difference.

He sat in the big leather reading chair by the fireplace and dialed the third. They had a cancellation. Or they were making a spot for him. Either way, he took the reservation. It only gave them an hour to get there. Hopefully, that would be enough time for Annabelle to get ready. He got up and walked down the hall to her room to let her know.

He paused at the sound of her voice coming through the closed door.

"Who's a good boy? Cappy is, that's who."

Hugh grinned. She was talking to her cat. There was something endearing about that. He knocked. "Annabelle? Our reservation is in less than an hour. Can you be ready in —"

She opened the door. "I'm ready now."

She wore the same sundress she'd had on earlier, minus the cardigan, and her hair was twisted up, revealing the exquisite expanse of her bare neck and shoulders. The few tendrils that drifted around her face only added to her loveliness. He didn't say anything for a moment, just enjoyed the view.

She plucked at the sides of the dress, pulling the lavender cotton away from her body and drawing his attention down to her shapely legs. The hem skimmed her knees. "Unless this isn't the right thing to wear. I can change." She glanced back in the room. "Not that I have that many other options."

"No," he said. "It's perfect." As was she. Not quite ready to break the moment, he gestured at the cat. The beast was sprawled on his back on the floor, legs akimbo, belly exposed. He looked like a fluffy throw rug. "How's Captain doing?"

She smiled. "He's having an awful time adjusting. As you can see."

Hugh laughed. "Does he like catnip? We could stop by the pet store and pick some up for him after dinner." Where had that come from? He couldn't remember a time in his life he'd ever even used the word catnip, let alone thought about buying any.

Her eyes lit up, setting them ablaze like emeralds in the sun. "There's a pet store? That would be awesome!"

"Then it's a plan. You look lovely, by the way. I should go get ready. I'll be back in a few minutes."

"Okay. I'm going to hang out with Captain until then."

"He doesn't have to stay cooped up in this room,

you know. He can have the run of the house. Unless you think he's going to shred the drapes and do his business on the rugs."

She made a face. "Captain would never do that."

"I didn't mean to imply—"

"He's fine in here."

So much for his attempt at nice. "How about tomorrow afternoon we take him outside and let him romp in the garden a bit? Before we go to the parade."

She smiled, her demeanor instantly softening. "That would be nice. Although don't expect too much romping."

"Got it." He gave her a nod. "Back as soon as I'm ready."

Which turned out to be sixteen minutes, twenty-nine seconds. He collected her, then drove them into town, but the only parking spot he could find was three blocks away.

He helped her out of the car without staring too hard at her legs. "We have a little bit of a walk." He pointed them in the right direction, and they set off.

She kept pace with him, easily matching his long stride. "Where are we eating?"

"The Poisoned Apple. Sort of a pub."

"You must feel right at home there."

"I can't say I ever went to places like that when I lived in England." Mostly because places like that didn't exist in 1665. "But their beer selection isn't bad."

"The town is even busier than it was last night."

"Wait until we come back for the parade." She'd yet to link her arm through his as she'd done before. He couldn't help but wonder why. He wanted to take her hand, but he wasn't going to push things.

When they reached the pub, he knew how lucky he'd been to get that cancellation. People stood around the door, pagers in hand as they waited for tables. He made a path to the door for them and got her inside. "I'll let them know we're here, but we're a little early. You want to find us a spot at the bar?"

She nodded. "What do you want to drink?"

"Guinness."

"Of course you do." With a smile, she headed deeper into the crowd as he went in the opposite direction to the hostess stand and gave his name.

Once he'd checked in and gotten a pager, he worked his way to the bar to find her. He stopped a few feet away as soon as he saw who Annabelle was sitting next to.

Piper.

Getting a seat at the bar had been pure chance, a matter of being in the right place at the right time.

Delaney focused on getting the bartender's attention, finally snagging him so she could place her order: a Guinness for Hugh and a white wine for her. She knew from her restaurant days that Guinness wasn't a quick pour, so she twisted in her seat to watch the crowd and put the back end of the bar behind her.

The people who came to Nocturne Falls clearly loved the whole Halloween vibe. A few of them wore masks, just the little Zorro kind that covered their eyes. Some of the women had their faces painted. Actually, so did some of the guys. One of them wore an eye patch and a pirate hat. It was impossible not to grin surrounded by such festivity.

She spotted Hugh on the other side of the pirate. She waved her hand. "Hugh," she shouted above the din. "Over here."

He stood there, looking like he smelled a barrel of week-old fish. Finally, he moved forward, coming around to her side. "We should go wait by the door."

"Our drinks aren't ready."

The woman behind Delaney leaned in. "Isn't this cozy?"

Delaney realized the barrel of week-old fish was the Barbie doll sitting next to her. And that Barbie doll was Piper. What a craptastic coincidence. Accompanying Piper was her friend Skipper, or whatever the other chick's name was. Apparently, it was girls' night out in Nocturne Falls.

If this town got any smaller, it would be the social equivalent of wearing Spanx.

Wine glazed Piper's gaze. "I see he hasn't broken up with you yet."

"Out with a friend?" Delaney's attempt to steer the conversation in a new direction was ignored.

"Piper, you made your point the first time we met. Enough." Hugh positioned himself between Delaney and Piper.

"Oh, you like telling women when stuff is over, don't you?" Piper gestured with her wine glass at Delaney, almost sloshing the wine over the rim. "He *will* break up with you, you know. It's only a matter of time."

"So you said, but your history isn't my future," Delaney answered quietly. "And you really need to stop blaming Hugh for *you* not being the right woman for him. The more you shriek about it, the more people are going to see his side of things."

Piper's jaw dropped. She started to get off her bar stool, but her girlfriend grabbed her arm and whispered something in her ear.

Having no desire to create more of a ruckus than they already had, Delaney slid off the bar stool and hooked her arm through Hugh's. Through a miracle of the karma fairy, the bartender delivered their drinks and check at that exact moment.

She turned to Hugh. "Take care of the bill, will you, sweetheart? I'd like to go somewhere else."

She smiled at Piper, who was still muttering, while Hugh gave a nod to the bartender and threw some bills down on the drinks they were abandoning. "You sure you want to go?"

"Yes. Now."

"You got it." Hugh grabbed her hand tight and started through the crowd.

"Bye, *Annabelle*," Piper called out over the crowd.

When they were out the door, she dropped the smile and took a breath. "Your ex is a real winner. It took you five months to figure out she wasn't the one?"

"I knew well before then, but she was pleasant enough. To me. I'm sorry about all that back there." Hugh's mouth curved into an appreciative smile. "That was quite the performance, *sweetheart*."

"Did I overstep? I'm sorry if I—"

"No, not at all." His gaze grew thoughtful. Then he leaned in and, right there on the street, kissed her on the mouth.

The kiss was over almost before it started, but it was still long enough to make her heart stutter in her chest. Wow, he smelled good. Masculine in a dark, earthy way. "What was that for?"

"We're supposed to be a couple, aren't we?" He winked at her. "Plus, I don't think I've ever had a woman stick up for me like that. You've done it twice now."

Delaney hiked the strap of her purse higher on her shoulder. "Maybe women don't stick up for you because what she said is true."

His smile dimmed a bit. "I realize that."

She inclined her head and smiled a little. "It might have been a tiny bit fun. I don't go in for confrontation much, but something got into me."

A curious twinkle lit his eyes. "Maybe tea with my grandmother? That woman is enough to push anyone to their breaking point."

"Maybe." That tea had given her a lot to think about. Like how close the dream of owning her own shop was, and how it was never going to happen. Because it couldn't without her doing things she'd regret later, but it was fun to dream. Her stomach rumbled. "Okay, despite asking to leave, I am really hungry."

He glanced down the street. "Town is packed tonight. I'm not sure where else we can get in."

"Do we have to get in somewhere? Can't we just grab a slice?"

"Of pizza?" His brows rose. "That's okay with you?"

"All day long. Then the pet store." Because while she was fine missing out on a snazzy dinner, she was not okay with Cappy being denied a new toy.

With a laugh, he nodded. "You got it." He offered her his arm.

She took it, and they started walking. By the time they'd stuffed themselves on pizza, which was shockingly good despite not being made in New York, and bought one of every kind of catnip creation the pet store offered (which Hugh had insisted on paying for), she'd had a great evening even with the rocky start.

Hugh was so easy to spend time with. Maybe once they got home, Stanhill would see how good a mood Hugh was in and she could finally confess her secret. The idea scared the cookies out of her, but he was too nice a guy to keep up the lying.

Hugh drove them home, the banter between them non-stop until he pulled into the driveway and uttered a curse.

An unfamiliar car was parked ahead of them, but it had Georgia plates so Delaney saw no immediate reason to panic. "Someone you know?"

He nodded. "Someone we both know. Unfortunately. Piper."

Hugh got out of the car and went around to open Annabelle's door. He'd had issues with some of his exes before, but nothing like this. He was going to put an end to this business with Piper once and for all, because if *he* was tired of it, he could only imagine what Annabelle must be feeling.

He helped her out of the car. "I will take care of this, I promise."

She nodded. "Be firm but kind. The poor woman is clearly not over you."

Stanhill met them at the door. "We have company."

Hugh frowned. "I saw her car. What room?"

"Library. I'll be in my quarters."

"I'd rather you come in with us," Hugh said.

"You would?"

"In case I need her bodily removed."

Stanhill gave a quick nod. "All right then."

Hugh led the way into the house, Annabelle behind him and Stanhill bringing up the rear. Hugh marched straight to the library and yanked the pocket doors wide. His ex stood there in all her tiresome, blond glory. "Piper, what are you doing here?"

She stood, oblivious to his irritation. "You may not want me, but you're going to want to listen to what I have to tell you."

Her expression reeked of accusation, but there was no wavering in her movements. If she'd been tipsy at the pub, she was sober now. "I did a little *investigating* on your new girlfriend. Found some very interesting things."

Annabelle stiffened. "You have no right to pry into my life."

Hugh held up his hand. "I already know what you're going to say."

Piper frowned. "You do?"

"Yes. Ms. Givens is a client of Eternamate, a match making agency. I know that because my grandmother is the one who contracted Eternamate to find me a match."

Piper's eyes rounded. "Oh, I *knew* about that. Not the part about Elenora setting it all up, though." Her drawl thickened when she was drunk, this time on power rather than alcohol. "That is rich, I tell you. Rich."

Annabelle tugged on his sleeve. She looked slightly green. "Hugh, we need to talk."

"As soon as I get Piper out of here, but if you want to leave, I understand—"

Piper's laugh cut him off. "This really is turning out better than I expected." She snapped her fingers at Annabelle. "Stay, sweetie, y'all gonna want to hear this."

She sauntered toward Hugh. "I wasn't talking about the match making thing, but that is a nice little tidbit. What I was referring to is your girlfriend here, this *Annabelle Givens*"—she made finger quotes around the name—"she's an impostor. A big ol' phony."

"Hugh." Annabelle's voice sounded on the verge of a sob.

"Enough of your games, Piper." Anger clouded Hugh's vision for a moment. He was sick of her petty jealous and ridiculous accusations.

She splayed her fingers over her chest and grinned. "It doesn't take a newspaper reporter to use Google, Hugh darling. You really ought to do a little more checking up on the women you invite into your home."

"I'd say," Stanhill groused. "Perhaps Annabelle and I should leave—"

"Stay, both of you. Piper wanted an audience. Now we can all see what a liar she is. Are you done, Piper? Because I am." Hugh was on the verge of throwing her out. Or maybe he'd call Sheriff Merrow and see if he could have her arrested.

"I'm not lying, Hugh." Piper's smile widened. "Annabelle Givens is from upstate New York."

"I already know that—"

"Where she is currently at *home*." Piper inspected her nails. "I know this because I spoke with her before arriving here. She told me all about Eternamate and how her match with you was canceled by the agency."

Her smile disappeared, and she pointed at Annabelle. "Which means this woman cannot be Annabelle Givens."

"I'm sure there's been some kind of mix-up." He looked at Annabelle. "Tell her she's wrong."

"I can't." Annabelle shook her head slowly, almost dislodging the line of tears clinging to her lower lashes. "I'm so sorry."

A pit opened up in his stomach. "What? Who the hell are you?"

She twisted her hands together. "I'd rather not say in front of—"

"Your name. *Now*." He could feel the darkness within him rising up, a heated wire coiling around his spine.

"Hugh," Stanhill started forward.

Hugh put his hand up to hold off his rook. "I'm waiting."

"Delaney. James."

124

Stanhill took another step. "Hugh, you need to—"

"Get Piper out of here." His gaze stayed fixed on the impostor who'd been taking advantage of his hospitality. "*Delaney* and I have a lot to discuss."

Stanhill's earlier admonition not to say anything to Annabelle about being a vampire came ringing back. He glared at his rook. "You knew about this."

Stanhill had Piper by the arm, but the woman wasn't putting up a fuss. She seemed to be content to go now that she'd dropped her bomb. He gave Hugh a nod, which was answer enough. "Don't do anything rash. I'll be right back."

Hugh returned his attention to Delaney. If that was even her real name. "You want to explain why the real Annabelle isn't here?"

She looked deflated but a little defiant, too. "She's at home, just like Piper said. I called her and pretended to work for Eternamate and canceled her match, also just like Piper said."

"Why? What's your game? Are you after my money?" Or worse, maybe she'd been sent by another vampire to steal his formulations. There were many who'd go to great lengths for the ability to walk in the sun. Except he wasn't there yet. Of course, with the amulet's power, it must seem to other vampires that he had indeed cracked the code.

The blasted thing was nothing but trouble.

She shook her head. "I didn't know a thing

about you except where you lived until I got here. You could have been a pauper for all I knew. And that's the truth."

"Then why?"

"To save her neck," Stanhill answered as he walked back in.

"So you did know," Hugh snarled. "Bloody hell. To think I can't trust you after all these years."

"You can trust me just fine. I only found out this afternoon. I told her not to tell you until I was sure you were in a good mood."

"Well, that worked out beautifully." He took a moment. "What do you mean to save her neck?"

Stanhill looked at Delaney. "Tell him exactly what you told me."

She inhaled before she began. "My boss shot a man and I saw the whole thing." She explained how she'd been in the kitchen of the restaurant she'd worked at and how the whole affair had gone down. Fear tugged at her mouth as she spoke. "He knew I was there."

She sat on one of the couches and wrapped her arms around her torso. "Stealing Annabelle's file wasn't a plan so much as a way out that presented itself. I was only thinking about staying alive. I apologize for lying to you. That was wrong and I'm sorry."

She put her head in her hands and sighed deeply.

Her story had taken most of the fight and the anger out of him. It certainly explained why she'd come with so few things and why she didn't seem in a rush to get married.

Stanhill went to her side to comfort her, and Hugh felt the slightest pang of jealousy. Which was just another type of chemistry.

Bloody hell.

"Stanhill, if you could give us a moment."

The man looked up, surprise in his eyes, perhaps at the softness of Hugh's tone. "Of course." He patted Delaney's shoulder. "It'll be all right, miss."

After he'd left and closed the doors behind him, Hugh approached. He sat on the coffee table in front of her. "In the time you've been here, have you been pretending about anything else besides being Annabelle?"

She looked up at him. "I'm not sure what you're getting at."

"Have you...been yourself? Or have you been the woman you thought I expected?"

She made a face. "Sorry, just me. I suck at lying. Usually." She sat back, her chest rising and falling with a slow inhale. "This whole mess is...I'm sorry. I wanted to tell you sooner but Stanhill told me to wait."

He nodded. "The thing is...if that really was you I was getting to know..." He couldn't believe what he was about to say. "I like that person."

Some of the angst left her eyes. "Thanks. I like you too. And since we're being honest, you're all right for a rich guy who doesn't seem to have an actual job."

"I have a job." It just wasn't one he could talk about.

She crossed her arms. "You mean filling in for Julian on occasion?" She shook her head. "You don't exactly strike me as the sexy vampire type. Sexy, yes. Vampire, no."

She thought he was sexy. He almost smiled but the thought of her reaction when and if she found out he really *was* a vampire stopped him. "Delaney suits you a lot better than Annabelle."

"That works out for me then, doesn't it?"

He wasn't quite sure where her attitude was coming from. After all, she was the one who'd been lying. "Is there something else going on that I don't know about?"

She stared at him for a long, hard second. "I'm just waiting for you to say whatever you have to say so I can get going. Finding a cheap motel that takes animals isn't going to be easy."

"You're not going to a motel. So long as you swear you're not lying to me about anything else, I see no reason you and Captain shouldn't stay here."

Her mouth opened slightly. "You mean that?"

He nodded.

"I swear I'm not lying to you about anything else." The honesty in her eyes confirmed that.

"Good. I do have one condition for you staying here."

She raised her brows. "And that is?"

"I expect you to stick to our pact. Thirty days."

She frowned. "Is that why you want me to stay? So you don't lose your inheritance?"

"I don't care about the inheritance. I don't need it." It wasn't the truth anyway, which was ironic considering he'd just asked her if she was lying about anything else. His omissions were far greater than hers.

He paused. And added to the lie. "I just want to make my grandmother happy." Actually, he just wanted keep his amulet. But the idea of Delaney leaving seemed far worse than losing his ability to daywalk.

He hesitated. That wasn't the only reason he wanted her to stay. "I also don't want you to get hurt."

Her mouth bent in the smallest of smiles. "Thank you."

"I'm going to call Sheriff Merrow."

The smile vanished and alarm bracketed her eyes "Why?"

He took her hand, reveling in the warmth of her skin. "Because I want to make sure you're not in any danger. You said you called the cops, but their apparent lack of response concerns me. This is a murder we're talking about."

"I know. Something should have happened by now. I've seen no report about a body. Maybe Rastinelli didn't really shoot that guy."

"No body. No evidence. That could explain the lack of action."

"They have some evidence. I sent them the video I took."

"Then your suspicion about Rastinelli having a man on the force is very likely correct. Even more reason to talk to Merrow about this."

Plus, it never hurt to have a werewolf in your corner.

Delaney gave Captain a kiss on the head and inhaled his sweet kitty smell. "We dodged a bullet there, Cappy." Which was a totally apropos statement considering the circumstances.

She was relieved that the truth was out. Hugh had handled it far better than she'd expected. Of course, he still needed her or he'd lose his inheritance. She was okay with that. She was using him. He might as well get something out of the deal.

His decision to call the sheriff on her behalf was unexpected. And caring. It made her feel even worse for lying to him in the first place. Maybe she'd find out from Stanhill what kind of sweets he liked and whip him up a batch of something. It was the least she could do.

"Delaney?" he called upstairs. "Sheriff Merrow's here. We're in the library."

She left Cappy on the bed and ran down the hall. "Coming."

When she got downstairs, Stanhill was serving coffee to a beast of a man barely contained in a cop uniform. Sheriff Merrow's resting face looked permanently unimpressed. His thick dark hair was on the long side of short. Probably as long as he could get away with, being a sheriff. She guessed if he smiled, he'd be pretty handsome. She also guessed smiling wasn't big on his list of things to do.

Hugh introduced her. "Delaney, this is Sheriff Hank Merrow. Sheriff, this is Delaney James."

Sheriff Merrow nodded and put his coffee on the side table as they all sat. "Mr. Ellingham tells me you witnessed a murder?"

"And recorded it." She explained everything she'd seen, heard and captured in as much detail as she remembered, including her less than satisfactory call to the Brooklyn PD. "That's really all there is to it. Anthony Rastinelli, my boss—"

"Ex-boss," Hugh corrected. "You're not going back to work for him."

She nodded. "That's for sure." She looked at the sheriff. "He's never done anything to frighten me before, but seeing that side of him scared me to death."

Sheriff Merrow nodded. "I'll find out everything I can about the man. Has he tried to contact you?"

"No—actually, yes. He texted me. Offered me a promotion."

Merrow snorted. "Anyone else tried to contact you since you've been here?"

"One of the girls I worked with at the restaurant, Samantha. She said if I didn't show up, Rastinelli was going to call the cops. And my ex-boyfriend."

"Your ex texted you?" Hugh's eyes narrowed.

"Yes. But I haven't responded to any of the texts."

"Good," Sheriff Merrow said. "I'd like the contact information and full names for those people as well. I'll need a copy of the video, too. Wouldn't mind looking at the texts, either. If this Rastinelli is involved in some kind of crime syndicate, you have no idea who's on his payroll."

The idea sent a new shockwave of fear through Delaney. "Wow. I never even thought about that." She stood. "I'll run upstairs and get my phone, then I can give you all that info."

Hugh and Sheriff Merrow both got to their feet as she left. She flew up the stairs and grabbed her phone, then hustled back down. It was nice to have powerful men like Hugh and the sheriff get all proactive about helping her out. It was a new feeling, and one she liked very much.

As she rejoined them in the library, another voice sounded from the front of the house. "What's going on? Why is the sheriff's car out front?"

Stanhill came in with Elenora in tow, his face a mask of consternation. "Your grandmother is here. In case you hadn't heard."

Sheriff Merrow stood.

Hugh got to his feet as well, sighing softly. "Good evening, Grandmamma. What brings you by?"

Without Hugh's asking, Stanhill slipped a tumbler of amber liquid into his hand. Whiskey of some kind.

Elenora lifted her chin in a very grandmother-knows-best sort of way. "I saw the patrol car. I was concerned."

Hugh's eyes narrowed. "How did you see the patrol car? You live miles away from here."

She pursed her lips in frustration. "Alice has a police scanner."

Sheriff Merrow rolled his eyes and shook his head. "Civilians."

Elenora put her hands on her hips. "She's the head of the coven. She needs to keep abreast of what's happening in the community."

The coven? As in witches? Did no one else think that was odd? Delaney glanced around. Nope.

Sheriff Merrow snorted. "You mean *you* need to keep abreast of what's happening in the community."

"Sheriff." Elenora's smile belied the warning in

her voice. "Let's not start the second vampire—"

"Grandmother," Hugh barked. "Enough."

"—werewolf war right here in my grandson's home." She frowned at Hugh. "What is the matter with you? Yelling at your grandmother that way. You're going to make Annabelle think horrible things about you." She returned her attention to Sheriff Merrow. "Now why are you here again?"

Delaney only vaguely heard what was being said as ice sluiced down her spine. Vampire-werewolf war...what? "Repeat what you just said."

"Which part, dear?" Elenora's smile once again brightened her face.

Delaney stood. Her heart pounded wildly in her chest. "Vampire-werewolf war?"

"It's nothing," Hugh said. His eyes were wide with apprehension. "Old inside family joke."

"Absolutely." Elenora waved a hand through the air. "I was just teasing."

Delaney didn't get the joke.

Stanhill tried to offer Elenora a drink, but she ignored him, oblivious to Delaney's rising panic. "The vampires and the werefolk put away their differences years ago."

"Didi." Hugh glared at her. "Enough."

Delaney stared at Hugh. "What the *hell* is she talking about?"

He started to speak, but Elenora cut him off. "I realize you're not actually a vampire yet, but when that day comes"—she smiled conspiratorially—"you'll have to learn our history. Of course, it'll be your history then too."

Hugh put his hand on Delaney's arm. "Delaney, listen to me."

She backed out of his grasp. "You have five seconds to explain."

Sheriff Merrow furrowed his brow. "I take it you don't know about Nocturne Falls."

She looked at him. "Know what?"

He went silent, his gaze shifting to Hugh.

Elenora clucked her tongue. "What's the meaning of all this? I was told the agency had informed you of exactly who we were."

On the verge of a very serious meltdown, Delaney looked at the older woman. "I'm not from the agency."

Hugh took her hand and whispered, "I can explain everything."

The plaintive note in his voice kept Delaney from bolting. She owed him at least a few minutes to make this madness right. Or to convince her she was dreaming. That's all this was. A weird, weird dream.

Elenora stopped smiling. "What?"

Hugh pointed at Stanhill. "Explain to her what's going on, please. As you escort her to her car."

Stanhill nodded and began herding Elenora out of the library. She went, protesting all the way.

Hugh turned to the sheriff. "Is there anything else you need from us?"

Us. The pronoun gave Delaney pause. Were they an *us*? It sure didn't feel that way.

"No. I'll contact you when I know more. I'll see myself out." The sheriff left, and she was alone with Hugh.

She pulled her hand out of his, and an involuntary shiver ran through her body. "This is just a thing you do, right? You and your family pretend to be vampires. Like Julian was the night we saw him in town? Tell me that's what it is. Because nothing else makes sense."

He took a breath. "It's not a ruse. What my grandmother said is true. I am, that is, *we* are vampires."

The room tilted slightly, and her ears rang with a tinny sound. She was on the verge of passing out. Or something. This was all really, really weird.

"I gotta go," she managed, and then she bolted for her room.

"Delaney!"

She ignored him, got inside then shut the door and locked it. Vampires. She didn't actually believe that, but then she didn't exactly not believe it. Hell, she didn't know what she thought except that Hugh and his grandmother were certifiable, and if she stayed here, bad things were going to happen.

No wonder Hugh needed a matchmaking service.

This had to be a joke, right? They'd started this town and then drunk too much of their own crazy kool-aid. That's all it was. Hugh and his family were mildly insane. That didn't explain the very real-looking fangs and strange silver glint Julian had sported.

A soft knock broke through her thoughts. "Delaney, we need to talk about this."

"I'm good, thanks." She had to get out of here. She opened a window and peered out. It was only a single-story drop, but what was she going to do with Captain? She couldn't exactly throw him out the window. Maybe if she shimmied over to the ledge, she could climb down the gutter—

"Delaney, please. I know how...surreal this must seem."

"Not surreal so much as crazy," she muttered to herself.

"I'm not crazy."

She froze. How had he heard that? Being crazy didn't give you superhuman hearing.

"You're also not in any danger. I swear to you."

"Okay, good to know." If he thought swearing to a thing like that was going to solve everything, he really was nuts. She grabbed Cappy's carrier bag and shoved him into it, which was like stuffing twenty-seven pounds of furry sausage into a two-pound casing, but so be it.

"Please open the door so we can talk."

"Let's talk in the morning. I need to sleep on this." She grabbed her purse and slung it over her shoulder, then hefted the strap of the carrier over her head and one arm and settled it cross-body style against her back. "Oof, Cappy, you're a beast."

Carefully, she climbed out the window and onto the ledge. Hugh had stopped trying to talk to her through the door. She took that as a good sign. Slowly, she inched her way along the ledge until she came to the gutter. It wasn't one of those flimsy metal types, but a sturdy column of concrete or stone or whatever it was that wealthy people used to get the rain off their house.

She latched on to the brackets with her fingers, then wiggled the toes of one foot into the set of brackets below those. Captain shifted, almost unbalancing her.

"Settle," she hissed. "This isn't fun for either one of us."

She got her other foot off the ledge and onto the downspout bracket. This was easily the most ridiculous thing she'd ever done. She was kind of out of choices, though. She could either do this and risk the chance that she'd fall and break her neck or she could go back inside and possibly be bitten to death by the very handsome lunatic who owned this house.

The calories in a single chocolate chip produce enough energy to walk one hundred and fifty feet.

If only her brain could come up with something more useful, like how to get out of here without dying. Teeth clenched, she shimmied her way down the gutter, losing her grip about halfway down.

She twisted to protect Cappy and landed in the grass without making too much noise, although he still let out a little yowl. "Hush."

She tiptoed to the front of the house. Sheriff Merrow's patrol car was gone. No chance she could sneak off with him. Although, if he actually was a werewolf, that wasn't exactly a superior option.

She pulled the cat carrier around so the bag was in front and more horizontal than vertical. Then she took off into the woods, hoping she'd hit a highway before anything else bad happened.

Hugh stayed in the shadows as he followed her, a little heartbroken that she was so afraid of him she'd choose to run as opposed to talk to him. He got it, though. Humans were programmed to be afraid of what they didn't understand.

A vampire in a romance novel was something very different than one standing in front of you.

They traipsed through the woods, her crunching

through the underbrush, him following soundless as a breath. She'd be angry if she knew he was there, but he wasn't going to let her come to harm because of what had happened.

She had enough to deal with already, what with seeing that man shot.

After about half an hour, she came to a stream. It was an off shoot of Wolf Creek, which was one of the main waterways that fed the falls. She sat beside the stream, took the cat carrier off and set it beside her, then put her head onto her knees.

He thought she was going to cry.

She didn't, proving once again how very different she was from the women he was used to. Instead, she talked to her cat.

"We're kinda hosed, Cap." She tipped her head back and sighed. "It's totally my fault." She was silent for a moment. "I screwed up our karma by stealing that woman's file and pretending to be her. I shouldn't have done that."

She unzipped the top flap enough to stick her hand in and scratch him. "I'm really sorry." Captain purred softly. That seemed to make her feel worse. She sniffed.

Maybe she was going to cry after all.

Then she took a deep inhale, blew it out and stared at the water. The moon bathed everything in a silvery light, but he doubted it was enough for her to see him if she turned around.

He crept closer, wishing he could comfort her in some way. Tell her it was going to be okay.

She petted Captain some more. "I'm not sorry I met Hugh. Or at least, I wasn't until he let his freak flag fly. A vampire. Can you believe that? And the grandmother thinks she's one too. And the sheriff is a werewolf. Add that Alice woman being a witch, and they make this town seem like a cover story for a whole lot of genuine weirdness."

He couldn't stand it anymore. He walked forward, crunching leaves underfoot to give her some warning. "That's because it is."

She grabbed the strap of the carrier like she was about to run again, her pulse ratcheting back up. "Don't come any closer."

"I'm not going to hurt you, Delaney. I have no desire to do that. All I want to do is help you understand." And keep her safe. And kiss her some more.

She stared at him. Her pulse evened out a little. "Why does your grandmother think you two are vampires?"

"Because we are." He pointed to the ground. "You mind if I sit?"

"It's a free forest."

Actually, it was Ellingham land, but telling her that wasn't going to buy him any consideration. He sat and crossed his legs. "We've been vampires since 1665."

Her lids lowered in that way a person's did when they thought they were dealing with an obvious lie. "So you're…" He could see her adding sums in her head. "You're three hundred and fifty years old?"

"Three hundred and seventy seven, to be exact. I was twenty-seven when Didi turned me."

Delaney's silent stare unnerved him, but at least she stayed put. "Didi was a vampire before you?"

He paused. He was about to share Ellingham history with her. The kind of information that could be their undoing if she decided to use it against him. "Lady Elenora Ellingham, Dowager Duchess of Sinclair, was known for keeping an eccentric court. One of her suitors, a strange, wealthy Frenchman by the name of Alard Desmarais had revealed himself to her as a vampire. She thought it was a parlor trick until she got to know him."

"What happened?" Delaney seemed rapt by the story now. Maybe he was making headway.

"In 1665, a plague struck London. It took my parents. Didi was bereft at losing her son and daughter-in-law. She refused to lose her grandsons as well. She begged Alard to turn us. He agreed on the condition that she would allow him to turn her as well."

"Obviously, she agreed."

Hugh nodded. "Then she turned us. I was the

first since I was already at court. Then Sebastian, then Julian." He blinked hard. Memories strobed through his brain, robbing his ability to speak for a moment. He'd never told this story to anyone outside of Juliette. There'd never been a reason.

"Are you okay?"

He was thrown by the compassion in her voice. It affected him almost more than the memories had. He looked away, unwilling to show her what he was feeling. "I'm fine."

He stood suddenly, ready for a change of topic. "I suppose you'd like proof."

She hugged the cat carrier to her.

"I didn't mean by biting anyone."

"That's excellent news." The slight quirk at the corners of her mouth told him she still didn't believe him. She put the carrier back on the ground.

"How about this?" His fangs shot through his gums, and he opened his mouth so she could see them. In full vampire form, his pupils would shine like an animal's, silvery white. He wasn't sure there was enough moonlight to make that happen.

"Those are pretty convincing, but you can buy amazingly real fangs at the mall around Halloween. Or, you know, probably all year round in this town."

He closed his mouth and sighed. "Maybe I should bite you."

"Hey now—"

He held up his hand. "I won't. Biting a person starts a process, and I'm not about to do that to you." But he needed her to know that he wasn't insane. They'd come this far. "What can I do to prove that I'm telling the truth?"

She frowned. "Hugh, it's clear you believe you're a vampire—"

"Because I am."

She raised her brows. "I've seen you outside while the sun was up. I'm pretty sure that's a big vampire no-no."

He ground his teeth together. He couldn't tell her about the amulet. They'd taken a vow as a family never to reveal that secret to anyone. "I can take a little sun." Bloody hell, that sounded false even to his ears.

She smiled in a sad, sure-sure kind of way. "You're a nice guy, Hugh. Maybe you should talk to somebody about this vampire thing—"

"Brace yourself." So help him, he was about to do something he swore he'd never do. It was so...tween movie. Unfortunately, he was out of other ideas.

"What?"

He lunged forward, took her into his arms and sped through the woods. She inhaled sharply, a deep shuddering breath that took the place of a scream. He dodged trees and leaped fallen logs as he made a wide circle and brought her back to the creek's edge a few moments later. They'd probably gone a mile.

He put her on her feet. "Now do you believe me?"

She wobbled her head in what he took to be a nod, then opened her mouth to say something and fainted.

Delaney woke up fully clothed on the four-poster bed. Even her shoes were still on. She blinked, getting her bearings. Soft snoring turned her head. Captain sprawled on the pillow next to her. The room was dark, but a little moonlight filtered through the curtains. She'd had the strangest dream.

It *had* been a dream. Or... She sat up and stared into the dimness, trying to comprehend the last thing she remembered.

Could Hugh really be a vampire? Vampires weren't real. Were they? He'd seemed so earnest. And not the least bit off his rocker. But then there was that speed run through the woods. There was no denying he was something...more than human. Which brought her back to whether or not he could really be a vampire.

Her hand went to her neck. No bite marks that

she could feel. She looked at Cappy. He purred as she checked his fatness for evidence of a bite. Nothing. Hugh had promised she was safe with him. As far as she could tell, he hadn't lied about that.

She swung her legs over the side of the bed and kicked off her shoes. She dug her toes into the plush carpet. The bedside clock said a little after one in the morning, but there was no way she'd be able to fall back asleep with all these questions keeping her brain spun up.

She left her room and went out into the hall. Muted voices carried up from somewhere below. The deep male tones sounded like Hugh and Stanhill.

She traipsed down the steps and found them in the spacious living room, Hugh standing beside the fireplace, Stanhill leaning against the back of one couch. They stopped talking when she came in.

Feeling a bit like an interloper, she smiled sheepishly. "Hi."

Hugh looked her over. "How are you feeling?"

"I fainted, right?"

"Yes."

"I feel okay."

Stanhill straightened. "How about a cup of hot chocolate, miss?"

"That sounds great, thank you."

When he left, she sat on the couch and tucked

her feet under her and took a breath. "We need to talk."

"I concur." Hugh came and sat across from her. "Where do you want to start?"

She stared at his knees. It was safer than having those piercing eyes of his derail her train of thought. "I don't know if I believe you're a vampire yet."

"That's okay. Are you afraid of me?"

She liked that he asked the tough questions straight out. There was a lot to be said for not dancing around the elephant in the room. "I didn't wake up with any bite marks, so…"

Mischief sparkled in his eyes. "Yes, but did you check the cat?"

She laughed softly as she looked at him. "I did, actually."

He groaned good-naturedly and scrubbed a hand across his face. "The curse of my kind."

"Speaking of, and I'm not saying I'm buying into this whole thing yet, but let's say there are vampires. Are they everywhere?"

He nodded. "Not just vampires, but shifters of all varieties, witches, fae, jinn—"

She held her hands up. "Okay, I get it. We are not alone." Seriously, though, that was a lot to accept. "So every town has these supernatural creatures?"

"Every town. Every state. Every country.

Humans just can't differentiate us from anyone else so we blend right in. Unless you happen to see our non-human side. Then you'd know."

"Non-human. That's putting a pin in it, huh? So you mean fangs and silvery eyes and what else? Do you fly? Turn into a bat? Please, in the name of all things sweet and sugary, do not tell me you sparkle."

One of his brows lifted indignantly. "No. No sparkling. Or turning into bats. Not in my family."

Stanhill came back in with her hot chocolate. Of course it was in a china cup and saucer on a silver tray. "Can I get you anything else, miss?"

"No, thank you." She took the cup and saucer and set it on the table separating the two couches. Talking about this was starting to make everything seem more real. "Are you a vampire too, Stanhill?"

"No, miss. I'm a…" He glanced at Hugh.

"Go ahead, tell her."

Stanhill nodded. "I'm Hugh's rook."

"What is that?" She sipped the chocolate, which was hot but delicious.

Stanhill tucked the tray behind his back. "A rook is a vampire's assistant. We do daylight errands. Protect the vampire while they're sleeping. That sort of thing."

"And in return you get what? I hope you at least have dental." She slanted her eyes at Hugh. "That wasn't a fang joke, I swear."

Stanhill lifted his chin. "My compensation is immortality. A boost to the senses, not as much as a vampire, but a nice bump. Faster healing. Lots of perks."

"No downside?"

He shrugged. "Can't be too far away from Hugh for any length of time. That's a bit of a drag, as I'm sure you can imagine." He winked at her.

"How do you get to be a rook?" She raised a hand. "Purely out of curiosity. I have no desire to become one."

"Almost the same way you become a vampire. Two bites in a set period of time."

She looked at Hugh. "You did this to him then?"

Hugh nodded. "He was my valet."

"Why not turn him into a full-fledged vampire?"

"I didn't want that, miss," Stanhill answered. "I'd been in service since I was a wee lad. I was happy to stay on in that regard." His jaw worked like he was fighting emotion. "Saved me from the plague, he did."

She studied Hugh, shaking her head slowly. "This is nuts. You know that, right?"

"I'll leave you to it then." Stanhill gave them a little nod and left.

Hugh said nothing for a few moments. "I know it must be hard to accept. And I'm sure you have more questions."

"Yes. Thousands. But I don't know where to

start." She drank a little more of her chocolate, buying herself time to sort the chaos in her head.

"What comes to mind first?"

"Is the sheriff really a werewolf?"

"Yes."

"Do your brothers have rooks?"

"Sebastian, yes. Julian, no." Hugh snorted. "Probably for the best. A rook would only cramp his style."

"Is that woman who lives with your grandmother a rook or a witch or what?"

"Alice is a witch. My grandmother saved her from being burned at the stake in Salem not long after we arrived in the colonies."

Delaney downed the last of her hot chocolate. Too bad the cup was so small. "Why aren't any of you married? Or is Sebastian married?"

"He was." Hugh seemed lost in thought for a moment. "She left him."

"Because he became a vampire?"

"No." Hugh's gaze pinned her. "Because she did."

He got up and walked toward the French doors. "This life holds a thousand temptations. She wanted to try them all and being married didn't fit into that plan."

Maybe that's why Hugh was in no hurry to get married. "I'm sorry for your brother. That kind of betrayal sucks. Hard."

Hugh turned to look at her. "You sound like you know that from experience."

She nodded and stared at her hands. She didn't tell a lot of people about her past, didn't want them to pity her for it, but Hugh wasn't just anyone. He'd already forgiven her lying to him and was now actively protecting her by letting her stay here. "My mother found out she had breast cancer when I was fourteen. Six months later, my father couldn't handle it. He was there one day and gone the next."

Hugh sat on the couch with her but kept his distance. "That must have devastated your mum. How did it affect her recovery? Has she remarried?"

Because he'd assumed her mother had lived, Delaney smiled, but her lips stayed pressed together. "She didn't recover. She died a month after my fifteenth birthday. My father was—is a defense contractor. He'd taken a job in Korea. Still lives there now. He didn't come home for her funeral."

"Sounds like a proper bastard."

"That's a pretty decent assessment." Her eyes were hot with tears. She blinked them away.

"What did you do after your mum died?"

"I went to live with my grandmother in Brooklyn. She passed away three years ago. It was a good life considering."

"Have you seen your father since?"

She nodded. "The summer after I graduated high school, he married a Korean woman."

Hugh's brows knit together. "Don't tell me you went to the wedding?"

"Yep. Purely for selfish reasons. He paid for the ticket and I really wanted to see Korea. I had a bit of an ulterior motive, though. When they got to the part of the service about anyone objecting, I stood up and told him exactly what I thought about him, his treatment of my mother and his failure to show up at the funeral."

"You didn't."

"I did." She smiled, but bent her head. "It's the moment in my life I'm probably most and least proud of."

His eyes shone with admiration. "I'm proud of you for doing it, and I've only known you a few days. That took courage."

"And a couple shots of *soju*."

He laughed. "That's some strong stuff. Even so, good for you." He stretched his arm along the back of the couch, his face going serious again. "Between your father and your cheating ex-boyfriend, you must not think much of men."

She lifted her gaze to see him better. "I know those two don't represent every man. But it's certainly given me a lot to think about."

"Understandable."

She sat up straighter and tipped her head. "Why aren't you married? You said you were twenty-seven when you were turned. Isn't that sort of old for a nobleman in the 1600s to be single?"

He went very still, his eyes focused on some spot on the cushion between them. "I was married."

That was…unexpected. But sensing he had more to say, she stayed quiet and gave him the time to find the words.

After a long pause, Hugh spoke again. "She died."

The cold, familiar bands of pain wrapped Hugh's heart, but Delaney deserved to have her questions answered. He just hadn't expected to breach this topic so soon.

"I'm so sorry, Hugh."

He nodded, the muscles in his jaw tensing against the ache in his soul.

"Was it the plague too?"

And there it was. The one question he most dreaded to answer. Because the full truth would frighten her away more than anything else he might say. "No."

Desperate to change the subject, he took her

hand. "If you're not sleepy, would you like to go into town?"

She frowned. "Won't everything be closed?"

"Not everything." He smiled. She was extraordinarily pretty. And open-minded enough to stay even after he'd confessed his true self. "Now that you know the secret of Nocturne Falls, there's a whole other side I can show you."

Intrigue danced in her eyes. "Like what?"

"There's a place called Insomnia. Horrible name, I know, but it's a members-only club, and the only members allowed are supernaturals. And guests of supernaturals."

"Not Piper then?"

"Definitely not Piper." In the name of all that was holy, please not Piper. He wasn't sure he could take another minute of that woman right now.

Delaney bit her pinkie finger, giving him a glimpse of her tongue. He was going to kiss her again before the night was over, that much he knew. "So...will there be other vampires there?"

"Probably. And shifters and fae and witches, and who knows what else. Interested?"

"I don't know."

"If a visit to Insomnia doesn't prove I'm telling you the truth, nothing will."

"It's not that. It's just..."

"Scared?" He waggled his brows, knowing

she'd take his assessment like he was daring her to back down.

Her eyes narrowed. His challenge seemed to have worked. "I'll go get changed."

It didn't take much for Delaney to get ready. Her wardrobe was sparse thanks to packing on the run and having no real clue what lay ahead. Fortunately, she'd brought one club-appropriate outfit. Skinny jeans, high-heeled black boots and a black strapless peplum top in leather. It wasn't something she'd ever have spent money on herself, but Mrs. Rastinelli occasionally brought hand-me-downs into the restaurant and let the girls pick through them. Mrs. Rastinelli was actually wife number two and dressed like she wasn't about to let there be a number three.

Most of the stuff she brought in was over-the-top sexy and verging on tacky, but somehow also expensive. Selling Mrs. Rastinelli's hand-me-downs on Ebay had become a nice little hobby for Delaney. Enough that she could afford to buy quality baking supplies.

Delaney had planned on selling the leather top on Ebay too. Until she'd tried it on. She'd never owned something so sexy and sophisticated. Clearly too sophisticated for Mrs. Rastinelli.

Delaney thanked whatever instinct had driven her to bring it along on this trip.

Hugh's mouth fell open as she walked down the stairs to the foyer where he waited. He wore a simple black suit with a white dress shirt open at the neck, no tie and looked pretty close to edible. "You look, uh…" He nodded. "This is a side of you I hadn't been expecting."

She'd smoked out her eye makeup, but she was pretty sure that wasn't what he was talking about. She stopped directly in front of him. "What side is that?"

"This, this…" He waved his hands at her outfit. "You look a little dangerous. In a good way."

She laughed. "I'm pretty sure that's not a word that's ever been used to describe me." But she liked it a lot. It made her feel powerful. And reckless.

Heady with his compliment, she did a little spin. "Is this okay for the club then?"

"Yeah. Yes. More than okay. Damn good."

In her heels, she was only a couple inches shorter than he was. Close enough to see the tantalizing shadow of stubble darkening his square jaw. The powerful, reckless feeling went to her head. She stared at his mouth. "Show me your fangs again."

If he really was a vampire, that shouldn't be a problem, right?

He stared at her for a second, then snorted softly before curling his lip back in a snarl. His canines were as sharp and pointed as any movie vampire's she'd ever seen. "Happy?"

She peered at them. "You swear those are real?"

His gaze rolled skyward. "Don't they look real?"

"Yes." She reached forward before she realized what she was doing. She snatched her hand back.

"You want to touch them? Go ahead. I promise not to bite. Just be careful, they're sharp."

"This is weird," she muttered.

"You started it."

"That I did." She reached out again and poked at one of his fangs. "Sure feels real."

She tested the point with a fingertip. "Ouch." She yanked her finger back. A drop of blood pearled on the tip. Sweet crispy crackers, what had she done? What if the blood drove him mad? She took a small step back, but nothing about him seemed crazed with blood lust.

"I told you they were sharp." He frowned and took her hand for closer inspection. "It's just a flesh wound."

Still holding her hand, he looked into her eyes. "May I?"

She knew what he was asking. She also realized that she was safe with this man. This man who could probably be very *unsafe*, if he really was a vampire. The irony was that she'd never felt half this secure with fully human Russell. Her realizations didn't stop her answer from coming out in a breathy wobble. "Y-yes."

He lifted her finger to his lips and tenderly sucked off the bead of blood. His mouth was warm and electric, and the contact shot straight through her. Like he'd put his mouth in a very different place.

"*Oh.*" Another breathy, trembling response. She took a deep inhale to erase the sudden light-headedness threatening to unbalance her, but there was no erasing the desire.

He turned her hand around. "See? All better?"

The blood was gone, but that's not what she was looking at. His eyes shone with the kind of luminescence of an animal's at night, but then she blinked and it was gone. "Thanks."

Her boldness was wavering, driving her to take advantage of it while she could. "Can you make your fangs go away just as easily?"

"Sure." He grinned to show her they were gone. "Too frightening?"

"No. Too hazardous." Then she leaned forward and planted her mouth on his.

He went completely still for a heartbeat, then his

161

arms were around her and his hands found homes, one on her hip, the other high on the middle of her back. He moaned softly as his mouth opened to tease his tongue across hers.

She wrapped her hands around his biceps, instantly distracted by the hard muscle beneath the fabric of his suit. Her head spun. She was either kissing a vampire or a crazy man and he really did seem way less crazy than a lot of the guys she'd known. Either way, she was okay with it.

Really, *really* okay with it.

When she broke the kiss and eased back, he smiled at her. "Does this mean you believe me?"

Did she? Maybe. "I...guess I do."

His expression softened. "No, you don't. Not yet. It's okay. I understand."

He stared at her throat for a few long moments, long enough that her hand went to her neck. "Okay, I get it, you're a vampire and my neck is bare."

"No, that's not what I was—yes, it is bare. I'll be right back." Then he was gone, only to return so quickly she didn't know how he'd done anything in such a short time.

In his hand, he held a large burgundy velvet box. "As beautiful as you look tonight, this is only gilding the lily, but if you would indulge me..." He opened the box.

Delaney sucked in a breath. "That's amazing."

Nestled on the burgundy velvet was a dragonfly worked in gold. Emeralds made up its body, but the wings were set with amethysts, sapphires and diamonds. The insect was strung on a new black velvet cord, but the patina of the gold and the cut of the stones spoke to the age of the piece.

He lifted it from the box and held it up. "May I?"

If this was his way of marking his territory, so be it. "On one condition."

He closed the box and set it on the entry table. "Yes?"

"Tell me about it. It looks old." She turned and lifted her hair so he could put the necklace on her.

"It is." He settled the piece around her throat, then held it there while she moved her hands. "It belonged to my mother."

His fingers brushed the back of her neck as he fastened the clasp, raising goose bumps on her skin and causing her to wonder what it would be like to have his hands on other parts of her. Or his fangs… "That's pretty old. It must be worth a fortune."

"There. What do you think?"

She looked in the foyer mirror, conscious of the fact that he hadn't answered her about the piece's value. "It's beautiful."

Their eyes met in the mirror. His held emotions she couldn't read, and his voice was low when he answered. "It suits you."

Her fingers went to the dragonfly as she turned to face him. "I know it's just a loan for the evening, but it's still very generous of you."

"It's nice to see it worn again." With the distance of memory lingering in his gaze, he opened the front door. "Shall we? I had Stanhill pull the car around."

Hugh drove them to the club, which wasn't far, but the trip covered some back roads that were new to her. When they arrived, she squinted at the place. Faded painted spelled out the name Caldwell Manufacturing on the old brick building in front of them. It looked like it had been new fifty years ago. "I've heard of industrial clubs, but this is hardcore. Are you sure it's safe?"

He nodded. "It's just a cover, I promise." He pointed at the fairly packed parking lot. "There wouldn't be cars here otherwise."

She peered up at the building. "What's this place supposed to manufacture?"

"Gaskets."

She stared at him. "For a second, I thought you said caskets. Hah! See what I did there? Caskets? Vampires?" He wasn't smiling. "Never mind."

He narrowed his eyes like he was seeing past her dumb joke. "We need some places of our own. The tourist side of things wears on you after a while."

"By 'we' I assume you mean supernaturals?"

He nodded. "Of which you are about to meet a large group." He jumped out of the car, a beautiful old Jaguar, and came around to her door and helped her out.

"Anything I need to know before we go in there?"

He shut her door and locked the car. "Trust your instincts. Just like in any club, there might be elements to avoid. But I'll be at your side the whole time."

He put his hand on the small of her back as they started toward the building, then leaned in to whisper in her ear. "Have I mentioned how ravishing you look?"

His warm breath tickled her skin, sending the most delicious shiver through her. "Not in so many words."

She linked her arm through his. "I have to say tonight you not only sound like James Bond, but in that suit, you look like him too."

"A high bar indeed." He opened a rusted steel door and let her in, then pulled it shut behind them.

Rows of worktables and machinery lined the vast open floor. The odors of dust and grease accompanied the utter stillness of the place. "Yeah, you're right, this is a happening joint. How was there not a line to get in?"

"Reserve judgment a moment longer." He

ushered her toward a freight elevator and punched a code into a shiny new keypad. The down button lit and the whirr of gears echoed through the warehouse.

When the doors opened, they stepped in and he pressed the button marked basement. When the doors reopened, Delaney's eyes went wide.

She stayed at Hugh's side, happy to follow him while she gawked.

The place was gorgeous, but dark. All that stood out immediately was the decor. Moody, industrial, and sleek, but plush at the same time. Leather seating, brushed metal accents, lots of blue neon, water features and the occasion blast of the smoke machine. "It's like a dream."

"That's the idea. Insomnia and all that." He led her toward the bar closest to them. "Let's get a drink and get comfortable."

The deep bass thump of club music rocked the place, but not at the ear-splitting level she was accustomed to. She leaned her back against the bar, too busy taking the club in to pay attention to ordering. "It's nice that you can actually talk in here."

Hugh tapped his ear. "Supernatural hearing. We don't need the music blasting."

"Neither do humans, but the clubs we go to seem to think we do. I take it you don't need as much lighting either. I can't see much more than what's under the spotlights." But as her eyes grew accustomed to the dim lighting, she started seeing the faces around her in more detail. Faces that were not quite human.

She inched closer to Hugh.

He put his hand on her arm. "You okay?"

"Just...adjusting."

"What would you like to drink while you adjust?"

"Wine. Red."

"Keep in mind that this place allows a certain amount of laxness most supernaturals would never adopt while in mixed company. What you're seeing are some half forms and some true ones."

Her gaze skipped from face to face. With some she could easily tell what they were. The werewolves had a very canine look about them. A few others looked more feline—cat shifters of some sort, she guessed. Another group had Hugh's luminescent eyes and fangs, so they were clearly vampires. The women who looked human might be witches.

Hugh placed their order with the bartender, then canted his head toward hers. "If you're uncomfortable, we can go. Just say the word."

"No, I'm fine." Even better since he'd said that. "It's just weird to be in a joint where being human makes me the minority."

"Don't be afraid. You're here with me."

She took him in: his gorgeous face and broad shoulders and the smile that seemed just for her. Her heart went a little achy at how beyond it all he was. *Don't go falling in love.* "So are you the BMOC around here, since you practically own the town?"

"The BMOC?"

She twisted to face him and rested her elbow on the bar. The move put his arm directly beneath her leather-wrapped chest. "Big Man On Campus."

He snorted. "I guess you could say that. I am one of the oldest supernaturals in this town."

"Not to mention one of the richest." Her fingers went to the dragonfly around her neck. He'd kind of skimmed that part.

"I don't know about that." Then the bartender arrived with their drinks and Hugh handed over a black American Express card.

She laughed. "They give those Centurion cards to just anyone these days?" Not even Rastinelli had one of those.

He handed her glass of wine over. "I've had plenty of time to get my financial house in order."

A gorgeous redhead in a simple black dress and patent heels came up to them. She carried a black leather portfolio and black leather clutch under one arm. Oddly business-like for a night club. "I'm sorry to interrupt, but can I have a moment of your time, Hugh?"

"Delaney, this is Pandora Williams. She's a

witch. Pandora, this is my guest, Delaney James. She's human."

"Thanks for the species update," Pandora said with a laugh and a wink at Hugh.

"Nice to meet you." And it was. Even if the supermodel-beautiful witch was being awfully familiar with the man Delaney had just been kissing.

Pandora smiled back. "You too. Great necklace."

"Thanks." Delaney wanted to say Hugh had given it to her, to make it clear what kind of relationship she was in with him, but then she reminded herself that the jewelry was only a loan, and she had no clue what kind of relationship they were having.

"Are you new in town? If you're looking for a place, I'd be happy to help you out."

Hugh smiled politely. "Pandora is Nocturne Fall's most-well-known Realtor. She caters to our kind."

Delaney grinned. He'd said *our* kind. Like she was a supernatural too. "Well, I'll store that away if the need to buy a town house pops up."

"Excellent." Pandora shifted back to Hugh. "Again, sorry to interrupt your evening out, but I was here talking to a client and saw you, so—"

Hugh shook his head. "If this is about Stanhill dating your mother, I swear I knew nothing about that."

Pandora laughed. "No. My sisters and I love Stanhill. Especially when he makes pancakes."

Hugh winced. "That was more information than I needed."

Pandora pinched her lips and nodded. "Got it. Keep the sleepovers to myself." She looked at Delaney. "Not that my sisters and I sleep over. We have our own places. But on Saturday mornings…" She made a face. "Sorry, rambling."

Hugh slid his arm around Delaney. It was a sweet gesture, but she still felt like a third wheel. His fingers rested on her shoulder and drew lazy circles. "What can I do for you, Pandora?"

"I see there's a vacant store across from the Hallowed Bean. That's your building, isn't it? Any plans to list it? With me? I don't usually do commercial, but I'd really love to broaden my reach."

Jealousy poked at Delaney, but that wasn't an emotion she had a right to. Before she did something she might regret, she put her hand on Hugh's arm. "While you two talk shop, I'm going to find the ladies' room."

Pandora pointed across the club. "Back corner."

Hugh caught Delaney's eye. "Be careful."

"I can go with you," Pandora offered.

"I'll be fine. You two carry on with business. Back in a sec." She grabbed her purse and started threading her way through the crowd, watching where she was going in a peripheral kind of way. Without Hugh's arm around her, without his fingers on her bare skin, it was easier to think.

Mostly about just how crazy over him she already was. *Stop being a fool. He only lent you that jewelry so you'd fit in.* Maybe. Maybe not. Her inner voice didn't know everything. When she went back to him, if Pandora wasn't still there, she'd ask him how he felt about…them.

There was a *them*, wasn't there?

The door to the ladies' room was in sight when she walked into the path of a mountain of a man. He peered at her, nostrils flaring.

"You're human." His eyes narrowed. "Tonight just got a whole lot more interesting."

Hugh watched Delaney disappear into the crowd, bereft she'd left him so easily. He hoped she hadn't left because of Pandora. If Delaney thought he was in any way interested in the witch, she was dead wrong. And now that she was out of his sight, a prickle of unease crawled over his skin. She was the only human here. "Excuse me, Pandora. Call Sebastian about the space. I have to go."

"But I—"

He left his drink and Pandora behind and went after Delaney. The crowd seemed to have grown in the few minutes they'd been inside. Where the hell was she?

He pushed deeper into the club. People tried to stop him, tried to talk to him. He turned them away.

Finally, he spotted her. A man he didn't recognize towered over her, blocking her path.

The edges of Hugh's vision went red at the thought that she might be in danger. He stormed forward, anger charging him for a fight.

Then Delaney threw her head back and laughed.

The color at the edge of Hugh's vision shifted from red to green, although his anger wasn't completely gone. She was chatting up another man? What had he said to make her laugh? With a cacophony of emotions bombarding him, Hugh sidled up to her. "Everything okay?"

She smiled at him and lightly touched his arm. "Everything's great. This is Nick Hardwin." She turned to the big man. "Nick, this is Hugh Ellingham."

Nick smiled respectfully. "I know who you are, Mr. Ellingham. Good to meet you in person, sir." He held out a hand the size of a Christmas ham.

Hugh's anger fizzled out. He shook Nick's hand but couldn't fake an expression to match his words. "Nice to meet you, too."

Delaney chatted on, oblivious to the fact that Hugh had been about to take the man's head off for a perceived transgression against her. "He's new to town too. He's a friend of the sheriff's, but he's not a werewolf, he's a *gargoyle*."

Nick nodded. "Merrow and I were in the same battalion. Shared a tour in Afghanistan."

"Which totally deserves a thanks," Delaney said.

Hugh grunted. "Thank you for your service."

"Anyway," Delaney went on. "He knew I was human right away and I told him I was here as your guest—Nick's a bouncer here and is supposed to keep tourists out on the off chance any manage to get in—and then we started talking and, short story, I still haven't made it to the ladies' room."

Nick seemed a little more aware of Hugh's mood. A quick glance at Hugh's face and Nick made his goodbyes. "I should get back to work. Nice to meet you, Delaney. Mr. Ellingham."

"Bye, Nick." She squeezed Hugh's arm. "I'll be right back, okay? Don't go anywhere."

Where did she think he was going to go? Before he could respond, she'd slipped away to the ladies' room. He leaned against the wall and considered what had just happened.

How he'd been driven by the need to protect her. Then driven by the need to have her for his own. He'd been jealous. Over nothing, really. But jealous all the same. He shouldn't have sucked that drop of blood from her finger. It was just a drop, and it wasn't like he'd actually bitten her, but maybe with her, a drop was all it took. He was walking a dangerous line.

The reality of what was happening couldn't have hit Hugh any harder than if Nick had punched him. He was falling for Delaney.

Hard.

Which also explained why he'd lied to her about the necklace.

That dragonfly hadn't belonged to his mother. It had belonged to Juliette. A gift on her twenty-third birthday. There was no other reason for why he'd wanted to see it on Delaney except that he'd wanted to mark her as his. To lay claim to her before bringing her here.

He couldn't remember the last time he'd felt that kind of base, primal need. Yes, he'd loved Juliette despite their marriage being arranged, but that had come sometime into the marriage. The guilt he felt over her death, a death he'd brought upon her, that was just an extension of his love. Wasn't it?

Another thought niggled at him. Perhaps there was *one* other reason he'd wanted to adorn Delaney with those jewels. To test himself. To determine if seeing another woman in his beloved late wife's jewels moved him in anyway.

It had. Just not the way he'd expected.

His first thought had been that the dragonfly had never looked as right on Juliette as it did on Delaney. A traitorous thought to be sure, but there it was. In Delaney's bright and unreserved light, Juliette's sainted memory had begun to fade.

He was utterly, hopelessly doomed.

Delaney suddenly appeared before him. Her lips were freshly slicked with gloss, and the scent of sugar teased at him. She grinned. "Miss me?"

"Desperately," he replied, covering his wretched state with an answer she would think a joke. The joke was on him. The answer was the bald truth.

"Well, I'm back, so you can stop moping. Where are our drinks?"

She was the anti-Piper. A girl who colored outside the lines and made no apologies or pretense about who she was. A girl who didn't care what was proper. A girl who didn't wait to be kissed. He pointed lamely. "At the bar. I'm not actually sure they'll still be there."

"Didn't you leave Pandora watching them?"

He frowned. That would have been a good idea. "No."

Delaney made a face. "You don't go out much, do you?"

He wanted her to have a good time. He *needed* her to. Needed her to fall in love with this town. That might be enough to make her stay. Another audacious thought. He waved down a passing server. "We need a table in the VIP section."

The girl nodded. "Sure thing. That just requires the purchase of a bottle."

He almost asked the girl if she knew who he was, but Insomnia wasn't one of the Ellingham properties. "Fine. Bring us a bottle of that Mouton Rothschild I saw on the wine list." If a fifteen-hundred-dollar bottle of wine didn't buy them a place in the VIP room, nothing would.

"Excellent selection, sir. If you'll just follow me."

He took Delaney's hand, happy to have her close again. "Will this make up for leaving the drinks behind?"

She laughed. "Uh, *yes*."

The VIP section was a tier of private seating areas two steps up and roped off from the rest of the club on the left side of the building. The server got them settled and went off to get their wine.

He sat next to Delaney on the white leather sofa.

She smiled at him. "This is cozy."

He reached over and pulled her in closer so that her backside was against his hip and they could both watch the crowd. "*This* is cozy."

She snuggled against him. "Any cozier and we'd have to get a room."

The thought filled him with as much wanton desire as her lush body pressed against his. He swept her hair off her shoulder and brushed a kiss on the curve of her neck, taking advantage of the closeness to inhale her perfume. That only made him want her more. How would she react if he scraped his fangs over her skin?

He kissed her again, but kept his fangs to himself.

She sucked in a breath only to let out a tiny mewl of pleasure on the exhale. She shifted and cut her eyes at him. "You're…doing things to me."

"Am I?" Not the things he wanted to be doing. He laughed softly, thrilled at the response he'd elicited from her. His hand stayed in her hair, running the silky strands through his fingers. "What do you think of the club?"

Her gaze turned to the crowd. The dance floor had started to fill up, and the music had taken on a more trance-like beat. "I like it. Reminds me a little of home. Not that I went out to clubs very much. And not that any of those places had this kind of crowd."

"I'd lay good money some of them did."

She smiled, her expression shifting into something coy. She stared at the small sliver of couch between them before looking up at him again through her lashes. "I believe you now. About who you really are."

He nodded. "And you're okay with that?"

She lifted her head to see him fully. "As strange as it is, yes."

Relief flooded him. "Thank you."

She canted her head. "For?"

"For not letting it frighten you away."

"It never bothered any of your other girlfriends."

She was so adorable. He snorted softly. "I never told any of them."

"Oh." Her smile faded. "I guess you wouldn't have told me either then."

"Except I thought you already knew. Well, Annabelle."

She nodded, her eyes clear and guileless. A few long moments passed before she spoke again, this time staring into his eyes. "What's happening between us?"

There it was. The question that had danced through his head all night. And as he thought the answer—we're falling in love—the realization that he'd forgotten one very important fact slammed him in the chest. Chemistry or not, he could not risk another woman's life in the turning. "We're enjoying each other's company. As friends do."

A delicate frown bent her pretty mouth. "You mean, we're just friends then?"

He nodded while the lie twisted his insides. "Just friends."

She cocked an eyebrow. "So when you left our drinks at the bar and showed up about to take Nick's head off, that was you just being friendly."

Ah. She'd noticed that after all. "I—"

"Also, *friendly* kissing rarely involves tongue. Just saying."

He hesitated. This was neither the time nor the place to tell her that his late wife's death was his fault and the fear of that happening again meant he could never give his heart to another woman.

She spoke before he could. "Look, I don't know

what kind of woman you think I am, but I'm *not* the friends with benefits type. At all."

That phrase was only vaguely familiar. He squinted at her. "Friends with benefits?"

Her mouth bunched to one side. "I don't sleep with men I'm not committed to."

He straightened. "I never thought...no, of course not." He frowned. "Is that what happens these days? Relationships have turned into friends with benefits?"

She shrugged one shoulder and went back to watching the crowd. "For some, I guess."

The server returned with their wine. It took her a couple of minutes to set everything up and pour them both a glass after Hugh approved it. Once he'd signed the check and they were alone again, he took Delaney's hand.

"Listen to me."

She set her wine glass down and turned to him. "Yes?"

"I'm not looking for benefits of any kind unless it's a mutual decision. As far as commitment goes—"

"I know. You're not looking for it." She smiled, but it didn't quite reach her eyes. "I wasn't trying to pressure you into anything or make you feel like—"

He cut her off with a kiss, not caring they were in public and the rumors it would start. He lingered over her mouth, allowing himself a long, languid taste of her. When he finally released her, she seemed a little breathless. "You drive me mad, Delaney. I haven't felt like this in a very long time, and the truth is, it frightens me a little."

It frightened him a lot. Her future with him could be a very short one.

She leaned her head to one side. "What are you afraid of? Getting hurt? That's part of life."

He just shook his head. "I don't want to talk about it here."

She studied him, the look in her eyes shifting to sympathy. "It doesn't matter. I don't even live here. And now that your grandmother knows the truth about me, I guess the thirty-day deal is off." She eased her hand out of his. "I should probably think about what I'm going to do next."

"Stay." He'd said it without hesitation.

She blinked. "Why? You don't want a serious relationship. And I'm not interested in being your live-in...whatever that would make me."

"Maybe...maybe I don't know exactly what I want except for you to stay."

She bit her lip. "Do you really feel that way or are you doing this out of pity for me and my situation?"

He picked up his glass of wine. "Keeping you safe has a lot to do with it, but it's because of the way I feel that I care about keeping you safe. Say you'll stay. Let's drink to it."

Her wine stayed on the table. "I can't just stay here indefinitely."

"Why not?" Indefinitely sounded just fine to him. Permanently sounded better.

"I don't live here."

"You could."

"I need a job."

"I can help you find one." Or he could just take care of her, but he had a feeling that suggestion wouldn't go over well. "Also, Captain loves it here."

She frowned, but there was a sparkle in her eyes. A second later she laughed and picked up her wine glass. "Bringing my cat into this is playing dirty." She clinked her glass against his. "You're a hard man to argue with."

"And I like to get my way."

"Gee, that doesn't remind me of your grandmother at all." She sipped her wine. "We need to set some rules if I'm going stay."

"Such as?"

"Honesty always. We started off with lies. No more of that."

"Agreed. What else?"

"We give this—us—a shot. A real shot."

His eyes narrowed. "What are you asking me for exactly?"

She hesitated. Gathering her courage perhaps. "That we both put our baggage aside and give this relationship a fighting chance. Otherwise, what's the point? We're doomed to fail if we don't."

He nodded. "I can…try."

"Good." She leaned in, beaming at him with the kind of naughty grin that curled his toes. "Because if you're willing to do that, then I think we can talk about adding some *benefits*."

Delaney enjoyed Hugh's stunned, open-mouthed response to her suggestion. She sipped her wine and took it all in, amazed that she could get that kind of response out of a centuries-old vampire.

Huh. Her boyfriend was a vampire.

He finally cleared his throat and found his voice. "What kind of benefits are you talking about?"

"Yeah, what kind of benefits?" Julian plopped down on the sofa next to them. He waved at one of the servers. "Hey, gorgeous, can you bring us another glass? Thanks."

With a grin, he put his feet up on the table and sat back. He gave Hugh a very pointed look. "Look at you, out at Insomnia of all places. And with a *date*."

Hugh's expression went stony. "I thought you preferred the human clubs, Julian."

Julian shrugged. "Even I need a break once in a while. Besides, I like to dip my toe into both sides of the river, if you know what I mean. Human, supernatural, I like 'em all."

Hugh grimaced. "If only it was just your toe you were dipping."

Delaney rolled her lips in to keep from laughing.

The server brought another glass and poured wine for Julian. He lifted the glass to them. "Here's to the happy couple then."

"We were just going home, actually," Hugh said.

Julian ignored the hint. "Before you do, I thought you should know I ran into Piper."

Hugh snorted. "There's a lot of that going around."

"She told me everything." Julian flicked his gaze toward Delaney before continuing. He gestured to her with his glass. "She's got it out for you."

Delaney waved her hand. "Tell me something I don't know about Psycho Barbie."

"It's handled," Hugh said.

Julian nodded. "And very well if the two of you are still a thing. I guess it also explains why you're here."

"What do you mean?" Delaney asked.

"I mean you two must have had a real heart to heart and dished all your secrets. My brother doesn't share his true nature with the women he dates." Julian fluttered his lashes. "The fact that he did that with you can only mean it's love."

"Julian—"

"It's too late to protest, brother dear." He tipped his head at Delaney. "You can't pretend otherwise when you've got this one wearing your dead wife's jewelry, now can you?"

Delaney's hand flew to the dragonfly. A chill ran through her, more because Hugh had lied to her—his mother's, indeed—than because of who it actually belonged to. Although that was a little creepy too. "This was your wife's?"

Hugh nodded. "Yes. I—"

"So much for honesty." If the piece weren't so valuable, she would have ripped it off and thrown it at him.

"I was going to tell you when we got home. There's more to the story, it's just not a conversation I want to have here."

Julian held his hands up. "Sorry about that. I figured if she knew you were a vampire, you'd told her all about Juliette too."

Delaney stared at Julian. "Why? What else is there to tell?"

"Say a word, Julian, and I will tear your throat out," Hugh snarled.

Julian refilled his glass then stood. He lifted the glass toward Delaney. "I'll just leave you to it then." And walked off.

Hugh was seething. Her anger over news of the dragonfly's true owner paled in comparison to whatever was going on with him. He hadn't been this enraged even when she'd confessed she wasn't who he thought she was. She wanted to touch him, to reassure him that whatever it was, it couldn't be that bad, but contact seemed like the last thing he'd welcome.

"Let's go home," she said quietly.

He continued staring after his brother, the muscles in his jaw tensing.

She took a breath. And put her hand on his leg. "Hugh."

Finally, he turned to her, and the luminescent anger in his eyes faded. He blinked once.

"Whatever it is," she assured him, "it's okay. Let's go home and talk about it."

Still no response.

"Or not." She pulled her hand back.

He grasped her wrist. His gaze dropped to the dragonfly around her neck, and pain took the place of anger in his eyes. "I killed her. I'm the reason she's dead."

She blinked. "You *killed* your wife."

He nodded.

A thousand scenarios played out in her head, all of them starring Hugh as the out of-control vampire and his late wife as the victim. She shivered. She couldn't really buy Hugh as a brutal killer, but she'd only known him a few days. Maybe he was a vampire Dr. Jekyll and Mr. Hyde. "You need to explain exactly what you mean by that."

Because staying here in Nocturne Falls no longer sounded like the best possible option. Even compared to Rastinelli and his gun.

He let her hand go and dropped his head into his hands. "I tried to save her from the plague."

"You mean by turning her into a vampire?"

He nodded. "I tried. She...didn't make it. The turning killed her."

More scenarios, this time Hugh clamping down on an unknown woman's neck and draining her until she died. Another tremor ran through Delaney.

Hugh turned his head to see her. "You're afraid of me now."

"No, I—"

"It's not a question. I can hear your heart pounding. The increase in your breathing." He moved away from her a few inches. "I would never hurt you, Delaney. Never."

Her heart broke a little for him. She went after him, sliding toward him on the sofa to close the gap he'd created. "I know."

And the truth was, she believed that. "How did the turning kill her? Did you...drink too much from her?"

His brow furrowed. "You think I...no, that's not how it works. She just didn't survive the process."

She blew out the breath she'd been holding. "Then you didn't really kill her."

He stared at her. "If it wasn't for my insistence, she never would have attempted the turning. I'm the reason and the cause of why she died."

"Hugh." She shook her head and put her hand on his shoulder. "The plague took your parents. What makes you think it wouldn't have taken her too?"

He shifted his gaze to the floor. "She could have survived it."

She took her hand off his shoulder. "And maybe she wouldn't have. It's been nearly four hundred years. You can't let this guilt color the rest of your life."

That brought his gaze back to her. "That's easy to say, but what if I kill another woman? I cannot live with that." His mouth set in a hard line. "I *will* not."

Delaney wanted to tell him everything would be all right, but platitudes weren't going to cut it. "I can understand why you'd be hesitant to plan a future with another woman, but if it's her decision to go through the process and she understands the risks, then what's wrong with that?"

No answer.

"It's too late, you know."

He looked at her. "For what?"

She took a breath, hoping her confession might bring him around. "For me to stop what I'm feeling for you."

A muscle in his cheek twitched. He stood. "We need to go home."

And just like that, the conversation was over.

Hugh had done more than enough talking for one night. Delaney made a little small talk in the car on the way home and tried to engage him, but when he didn't answer, she went silent. He wanted to think and she understood that he needed some time to deal with her confession and his memories and get his head straight.

Before they arrived home, she'd fallen asleep, reminding him that she was still very much human. He parked in the garage, then carefully opened her door, lifted her into his arms and carried her into the house.

She turned into him, snuggling her face against his shoulder. He fought not to kiss her, not to bury his nose in the bend of her neck and inhale her fragrance, not to indulge any of the urges that he no longer felt he had the right to. He'd shut her off after she'd declared she had feelings for him.

There would be repercussions for that. She

might leave after all. And he would have to let her go because responding in kind, even if it was the truth, would only end up hurting her more. He couldn't offer her a future. Not the kind of future it seemed that she wanted. One that might lead to her willingly undergoing the process of becoming his vampire bride.

He carried her into her bedroom and laid her gently on the bed. Her cat was nowhere to be found, but she'd left her door open. No doubt Captain was exploring the house.

Hugh tugged her boots off, trying not to wake her. He thought he'd managed it until, as he stood at her bedside, studying the woman he was undeniably falling for, she murmured his name.

"Hugh."

"Shh. It's very late. Go back to sleep." He sat on the edge of the mattress and brushed her hair off her face. He hadn't turned the lights on, but he didn't need them to see how beautiful she was.

"Are you mad at me?" Her voice was a sleepy whisper.

"Mad? No. Not at all."

"You weren't talking to me."

"I didn't know what to say." Or how to say it, or how to explain what a mess his head was.

"Do you want me to leave?"

"No." Emotion clogged his throat. Damn it.

Her hand found his. She slipped her fingers

through his and held on. "Then what are we going to do?"

"About?"

"Me. Falling in love with you."

He sat very still, unable to think or move or process. "Delaney, you can't—"

"Too late. I am." She released his hand and rolled to her side. "Don't worry," she whispered, the tiniest sob clinging to her voice. "I'll get over you. Eventually."

Anger at his own inability to respond finally took hold of him. He had to say something. "Delaney…" Sweet, beautiful Delaney.

She rolled back over, squinting at him.

He knew she couldn't see him in the dark the way he could see her. "I cannot ask any woman to risk her life for me. You must understand that."

"You're not asking me. If we get to that point, I will either make that decision or I won't. But it will be my decision. Why can't you understand *that*?"

"Because…" He swallowed. "Because I am a fool."

She smiled and even in the dark room it felt like he'd been granted a moment in the sun. "Good thing I have a soft spot for foolish men."

He bent his head to her stomach, the earthy scent of her leather top mingling with her sweet fragrance. Losing the presence of her light and joy in his house was an unhappy thought. "Don't leave me."

Her fingers threaded through his hair. "I can only stay if you promise not to shut me out anymore. I know I'm only human but—"

"No." He lifted his head and turned his face to kiss the inside of her wrist. "Don't say you're only human. There's nothing wrong with that. With who you are. Nothing at all. I won't shut you out again. Will you stay?"

She nodded. Then smiled. "Can you see me? That I nodded?"

"Yes." He slid his hands to her rib cage, his emotions raw and lying on the surface of his soul. "You scare me, Delaney."

"I scare you?"

He tugged her closer. "The way you make me feel."

She put her hands on his shoulders, her voice still breathy but very awake. "Which is?"

"Vulnerable." He kissed the soft curves of her body that spilled over the edge of her leather top and was rewarded with a small purr of pleasure. "Predatory." She was warm and delicious. His mouth found the hollow of her throat. Her fingers dug into him. "Protective."

She arched beneath him, sighing.

Each kiss brought him nearer to her mouth, but he teased her, refusing to come closer than the line of her jaw or the corner of her lips. It was the kind of torturous pleasure he'd never indulged in with any other woman beside Juliette, preferring to keep those relationships as emotionally unattached as possible.

She growled softly when his lips brushed the soft spot behind her ear, then pulled away suddenly. "I can't do this. I can't do this with a man who isn't willing to fully commit to the possibility of love. It's the surest way I know to get my heart broken. And you said you'd never hurt me."

He looked her squarely in the eyes. She was wily, this one, to use his own words against him, but she was right. "Delaney, I want no one but you. And if that means someday we have to face the very difficult decision about what a future together means then...I'm willing to take that chance. Even though you know where I stand."

"And you know where I stand."

"I do."

She hesitated. "So, basically, we've got a big fight coming up."

He laughed softly. "Yes, I suppose we do."

She pushed his jacket off his shoulders. "Then I guess we'd better enjoy the honeymoon phase as much as we can."

Delaney was still asleep when Hugh planted a kiss on her temple and crawled out of her bed. He let her sleep, especially since she hadn't gotten much of a chance to do that last night. With a grin he couldn't shake, he showered and dressed and went downstairs for coffee.

Captain and Stanhill were already in the kitchen. Captain was eating scrambled eggs and smoked salmon off one of the good china saucers while Stanhill read his paper.

Stanhill flipped his paper down and stared at him. "You had sex."

"Don't be vulgar." Hugh poured a cup of coffee. "We're two consenting adults."

"I was just stating a fact based on your appearance. Can't say I've ever seen you *glow* before. But then I suppose Corette has the same effect on me."

That took the smile off Hugh's face. "I don't need to hear about your exploits with your witch paramour and I'm not glowing. I'm happy." Which wasn't a word he'd used honestly in a long time.

"Whatever you say. I'm surprised Delaney was so willing."

Hugh glared at his rook. "Are you implying I forced her?"

"Not at all, just that she seemed like the type to want some sort of commitment first, and we all know that's not your style."

Hugh sat at the table. "Maybe I've changed."

Stanhill barked out a laugh. "I doubt that." He calmed. "Are you saying you're committing to her? That marriage is on the table?" He sat up a little. "That you would turn her?"

Hugh bought some time by drinking his coffee. "We've agreed to have that discussion when the time comes."

"Well, you have made progress."

Hugh watched Captain. The cat was not a delicate eater. "Speaking of progress, when did the cat start eating off the Wedgwood?"

Stanhill flipped his paper back up. "You'd better not break her heart."

Hugh sighed and drank his coffee. He would never intentionally hurt Delaney, but he still couldn't see agreeing to turn her into a vampire. If it came to that.

Three rapid knocks sounded on the front door.

Stanhill put the paper down. "I'll get it."

He returned a moment later with Sheriff Merrow in tow. "Coffee, Sheriff?"

"Sure." He took a seat at the table across from Hugh. "Did some digging on Delaney's boss."

Hugh nodded. "And?"

"He's bad news. Racketeering, tax evasion, money laundering...and at least two suspected murders for hire, but they haven't been able to nail him on anything. He's like John Gotti, a real Teflon Don."

Hugh's gut clenched at the thought of a villain like that after Delaney. "Damn. She could very well be in danger then."

Stanhill put a cup of coffee in front of the sheriff. Concern bent Stanhill's brows, but he said nothing.

Merrow nodded. "If this guy finds out where she is, yes." Merrow shook his head. "I don't want to cause panic, but Bridget had a couple of out-of-towners at the bar last night and—"

"You told Bridget?" Merrow's sister, Bridget, ran Howlers, a very popular local dive bar. The name was rather tongue in cheek seeing as how she, like both her brothers, was a werewolf, but the place was a Nocturne Falls landmark.

"I wanted her to be on the lookout since she gets a lot of traffic." He drank his coffee. "Like I was saying, she had a couple of fellows in last night from New York. They paid cash, so she didn't even get names."

Hugh frowned. "I'd imagine New Yorkers aren't that uncommon." He also didn't want to cause Delaney any unnecessary stress.

"No, but these guys were asking if there were a lot of other New Yorkers in town. Where they hung out. Where was the best place to catch a Yankees game on TV."

Warning bells went off in Hugh's head. "You think they were looking for Delaney?"

Merrow shrugged. "Don't know, but it's worth keeping an eye on them. I've asked Bridget to look through her security cams and see if she can find clear pictures of them. Just in case. Either way, thought you should be aware of this possible situation."

The thought of Delaney in trouble made him want to chew nails. "I can protect her."

"I don't doubt that," Merrow said. "I also don't really want to do the paperwork on a double homicide."

"I promised her we'd go to the Panic Parade."

Merrow took a thoughtful breath. "Doubtful they'd try something in a crowd, but keep her close." He drained his cup and stood. "Thanks for the coffee. I'll let you know if I find anything else out."

Hugh got to his feet. "Maybe it's nothing, but

Piper knows Delaney's full name and that she came here to hide out. Julian said last night that Piper made it clear to him that she's 'out for Delaney,' for what that's worth."

Merrow rubbed a hand slowly over his mouth. "I hate to stir that pot if I don't have to."

Hugh nodded. No one liked to cross the Hodges. They loved to get their revenge in print. "I'll talk to Julian. See if I can get something concrete."

"Or…" Merrow's brows lifted. "You might want to talk to Piper yourself. She may tell you more than she told your brother. And at least it wouldn't be secondhand."

"You know what you're asking me?"

Merrow nodded and headed for the door. "I'll let myself out. Call me after you've seen her."

Hugh groaned as the door shut. He looked at Stanhill. "Piper."

Stanhill put Merrow's cup in the sink. "It's for Delaney."

Hugh grabbed his coat. "That's the only reason I'd do this. I'll be back as soon as I can."

The only male in Delaney's bed when she woke up was Captain. He stared at her from the other pillow, judging her in the silent way of cats. She propped herself on her elbows and wrinkled her nose at him. "Be quiet. I'm a grown woman. I can sleep with whoever I like. And I like Hugh."

In fact, she liked him a *lot*.

Captain licked his chops and burped a sulfurous, fishy cloud at her.

"Ew. What have you been eating?"

He put his head down and closed his eyes.

"Fine, go to sleep. Your stinky cat breath isn't enough to ruin my mood." Not when she and Hugh had reached a mutual agreement about giving a relationship an honest try.

She kissed him on the head then lay back down and grinned as a sense of nutty wonderment filled her. She was in a *relationship* with a *vampire*. She put her hand to her throat, but the dragonfly was gone.

Bolting upright, she started patting the sheets. Crap. If she'd lost that…then she saw it on the nightstand. A simple ivory note card was propped next to it.

She snatched it up and read.

Had an errand. See you soon. Miss you already.

-H

She read it again, still smiling. "Miss you too," she whispered to the note. She looked over her shoulder at Captain. "Your mother is gone, you know that? Gone hard."

With a laugh, she hopped out of bed and

climbed into a long, hot shower that felt almost as good as last night. Hugh had been nothing short of amazing. Sweet, tender and utterly devoted while somehow dominant and demanding at the same time. He'd left her exhausted in the most pleasurable way possible.

She rinsed the shampoo from her hair. No wonder Piper hadn't wanted to let him go.

A few more minutes of luxuriating under the hot spray and she got out, wrapped herself and her hair in towels, then tried to figure out what to wear. Her clothing options were getting more limited by the day. She ended up pulling on jeans and a T-shirt.

If she was going to stay here, which she was, at least for a few more weeks, she needed more things to wear. She hadn't spent a dime since she'd gotten here so she could spare a little bit. Maybe she'd drive into town and check out the boutiques she'd seen.

She grabbed her purse and headed downstairs. She poked her head into the kitchen. "Stanhill?"

No sign of him. Maybe he'd gone with Hugh. She checked a few other rooms, but couldn't find him. She went back to the kitchen and left him a note, promising to be back in an hour or two.

The drive into town wasn't bad, but parking took her longer than expected. Finally, she snagged a spot and hit the sidewalk. The streets were busy, probably because of the parade tomorrow. Signs were posted showing the parade route. That would be fun.

She walked past the park. The gargoyle at the fountain was telling jokes to the kids gathered around. She stopped for a moment as the realization struck her that the gargoyle was pretty real and not animatronic, like she'd first thought.

On the other side of the park was one of the little clothing stores she'd seen. She stopped in and poked around, but the styles and prices were a little too upscale. "Is there a secondhand store in town?" she asked the clerk.

The woman nodded. "A block down and turn right. It's across from the Tombstone."

"The Tombstone?"

"The newspaper building."

"Oh, right. Thanks." The newspaper Piper's family owned. Delaney followed the woman's directions and found the shop easily, but did her best to ignore the building on the other side of the street. A chance meeting with Piper was not on her agenda.

The store's selection was great, and she had an armful of selections after only a few minutes. Jeans, a few tops and a new sundress, plus a vintage candy mold she didn't need but couldn't resist. She paid and, bag in hand, left the little shop behind.

She stopped outside the door and stared.

Hugh was leaving the Tombstone building. What errand had he been doing, exactly? She could just make out the image of the woman watching him from inside the lobby. Tall, blonde and unmistakably Piper.

Betrayal gut-punched her. This was shades of Russell all over again. And after what had happened last night...she shook her head. She was jumping to conclusions.

Hugh got in his Jaguar and drove off. He didn't look happy. That might be a good sign. If he'd just had a happy meeting with Piper, he'd have a smile on his face, wouldn't he?

None of that erased the sick feeling in her belly. She walked slowly back to her car, her thoughts continuing to spin out possibilities. Maybe Piper had called him about something. Maybe she was trying to blackmail him over Delaney's real identity. Except her real identity was basically public knowledge now.

Forcing herself not to freak, she drove back to Hugh's and went inside.

He and Stanhill were in the middle of a heated conversation in the living room. The last thing she heard was Hugh saying, "I don't want to tell her any of this yet."

That didn't sound so great. She walked in, not caring if she was interrupting. "You don't want to tell me what?"

Hugh looked relieved to see her. "There you are. You shouldn't have gone into town alone."

His concern wasn't nearly as touching as it should have been. "Why? Because I might see you meeting with Piper?"

He frowned, then shook his head. "No, but about that—"

"Yes, please explain. I'm dying to know why you didn't tell me you were going to see Piper. I thought we were going to be honest with one another now? Especially after we just slept together." She dropped her bag on the floor and took a seat on the sofa, kicking her feet up on the coffee table and settling in.

Stanhill made for the door.

She pointed at him. "You. Stay."

He cleared his throat and took a seat in one of the occasional chairs.

Hugh sighed. "Our sleeping together had nothing to do with me going to see her. Not directly anyway."

"Then why'd you go?"

"Because she threatened you." His eyes took on a predatory gleam. "And I am *not* okay with that."

"What?" All traces of frustration vanished from Delaney's gorgeous face. "What do you mean she threatened me? How?"

Hugh sat near her on the sofa. "First things first. I know you're mad I went to see Piper."

"No, I'm mad you went to see her without telling me and that I had to find out about it on my own. But maybe that's just my own insecurity talking and maybe I don't have a right to that with you. Not yet."

"No, you do. I know your last boyfriend cheated on you. I am not that man. Nor will I ever be." He never wanted her to feel betrayed again, especially not because of something he'd done.

"Even better." Her smile broadened. "Now tell me about Piper threatening me."

"Remember when we were at Insomnia and Julian said Piper was out to get you?"

Delaney nodded. "Sure, but that's not really a threat."

"I didn't think that much of it either, until I talked to Sheriff Merrow again—"

"When was that?"

"Right before lunch. You were still asleep." Still lounging in the bed they'd shared. A bed he wished he'd stayed in longer. "Merrow came by to give me an update. His sister, Bridget, runs Howlers, a local dive bar in town and—"

"Wait. Is Bridget a werewolf too?"

"Yes."

"Howlers? That's not a little on the nose or anything." Delaney grinned. "Go on."

"Bridget had some customers come in who caused her some concern."

"I'm not following."

"Sheriff Merrow told her about your situation. That family is pretty close, and because of Howlers, Bridget has her finger on the pulse of this town."

"Got it. So what about these customers?"

"They were from New York and asked where other New Yorkers tended to hang out in town."

Delaney froze. "You mean like they were looking for me?"

He nodded. "Maybe. They paid cash so we don't have any names, but Bridget is looking through her security footage to see if she can find a clear picture of them."

Delaney hugged her knees to her chest. "Where does Piper fit into all this?"

"Merrow wanted me to talk to her after I told him what she'd said to Julian. He thought she was more likely to tell me what she might have done than anyone else."

"And?"

It wasn't good. But Delaney deserved to know. "Piper heard your name during the confrontation we had here. She researched you and found out there was a missing-persons report on you in New York."

"What?" Delaney pressed her hand to her forehead. "That piece of—one of my co-workers texted me to say that if I didn't show up, Rastinelli was going to call the police and tell them I'd gone missing. I thought it was just a scare tactic. I never thought he'd actually do it."

Hugh shoved a hand through his hair. "Sounds like another indicator that he's got some dirty cops on his payroll. Bloody hell. Those men at Howlers might actually be here looking for you."

Hugh's phone buzzed. He pulled it out to see a text from Sheriff Merrow. He opened it. "Bridget found some clear shots of the men. Merrow wants us to come down to the station so you can see if either of them are familiar."

"Okay." She reached out and grabbed his hand. "What if they come after me?"

He kissed her knuckles and smiled. "Sweetheart, I don't care how dangerous those men think they are, they're nothing against an aged vampire and his rook."

"Damn straight," Stanhill chimed in. "They won't get a chance to lay hands on you, miss."

She smiled.

Hugh squeezed her hand. "I want you to feel safe."

"I do." Her smile faded a bit and her gaze turned wistful. "I guess this means no parade, huh?"

He knew she'd be disappointed, but there was nothing he could do. Her safety was more important. "Probably not."

"That kinda sucks." She took a deep breath. "Let's go see the sheriff. Get this over with."

Stanhill stood. "I'll bring the car around." He grinned at her. "If it's all right that I leave."

"Yes." She laughed. "Sorry about ordering you around like that."

He winked at her. "I assure you, I'm used to it."

"Oh please," Hugh said. "Just go get the car."

"See?" Stanhill shook his head as he walked out of the room.

Delaney's soft laughter continued. "You two are quite a team."

Hugh looked after his rook. "He's a good man."

She took his hand. "So are you. I'm sorry I gave

you such a hard time about going to see Piper. That wasn't fair of me."

He pulled her close. "Considering your history with men not being honest, I'd say you get a pass." He brushed her bottom lip with his thumb and heat spiraled through him at the thought of having her in his bed again. "I will never intentionally hurt you, Delaney. If I have to tell you that every day, I will."

He sealed his promise with a slow kiss. "And I will never let anyone else hurt you." He looked into her eyes. "If these men come after you, they will have to go through me. If they attempt to hurt you, I will kill them."

She swallowed. "It's totally wrong of me to be turned on by the thought of murder, but that's kind of hot."

Her words caught him off guard, and he laughed out loud. "You never fail to surprise me, woman. For someone of my age, that is a rare and outstanding quality."

Two quick honks broke the mood. "Stanhill," Hugh growled as he got to his feet. He raised a brow at Delaney and offered her a hand up. "That impudence is all for your benefit, I hope you know. He likes you. And he's a tough critic."

She smiled and took his hand as she stood. "I like Stanhill, too. When I first got here, I thought he was you."

Hugh frowned. "You seem as though you would have been okay with that."

"He's a very handsome man, but he's a little old for me." She pursed her lips and leaned into him. "Of course, that was before I knew you were three hundred and seventy-seven."

He started to argue that vampires aged differently, but she pressed a finger to his lips and smiled slyly. "Who knew I had a thing for older men with really sharp teeth?"

Fifteen minutes later, they were sitting in the sheriff's office. It was a block off Main in a pretty brick building with a small front parking lot. Sheriff Merrow's office sat just beyond the receptionist's desk, which is where she and Hugh sat now. When they'd come in, she'd seen a smaller, second office, maybe an interrogation room, and a hall with a sign above it that said "Holding," but not much more than that. Apparently, when your town's sheriff was a werewolf, crime wasn't that big of an issue.

"Appreciate you coming in," Sheriff Merrow said.

He was about to close his office door, when the receptionist barged in. "Can I get y'all a Coke? We have bottled water too. Or coffee."

He glowered at the woman. "Mrs. Caruthers, I am trying to—"

"You hush, Hank. Where are your manners?

And for Pete's sake, call me Aunt Birdie." She shook her head and looked at Delaney. "I changed his diapers, you know. And his brother Titus's."

"Mrs. Ca—*Aunt* Birdie." Sheriff Merrow pointed out the door. "Back to your desk *please*."

Delaney hoped her shock wasn't registering on her face. She could not imagine changing a werewolf's diapers. "I would have thought it was more of a housebreaking situation," she muttered under her breath.

Hugh coughed and shot her a pointed look.

"What was that, dear?" Mrs. Caruthers asked as she soundly ignored Sheriff Merrow.

"Nothing," Delaney said. "We're good on the drinks."

Mrs. Caruthers's grin widened. "If you change your mind, just let me know. And y'all can call me Birdie."

Sheriff Merrow pointed with greater enthusiasm.

Birdie left.

He shut the door. "Sorry about that. She's a force of nature, that one."

"Is she really your aunt?"

Sheriff Merrow's nostrils flared. "Yes."

Delaney stifled a snort of laughter. "I like the pushiness of Southern hospitality, although it's going to take some getting used to."

Sheriff Merrow sighed, opened a file and

pushed it across the desk toward her. "Pictures are grainy, but it's the best Bridget could do. Resolution on her security feed isn't great."

She studied the pictures, finally pushing the file back toward him. "Sorry, neither of these men look familiar, although they do look like the type of guys that Little Tony—that's Anthony Rastinelli's son—hangs out with."

Sheriff Merrow closed the file and moved it to the corner of his otherwise pristine desk, then looked at Hugh. "What did you find out from Piper?"

"Not much," Hugh said. "Just that she found a missing person's report on Delaney."

Sheriff Merrow tapped a finger on the file. "That doesn't help me eliminate these two at all."

"Probably makes them even more suspicious, huh?" Delaney sighed. "Hugh said we probably shouldn't go to the parade tomorrow with those two in town."

"Actually…" Sheriff Merrow sat forward. "If you went, we might be able to draw them out. If they are indeed in town after you."

"No," Hugh said. "We're not using Delaney as bait."

She put her hand on his arm. "Wait a minute. If it means getting rid of these guys—or maybe finding out there's no one here after me—then why not?" She looked at the sheriff. "I'd be totally protected, right?"

"Absolutely."

"By you and two deputies?" Hugh snorted derisively. "I wouldn't call that totally protected."

Sheriff Merrow's already squinty-eyed gaze got a little squintier. "We're all werewolves. And I'd assumed you'd be at her side the whole time. Are you saying you plus three of us wouldn't be enough?"

Hugh leaned forward, clearly not amused, considering the stern set of his mouth. "I'm saying I don't want to put her into any more danger than she already is."

"The thing is," Delaney started. "We don't actually know if I'm in danger or not. This would be a good way to figure that out."

Hugh shifted his gaze to her. "I don't like it."

"I'm not madly in love with it, but it's a solid plan." She nodded at Sheriff Merrow. "I'm willing to give it a shot."

Hugh frowned. "What about your new friend, the gargoyle? You think he'd be up for helping out? Just to add a little sheer brute force."

"I talked to him for five minutes. I have no idea." But it was nice to know Hugh was over being jealous of Nick. She looked at the sheriff. "He said he knew you from the Army. Nick Hardwin?"

Sheriff Merrow's head did a slow bob. "Nick Hardwin. Good guy. Just into town. I could deputize him if it makes you feel better."

"Yes, it would." Hugh stared at Delaney. "Are you sure you're all right with this?"

"With three werewolves, one gargoyle, one vampire and Stanhill? I can't think of how I might be safer."

"I can," Hugh groused.

"Yes, I know. If I wasn't there at all." She bit back a laugh. "Sheriff, what about the possibility that these men don't even see me at the parade?"

"In that crowd, they may not. If nothing happens tomorrow, we'll have to reevaluate." He thought for a moment. "You two should go out to Howler's tonight. Talk about going to the parade. It'll be packed, and there's a good chance our guys will be there."

Hugh growled softly.

Sheriff Merrow nodded. "I get it, Ellingham. I wouldn't want my woman to be in danger either, but we need Rastinelli to act first. Without provocation, we've got nothing. That's why he's not already in jail."

"What about the video of him shooting that guy?" Delaney asked. "Why haven't they acted on it?"

The sheriff frowned. "I have a feeling whoever Rastinelli owns in the police department made that disappear."

"Well, that sucks."

"It's just more reason for you two to go tonight and set this plan in motion."

She grabbed Hugh's hand. "C'mon, it'll be fun to go out and...have fun."

"Fine." Hugh laced his fingers with hers as he looked at the sheriff. "But if I have to rip someone's heart out, I will."

The sheriff sighed. "I'd rather not know about that. But I'll still tell Bridget to expect you."

Howler's was Hugh's idea of hell. Wall-to-wall human tourists, loud music, cheap alcohol and questionable bar food.

"This place is crazy," Delaney exclaimed with a happy grin. "Ooo, I see dart boards in the back room. I love darts!" She hooked her arm through his. "You want to put our name on the list to play?"

Maybe Howler's wasn't that bad. Especially not with Delaney at his side. Somehow she made jeans and an off-the-shoulder T-shirt look as provocative as a lace teddy. Bloody hell, she turned him on. "You don't want to play darts with me. My accuracy won't make it much of a game, I'm afraid."

She pretended to be upset with him, but her eyes sparkled. "We could shoot some pool."

"Same thing."

"Shuffle bowl?"

He frowned. "I don't even know what that is."

"It's like bowling but on a table with a puck." She leaned in and whispered in his ear. "Your Lordship needs to get out more."

He snorted. "And you need to spend less time with Stanhill." Although he couldn't deny his honorific title coming from her lips sent a jolt of heat through him. He kissed her, laughing as he did. This woman made him happy beyond description. He wanted to shower her with gifts, to spoil her in a way he imagined she'd never experienced.

Howler's wasn't the place to do that, but if she was having a good time, he would too. All while keeping an eye out for anyone paying too much attention to her.

Bridget waved at them from behind the bar. "Hugh, Delaney, over here." She pointed at two bar seats that were opening up.

He'd met Bridget a few times before, but he couldn't say they were more than acquaintances.

Another couple made a beeline for the stools, but Bridget bared her teeth and barked at them. The couple scurried away.

"All righty then," Delaney muttered.

"Exactly." Hugh took her hand and pushed through the crowd to claim the seats.

"Hank told me you guys were coming." Bridget smiled. She was a little wild looking with all that auburn hair and those big gold eyes, but attractive enough if you went for that type. Which he didn't.

Bridget stuck her hand out to Delaney. "Bridget Merrow, nice to meet you."

Delaney hopped into the seat and shook the woman's hand. "Nice to meet you too. Anyone in here we ought to know about?"

"Not yet. But I'll keep you posted. I've got my staff on the lookout for them too," Bridget answered. She waggled her finger between them. "What'll it be to drink?"

Hugh took the seat beside Delaney, letting her answer first.

"White wine."

"Whiskey," Hugh responded. "Best you have. For both orders." Which still didn't offer much hope.

Bridget's brows shot up. "You want the best white I have, I'm going to have to open a bottle."

"Fine," Hugh answered. At least that way Delaney wouldn't end up with something that had been open too long and gone vinegary, although he imagined this establishment went through alcohol pretty quickly.

As Bridget went to fill their order, Delaney twisted her chair toward him and wiggled into position so that one of her knees was between his. He didn't really need a drink. Her grin was intoxicating enough. She leaned forward, clearly enjoying herself. "You hate this place, don't you?"

"What makes you say that?"

She shrugged. "What doesn't make me say that? It's loud, it's full of tourists…" She glanced down. "I think there's sawdust on the floor."

He slid his hand up her leg, reveling in being able to touch her. "I hadn't noticed."

She laughed. "I don't believe that for a second."

"Maybe I was too distracted by you." He gave her thigh a squeeze.

She blushed a little, but then seriousness came over her. "Thanks for doing this."

"For having a feel in a public place?"

She smirked. "You know what I mean. For coming to Howler's. And for agreeing to do the parade tomorrow." As her expression sobered again, she traced a circle on the back of his hand, which still rested on her leg. "There has to be an end to this. I can't live the rest of my life looking over my shoulder."

"No, you can't. Doesn't mean I like what we've decided to do, but I want you to be safe and happy." As happy as she made him.

"I am happy." Her smile reappeared. "More than I could have imagined. Are you happy?"

He swallowed. "I am." So much it scared him.

Bridget returned with their drinks. "Don't go look now, but the two guys that were in here before are now in the back room at a booth. There's a third guy with them."

Delaney's leg twitched beneath his hand. He gave her a reassuring pat but kept his eyes on Bridget. "Have they seen us?"

She smiled like they were talking about something completely unrelated. "I don't think so. They probably came in through the rear entrance. Most people use the front door, but there's a little overflow parking lot in the back. Anybody who parks back there usually comes in that way."

"Thanks. Text your brother, let him know. In fact, ask him to wait for us in that back parking lot. We might be able to draw them out."

Delaney twisted her wine glass in place on its paper napkin. "I thought we were just supposed to let them overhear us talking about going to the parade tomorrow."

"We're going to do that. Then we're going to take it a step further. See if we can wrap this business up this evening." Then he could take her to the parade without the distraction of this threat.

"I'll let Hank know." With a nod, Bridget headed back to the kitchen.

The joy had left Delaney's face, although she was clearly trying not to look frightened. "I'm not sure I like this."

"Sweetheart, I promise I can protect you if something happens." He lowered his voice, not that anyone could hear him over the ruckus in this place. "Three humans against one vampire is not much of a fight."

She managed an almost convincing smile, and he hated that she was afraid. For that alone her former boss deserved to be punished. "What's your plan then?"

"Have you ever done any acting?"

"Does a school play count?"

"Absolutely."

"Then yes."

"Excellent. Here's what I'm thinking…"

Drinks in hand, Hugh and Delaney stumbled their way into the back room. There were enough people in the place that there was no way Rastinelli's guys would try something in the bar. She pointed at one of the dart boards. "That one's open," she declared, hoping she'd gauged the perfect acceptable level of loudness for a supposedly drunk person.

Hugh raised his whiskey to her. "You wanna play darts, me love, we're gonna play darts."

Not only had his accent thickened, it had gotten less sophisticated. She threw her hands up into the air, spilling a little of her wine. "Yay!"

"I'll be right back." He left his drink with her and went to see about getting darts as planned, while she leaned against the back wall and used one of the bar mirrors to check on her new friends in the booth.

They were definitely Little Tony's sort of crew. She could practically smell the garlic on them. And judging by the direction of their gazes, they were sizing her up as well. It kind of terrified her to think that these men might be here to kidnap her and take her back to Rastinelli.

Or worse.

She covered her shudder by having a sip of wine and remembering she was supposed to be tipsy. Then Hugh returned to her, darts in hand, and her thoughts shifted back to the fact that she now had a very dangerous boyfriend. Who was a mother-freakin' vampire. Let the bad guys come after them.

"Hello, lover," she purred at him.

"'Ello, angel." He wrapped his arms around her and pulled her close to nuzzle her neck. "They're watching us," he whispered into her ear.

She laughed like he'd just said something very naughty. "Mm-hmm."

"Let's drop the hint about the parade, then see if we can get them to follow us out." He leaned away and leered at her before announcing, "And that's not all I'm going to do to you."

"You're a bad man." She swatted at him playfully, missing on purpose.

Leaving their drinks behind, he walked them

toward the dart board and closer to the trio of thugs. "I might be bad, but you'd better be a good girl or I won't take you to the parade tomorrow."

She stuck her lip out in a pout. "You promised. I want cotton candy."

He tossed the darts onto a table, the glow in his eyes positively devilish. "I've got something for you that's even sweeter."

She bit her lip and did her best to look overcome with desire. Not that hard to do considering she knew *exactly* what he had for her. "I don't want to play darts anymore."

"Brilliant." He grabbed her hand. "Neither do I, love."

She bumped the back door open with her hip, and with their hands and arms entangled, she and Hugh spilled into the dark parking lot like a pair of crazed lovers oblivious to the world.

Hugh gestured with a nod. "Over there where the light's burned out. Against that wall."

She did a quick scan of the parking lot. "Okay, but I don't see the sheriff."

"He's close. I can smell wolf."

That was slightly reassuring. She let Hugh guide her to the spot he'd indicated, and then he pushed her against the wall and started kissing her. His hands roamed her body with reckless abandon. The brick was rough on her back, but the soft heat of his mouth made up for it. She gasped at the urgency of his affection. He might be acting, but her moans and writhing were one hundred percent genuine. The man had no idea what he did to her.

His mouth strayed to her ear. "Back door just opened. They're coming."

She tensed, her breath coming in gulps. She hadn't heard a thing.

"Don't be afraid," he whispered.

Then she caught the sounds of shoes scuffling on pavement, but it was dark and Hugh blocked most of her field of vision. A dark shape moved behind him.

A bottle crashed down on his head a second later, showering them both with shards of glass and drops of stale beer. Before she could scream, Hugh jerked his elbow back and caught one of the thugs square across the nose. He went down with a grunt.

Hugh twisted to slug the second one and Delaney ran, a gut reaction. But not a good one. A hand grabbed her from behind and another hand clamped down on her mouth.

"You're going with me," the thug holding her said. "Sorry your boyfriend can't come with us, but—"

A loud crash was followed by a car alarm going off, and then somehow Hugh was standing in front of her. "You're not taking her anywhere."

The thug pulled her to his left, then threw a right hook at Hugh.

Hugh caught the man's fist and squeezed until bone crunched. The man howled in pain and let go of Delaney, curling his uninjured hand into a fist.

Before he could swing, Hugh shoved the heel of his hand into the man's solar plexus with such force that the thug went flying into the wall. He collapsed onto the pavement.

"You didn't leave much for me." Sheriff Merrow walked toward them.

"Thought you'd be here sooner," Hugh answered.

"You had it handled."

"Yes, I did." Hugh smiled at Delaney, turning her insides to warm, gooey appreciation. "Are you all right, my darling?"

She nodded, not quite capable of speech.

The sheriff walked over and clamped handcuffs onto the unconscious thug who'd accosted her, then he squeezed the walkie-talkie at his shoulder. "I need another squad car at Howler's."

Hugh took Delaney's face gently between his hands. "Are you sure you're okay? You look pale. I'm sorry he put his hands on you."

She tried to smile. "I'm fine. A little shaken up, but that went way faster than I expected."

"Better that way. Less time for something genuinely awful to happen."

"How's your head?"

"My head?" He looked puzzled. "Why?"

She laughed. "You got hit with a beer bottle."

He ran a hand through his hair, sending a few pieces of glass flying. "Hard vampire head. No damage done."

A squad car careened into the parking lot, and a deputy jumped out. "Bar fight?" he asked Sheriff Merrow.

"Something like that. There are two more perps by the wall where the light is out." Sheriff Merrow hauled his semi-conscious thug to the car, threw him over the trunk and started patting him down. He pulled out a handgun. "Bet you don't have a permit for this, do you?"

Before the thug could answer, the sheriff shoved him in the squad car and shut the door. He held up the gun. "I'm going to need you two to come down to the station and make a statement."

Hugh nodded and put his arm around Delaney. "We'll be right there."

18

An hour and a half later, they were finally home. Hugh considered the evening a success. Delaney was no longer in immediate danger, and the arrest of Rastinelli's men would send a message. He hoped. He wasn't so foolish to think that this was one and done, but it would take at least a day for Rastinelli to get more men down here, unless they were willing to fly, which meant a record of the trip and no easy way to bring firearms.

The upside was Delaney seemed at peace again, which made Hugh happy.

Stanhill greeted them as they walked in. "How did it go?"

Hugh gave him the recap.

"Bleedin' amateurs." Stanhill nodded at Delaney. "You all right then?"

She tucked a strand of hair behind one ear. "I am. Hugh took care of them like *that*." She snapped her fingers. "Although…I'm kind of hungry."

"We never did eat dinner." So much for taking care of her every need. He looked at Stanhill. "What have we got?"

"Bits and bobs." Stanhill shrugged. "What do you feel like, miss?"

She put her hand on her stomach. "Thai food, but I don't suppose you have that in Nocturne Falls."

"Ah, but we do." Stanhill raised a finger. "Follow me."

Into the kitchen they went, where Stanhill produced a paper menu from one of the kitchen drawers. "Open until eleven p.m., so you have half an hour to order. They don't deliver, but I'll run into town and pick it up."

"Thank you!" Delaney let out a little squeal of delight. "I want all of it." She laughed. "Gimme a sec, and I'll narrow it down." She pored over the menu. "Hugh, what are you getting? You must be starved."

"I am, but my needs right now are a little…different."

She looked up from the menu, her brows furrowed. "What do you mean?" Her mouth rounded. "Oh."

He nodded, knowing then that she understood he needed to feed. He'd held off for a few days—actually, he hadn't given it much thought he'd been so preoccupied with her—but especially now after the exertion of power during the fight, he needed blood. "I'll just slip downstairs and—"

"I want to go with you." She straightened, a very determined look in her eye.

Stanhill made a small noise in the back of his throat. "Miss, I don't think—"

"We said no more secrets." She kept her eyes on Hugh. Almost challenging him.

"Delaney, this isn't a secret I'm keeping from you. It's just not something I share with anyone."

She crossed her arms. "So I'm just anyone?"

"I didn't say that."

She looked at Stanhill. "Shrimp pad thai, spicy, and an order of spring rolls."

"Very good," he answered. He snatched keys off a hook by the door and zipped out. Undoubtedly, Hugh would have to tell Stanhill what was about to happen when he returned. Hugh knew his rook too well to think he'd let this one lie.

Hugh rolled his shoulders. "Sweetheart, what you're asking is—"

She strode toward him, resolve shining in her eyes like a flame. "What I'm asking is to be included in one more part of your life. You wanted me to believe you're a vampire, and I do. You wanted me to stay, and I've agreed to that too. If we're taking a chance on this relationship and looking toward the future, then this is just one more thing you can share with me to help me understand your world."

He couldn't really say no to that. "It's a very intimate act."

She slipped her arms around his neck and gently nipped his jaw, the scrape of her teeth sending a jolt of pleasure spiraling through him. She kept her mouth against his skin as she spoke. "I can't imagine it's more intimate than some of the things we've already done."

He closed his eyes and groaned softly, powerless to keep his hands from sliding down her rib cage to rest on the crest of her hips. He almost forgot what they were talking about. "No, I suppose not."

She pressed into him, her breath a warm caress that was followed by her tongue. "Then share this with me. Please. I really want to understand your life and what it's like to be you."

"A lot of women faint at the sight of blood." A weak argument, but all he could come up with against the onslaught of her affections.

She leaned back, canted her head and tightened her mouth into a firm line. "I'm not most women."

"No, you most definitely are not." He sighed, defeated. But he couldn't get his feet to move.

"There's something else bothering you, isn't there?"

He narrowed his eyes. "I suppose there is. I can't

help but think you'll see me differently after this. It's something akin to having the wizard's curtain drawn back."

She shook her head. "What I feel for you can't be changed that easily."

"That's reassuring." But they'd see about that soon. Knowing a truth and seeing it demonstrated were two very different things. "Downstairs we go, then."

He led her to the basement door and unlocked it, then stopped on the first tread. "I'll lead. I know where the light switches are."

She followed him down into the dark, her steps careful but never hesitant. She was as brave as she was beautiful.

That didn't mean he was free of misgivings, but he was too besotted not to indulge her. He flicked on the light. "Welcome to my sanctum sanctorum."

She looked around, nodding slowly. "This is very cool. Your grandmother said she isn't allowed down here and has no idea what you do in this place." She gestured at the tables full of equipment and the tall cabinets stacked with supplies. "What is all this?"

"My lab." He stood between the two main work tables.

"So what kind of stuff *do* you work on in here?"

"I…" And then he realized he had one secret left

to confess. "It's occurred to me that I haven't told you the whole truth."

A tentative look crossed her face. "I'm almost afraid to ask."

"It's nothing bad, I swear." He pulled the amulet from beneath his shirt. "This is how Didi persuaded me to agree to Annabelle's visit. I have enough money that the loss of any inheritance makes no difference."

She came to stand beside him, staring at the amulet. "What is it?"

"Our most secret of secrets. No one outside my family knows it."

She stopped, her eyes widening. "Are you sure you want to tell me?"

"You said yourself there can be no secrets between us if we have any chance of making things work." He held up the amulet. "This is what allows me to walk in the sun. Without it, the sun would kill me. The magic that powers this was created by Alice Bishop, my grandmother's companion. In thanks for saving her life, she found a way to protect ours."

Her mouth rounded. "Really?" Her gaze went from the amulet to him then back again. "That's why your grandmother wears one too."

He nodded. "As well as both my brothers."

"But not Stanhill?"

"No, as a rook, it's not required."

232

Her fingers brushed the amulet, then she wrapped her arms around her torso and leaned back against one of the work tables. "Why are you telling me this? That's a pretty big thing to reveal to someone you've only known a short time."

"Because I love you." What was the point in pretending otherwise? "And I don't want anything between us."

"You...love me?" She paled, looking very fragile and human in that moment.

"Yes." He put his hands on her arms and drew her in, holding her loosely against him. "Does that frighten you?"

Her response came in a breathy whisper. "No."

"Good. Because I am utterly lost in you, Delaney. I know it's only been a few days, but I cannot imagine myself with another woman. You're my last thought of the day and my first thought when I awake."

Her chest rose and fell with her breaths. "What about not wanting to be married? About not being over Juliette?"

He bent his forehead to hers, needing to connect himself to her as much as possible. "What I'm not over is the guilt of her death. I may never be over that. Losing her devastated me and my fear at feeling that kind of pain again has kept me from loving anyone else." He smiled, his memories of Juliette more sweet than bitter. "She would be angry at me for not giving another woman a chance. But then, she's not the one who's had to bear the burden of her death.

He sighed. "You know, we married out of a sense of duty. It was expected of us, but I know if given the chance she would have married another."

"Did she love you?"

He turned away. "She was a good wife." That's all he could say. Because the real answer hurt too much.

"That's really why you feel so guilty, isn't it? Because she chose to be turned out of duty to you, not because she loved you."

He nodded, seeing only the lab before him. "Her entire life was sacrificed upon the altar of Lord Ellingham."

"But she could have died from the plague. It was her *choice* to be turned."

He laughed brusquely. "I wish that were true."

"What do you mean?"

"I was her lord and husband." He shook his head. "It was a very different time. Women had less say in things. And I was a man trying very hard to overcome my place in the world as my father's second son. I'm not sure you would have liked me then."

"Maybe not, but...but I love you now."

Her words were a whisper, but they rang

through him like the peal of church bells. He twisted to see her face. "You do?"

She nodded, her eyes glittering in the lab's spotlights. "It's crazy. But then again, maybe that's who I am. The crazy cat lady in love with the vampire."

He swept her into his arms and spun her around, kissing her face as she laughed. "That's exactly who I want you to be."

"Put me down, you're making me dizzy."

He set her feet on the floor and kissed her again for good measure.

She gently pushed him away with her hands on his shoulders. "Why did you tell me all that about the amulet?"

He looked around. "You asked what I do down here. There was no way to answer you truthfully without the rest of it coming out. My work down here has been a struggle to find a formula that would take the place of the amulets."

"But why? If you have them, why do you need something else?"

"Because since Alice created them, my grandmother has used them to bend us to her will. Sebastian would very much like to leave Nocturne Falls and hunt for his estranged wife, but my grandmother refuses to grant him permission, threatening to have Alice revoke the amulet's magic if he does."

"There are other witches in town. Have one of them make you a new amulet."

"If only it were that easy. Alice's magic is something more than what modern witches have." He raked a hand through his hair. "When my grandmother saved her from death in Salem, Alice somehow managed to harness the souls of her sisters murdered before her. Those souls strengthened her as if she had the power of ten witches instead of one, and she channeled those souls into the magic of the amulets."

Shock brightened Delaney's eyes. "That's some serious magic."

"Exactly."

"I can imagine you also wouldn't want to tell another witch either, because like you said, the amulets are a source of vulnerability." She frowned. "What would happen if someone were to yank that off you while you're standing in the sun? Would you really burn up like vampires do in books and movies?"

An image of the one vampire he'd seen face the dawn filled his head. "If I could not find cover, I would burn to ashes in a matter of minutes."

She covered her mouth with her hand. "That's horrifying."

"Indeed. Not something I'd like to experience."

"Is there anything I can do to help?"

He smiled, her willingness gift enough. "No, my

darling. I have collected and studied every text that holds even the slightest hint of promise. Someday I will unlock the secret."

"Baking is kind of like science. You never know, I might be able to help."

A new urge to kiss her arose. "This is not so much science as it is part alchemy and part witchcraft. Not that I am so talented in either, but I've taught myself a great deal over the years."

"Thank you for confiding in me. For trusting me." She walked around the closest work table, studying the things laid out on it and trailing her fingers around the edge as she made the loop back to him. "We're both still hungry and my food will be here soon. You should feed. It's what we came down here for."

"Yes." Doing this in front of her went against his grain, but the time for protesting was over. He went to move past her, gesturing toward the far bank of cabinets. "I need to get to that refrigeration unit."

She hopped up onto the work table and propped her foot on the one across from it, blocking his path. "No, you don't."

"If I'm going to feed, I do."

She swept her hair over to one shoulder, and color flooded her cheeks. "You have a source right here."

Heat rushed through him in such a surge he saw

stars. He'd already had a taste of her when she'd pricked her finger on his fang, but to drink from her…that wasn't something he could allow. He was in love with her, and any vampire who drank from the mortal they loved risked hurting that mortal. He refused to put her in that precarious position. "No, absolutely not—"

"Why? Will it turn me into a vampire?"

"That's not how it works."

"Well, how would I know? You haven't explained that part to me."

"It takes three bites on consecutive nights to turn a mortal into a vampire. Two to make a rook. One has no effect."

"Which explains why the world isn't overrun with you fanged types."

"Yes." Her leg still blocked his path. "Now if you'll excuse me—"

"Will it hurt? I'm not afraid. Just curious."

"I'm not biting you."

She made a face, her voice carrying a teasing tone. "Is it because your fangs aren't sharp enough?"

"You know my fangs are perfectly—you can't prod me into this, Delaney."

She leaned in, close enough to kiss. "Are you afraid you won't be able to stop?"

Terrified. "Delaney, I'm not doing this."

"Then what?"

How did he explain the spell her blood would weave over him? The way he would come to crave her more and more. The way he would be unable to think of anything but drinking from her until she had nothing left to offer. If he didn't physically exhaust her first. Then turning her would be the only way to save her. "Because of the risk involved."

"I already know. I might not survive the turning."

"Not that risk."

She jerked back. "There's another?"

"Yes, but I don't wish to discuss it." She'd only push harder if she knew the details.

She wrinkled her nose. Disgustingly cute. "No secrets, remember?"

He said nothing, just stared at her.

She huffed out a breath and let her leg swing down. "Fine. Go get your gross old bagged-up blood. That is what's in there, right?"

Relief surged through him. "Yes. Gross old bagged-up blood." Which would now forever pale against the knowledge of what he could have had.

Still, he barely managed not to laugh as he brushed past her. He put his back to her and bent to open the cold storage unit.

The tinny scrape of metal on metal reached his ears. Then Delaney's voice.

"Ow! Crap."

The sweet metallic tang of blood filled his nostrils. He straightened and turned to see what she'd done, but he already knew.

Blood spilled from her hand.

She held it out in front of her. "I didn't know that little blade was *that* sharp."

His gaze fixed to the slice across her palm. "It's a *scalpel*."

She lifted her hand, examining her wound. "Why on earth do you need a scalpel?"

Tissue samples, but that wasn't important now. Unable to control his growing hunger any longer, he felt his fangs punch through his gums.

She lifted her eyes to his and held her hand out to him. "We should do something about this."

Need fogged his thoughts. Blood dripped onto the floor. "You did that on purpose."

"Yes and no. I only meant to nick myself, not cause arterial damage."

"There's no artery there," he muttered. Somehow he was standing next to her.

"You won't even have to bite me now." Her voice held innocence, but determination edged her gaze.

Upstairs, the kitchen door opened and closed, accompanied by familiar footsteps. The pungent aroma of Thai food wafted down. His rook had returned.

With a staggering amount of control, Hugh

shouted for the man. "Stanhill. Bring the first aid kit immediately."

"Hugh," Delaney pleaded.

"No. Don't press me on this again."

As Stanhill started down the stairs, Hugh strode up them and away from Delaney. Another second and he'd succumb. "Bandage her hand. I'll be in my quarters. I did not yet feed."

Stanhill raised a brow. "Understood."

Hugh retreated to his room, his restraint tested nearly to the breaking point. He closed the door and bolted it, realizing the foolishness of that action even as he did it. A powerful, aged vampire, and he was locking himself away from a *mortal*.

He closed his eyes. He'd never been so affected by a woman this way before. There was no doubt in his mind that Delaney would want to be turned into a vampire. Especially now that she'd professed her love for him.

He loved her as well, which only strengthened his refusal to turn her. But she would talk him into it somehow, like she'd talked him into letting her be bait for those thugs at Howlers. He would never be able to refuse her. Not when he already knew he would kill for her.

And he could see only one way out, one way to preserve her life. She had to leave.

To keep her alive, he had to break her heart.

19

"You can't force him, miss." Stanhill dabbed the slice on her palm with a cotton pad dampened with something that stung.

Delaney sucked in a breath. "I know." But the sting of the cleanser was nothing compared to the ache in her heart over the foolishness of what she'd done. "I feel like an idiot."

Stanhill smiled as he took a bandage from the kit. "He makes us all feel that way sometimes."

"Why is it such a big deal? I thought I'd be the better option over blood in a bag."

Stanhill peeled off the paper backing. "You are. In theory. But in practice, it's a much different thing."

She held her hand still while he fixed the bandage over her self-inflicted wound. "Why, though? I don't get it."

"You'll have to get that answer from him, miss." He snapped the kit shut. "There you go. All better."

She held her hand up with the enormous bandage on it. "Yes, this looks normal. Not at all like I did something stupid."

He laughed. "No one but you and I know how that happened."

"And Hugh." She sighed and hopped off the table. "I'm not sure I can look him in the eyes again after humiliating myself that way."

"Come eat. You'll feel better. Food's on the table upstairs."

"Maybe you're right. Not that I'm very hungry anymore." She started for the stairs, but Stanhill made no effort to leave.

She stopped on the landing. "You're going to take blood to him aren't you?"

"Yes, miss."

With a sad smile, she trudged up to the kitchen. A white plastic bag filled with takeout containers sat on the table. It smelled great, but her appetite was gone. Stanhill had gone to the trouble, though, so she pulled out the container, unwrapped a pair of chopsticks and sat down to eat.

Stanhill came through the basement door, shutting it firmly behind him. She didn't need to look at him to know he had a plastic bag of blood tucked under his arm. "Everything to your liking, miss?"

She forced a smile. "Great, thank you for getting this for me."

"You're welcome." He walked toward the house's interior.

"Stanhill?"

He stopped. "Yes?"

"Tell him I won't do that again. Please. I promise."

Stanhill nodded. "I will, but I think he'd like to hear that from your lips himself."

She sighed and stared at her food. "Tomorrow."

"Tomorrow." Then he left. A moment later, she heard footsteps on the stairs.

First thing in the morning, when they were both up and the sting of the humiliation had worn off, she'd apologize to Hugh. If she didn't, the tension between them would ruin what promised to be a very fun day at the parade.

After all he'd done for her—letting her stay, protecting her from those men—he deserved a face-to-face apology. She loved him and he loved her. That was enough for now, wasn't it?

She poked at the pad thai with her chopsticks. Maybe as things progressed, he'd change his mind. How could he not, really? Because their relationship would either lead to them breaking up or deciding to spend the rest of their lives together.

Which for her, would mean making the literally life-changing decision to become a vampire. A little half smile bent her mouth. Delaney James—no,

Ellingham—confectioner and vampire. She stuck a shrimp in her mouth and chewed.

What a one-eighty her life had made in these last few days. She got up and went to the fridge to get a bottle of water. What would it be like to be a vampire? Would Alice make her an amulet too? Delaney dreaded the thought of going without sunlight for the rest of her days. Or nights, as the case might be.

No more lazy days off spent by the pool. Or the beach. Or the park. But of course, she'd have Hugh, and his company would help make up for that.

She spun some noodles around her chopsticks and took another bite. Tomorrow, Hugh would have his apology, and she'd let things between them take their natural course.

In her heart, she knew exactly where that natural course was going to lead, so sooner or later, she'd end up becoming a vampire and none of this would matter anyway.

"I know *why* you refused her," Stanhill said as Hugh let him in. "But she doesn't, and so she's down there feeling like a right idiot and wondering where she went wrong. You'd be lucky if she stays after all this."

"Maybe it would be better if she didn't stay. If

that was her decision." Hugh's heart was heavy, saddened by the inevitable split that would be required to keep Delaney safe.

Stanhill held out the bagged goods. "What the bloody hell are you talking about?"

Hugh took the bag and shook his head. "I will not turn her and risk her life."

"But you love her."

"Which is exactly why I won't turn her."

"Maybe *you're* the right idiot." Stanhill scowled. "She could come through the turning right as rain."

Hugh scowled right back. "And it could kill her. Would you take that chance with Corette's life?"

Stanhill's expression softened. "I...I don't know."

"Exactly."

Stanhill sighed. "But you love her. Don't you want to spend the rest of your life with her?"

"I do. But I will *not* have her death on my hands."

"So you're going to break both your hearts on the chance that something might go wrong. Trade an eternity of happiness for an eternity of sorrow. Over a *chance*."

"She'll get over me."

"Will she? Or will she go to her grave wondering what might have happened?"

"Enough, Stanhill."

He snorted softly. "And you. You'll have centuries to think about her. At least her suffering will end with her death. You don't have that option. Unless you slip out of that amulet and into the sunshine."

Hugh punched him.

Stanhill staggered back, arms out to keep his balance. "Bloody hell, what was that for?"

"For not shutting the hell up when I said enough. I know what I'm doing."

Stanhill rubbed his jaw, eyes blazing with indignation. "No, you don't. Or you wouldn't be doing it."

"You'd have me do what then? Marry her? Turn her? What if she dies? What then?"

"It might not happen that way."

"But if it does?" Hugh stared at him, feeling the pain of that possibility like a dagger to the heart. "Do you know what losing her that way would do to me? I can't be responsible for that. It would...it will kill me."

Stanhill's stern expression remained. "Either way, you lose her. And either way, you're responsible. Is this the end of you then? Will you wait until she's gone before you meet the dawn, or do you plan to head out tomorrow at sunrise and get it over with?"

Hugh went very still. He hadn't thought about it in those terms. He sank into a nearby chair. "I'm damned if I do, damned if I don't."

"It's better to have loved and lost than never to have

loved at all is a cliché for a reason. It's true. You're a bleedin' vampire. Top of the food chain. And yet you're ruled by fear."

Hugh knew he was right. He said nothing.

Stanhill worked his jaw back and forth. "Think long and hard before you make a decision you will regret for the rest of your very long life."

"All I can do is think."

The rook left, shutting the door firmly behind him.

Hugh stared at the bag in his lap as he slowly went numb from the impending loss. His bones felt as heavy as lead, his muscles watery, his brain mush. The only thing good in his life was sitting downstairs, feeling like she'd done something very wrong and not knowing why.

Maybe he deserved to be alone. Certainly Delaney deserved someone better than him. Someone who couldn't hurt her. Someone who could return her love with his whole heart, unshackled by the fear that his love would end in her demise.

Starting tomorrow, he'd begin the process of widening the gap between them. Eventually, Delaney would leave him and truly be safe.

His hand went to the amulet, his fingertips tracing the ancient carving on the stone. Whatever decisions he made after she was gone would be his and his alone to deal with.

Morning for Delaney came around eleven a.m. She slipped out of bed, pulled the curtains back and stared into the garden. Blue sky, lots of sun, all in all, a gorgeous day for the parade.

And an apology.

She walked out into the hall and, based on the quietness of the house, decided Hugh was still asleep. That would give her time to get ready and figure out what she was going to say. She went back into her room and shut the door.

Captain had jumped onto the window sill and was basking in a warm ray of sun. She scratched him on the head. "You probably want a little outside time, huh?"

He leaned into her hand and purred. If only Hugh was that easy. She laughed. Actually, that would be boring.

After a shower, hair and makeup, she dressed in

one of the tops she'd bought at the secondhand store, a pair of cuffed boyfriend jeans and some cute flats. Little gold hoops, the moonstone ring that had been her mom's and she was done. Well, except for a fresh bandage on her cut hand.

This time when she walked into the hall, faint kitchen sounds greeted her. Stanhill was making breakfast.

Hugh rarely slept longer than it took to brew the first pot of coffee.

She walked down to his room and knocked tentatively on the door. She was a little nervous, but this needed to be done. They'd both feel better afterward, and they'd be able to enjoy their day out.

She was about to knock again when he answered, wearing only a towel and a few droplets of water. *Oh my.* She smiled. "I hope I'm not interrupting, but—"

"I just got out of the shower. What do you need?"

Okay, so maybe he was still mad. "I wanted to apologize for last night. I'm sorry for trying to force you to do something you didn't want to do. That was wrong. And I'm sorry." She'd said that twice. Stupid nerves.

A flicker of something passed through his eyes, then was gone. "Good. Don't do it again."

"I won't." She blinked, trying to find the man

she'd fallen in love with, because the one in front of her was so cold and distant she didn't recognize him. "Do you still want to go to the parade or should I go by myself?"

"I said I would take you."

He hadn't smiled once. What the hell was wrong? "Okay. Thanks. The parade starts at one. I'll be downstairs whenever you're ready to go."

He nodded and shut the door.

She stared at the paneled wood, unable to process what had just happened. Clearly she'd upset him more than she realized. Finally, she trudged downstairs. Maybe he just needed coffee. She sure did.

Stanhill was in the kitchen. He stood as she came in. "Breakfast?"

"Um, sure, I guess." She plunked down in a chair.

He poured a cup of coffee and put it in front of her. "Something wrong, miss?"

She stared into the dark liquid. "I apologized to Hugh this morning, but he still seems really upset by what I did last night. I thought he'd be over it by now. Or at least after I said I was sorry."

He placed the sugar and creamer beside her cup and sighed like he was worn out. Or frustrated. "Don't let him upset you too much. He can be like that. Too many years of navel gazing and what have you. He'll get over it. Just be yourself. You've apologized. That's all that's required of you."

She hoped he was right. After all, he knew Hugh better than she did. She dumped some sugar and cream into her cup and drank.

"Omelet okay?" Stanhill asked. "I can do ham and cheese."

"Great, yes. Thanks." She sipped her coffee.

"Are you still going to the parade then?"

She nodded. "I asked him that too. He said he was going to take me so…" She shrugged.

"You'll have a good time. It's quite a laugh what some of the floats get up to." He cracked eggs into a bowl. "The theme of panic has come to mean what scares you, so most of the floats try to pick a fear and run with it."

Stanhill was a little chattier than usual today, but she was glad for it. Better than obsessing about Hugh and his cold shoulder. The look of sympathy in Stanhill's eyes didn't go unnoticed, but by the end of breakfast and her delicious omelet, she was feeling better.

Until Hugh came downstairs. She met him in the foyer. It was clear his mood hadn't changed.

He looked handsome in his jeans and button-down shirt with the sleeves rolled to show off his toned forearms, but the seemingly permanent scowl on his face made him look intimidating. He'd added a pair of dark sunglasses, making it even harder to judge his disposition. "Are you ready?"

"Yes." She nodded. Stanhill said just to be herself. She focused on that and smiled brightly. "This is going to be fun, huh?"

He said nothing.

Stanhill stuck his head out of the kitchen and looked at Hugh. "Can I see you a moment?"

Delaney stayed by the door. The harsh, muted tones told her whatever they were discussing wasn't for her ears.

When Hugh returned, his mood was unchanged. In fact, all the way there, he said nothing. Not until they'd parked did he finally speak. "Stay close. Don't wander off."

She narrowed her eyes at him. "I'm not a child."

"No, you're not. But you're also not out of danger yet. I doubt Rastinelli has had time to get more men down here, but you need to be careful all the same."

She gave him a little salute, realizing the bit of sass probably didn't help his mood, but she couldn't help herself.

People were everywhere. She chalked up their decent parking spot to Hugh's knowledge of the town. They got out of the car and followed the others walking to Main Street. Crowds already lined the street, which had been roped off. Vendors in Keller's Sweets-n-Treats T-shirts strolled the street on the insides of the ropes selling popcorn, cotton candy, and enormous pinwheel lollipops.

"You want cotton candy?"

Hugh's question almost knocked her over. It was the first nice-ish thing he'd said to her all day. "I'd love some, thanks."

He waved the man down and handed him a few dollars. Delaney picked traditional pink, and the vendor handed her a cloud on a stick. She pulled the cellophane off, wrapped it around the stick for later (like there would be any left) then unwound a gossamer strand of sugar and stuck it in her mouth.

"Mmm." The sugar hit a second later, sweet and melty and delicious. She offered the huge ball of floss to Hugh. "Want some?"

He shook his head.

"C'mon, have a little. You paid for it. Besides, it might sweeten you up." She shot him a pointed look, tired of pretending there wasn't something going on.

He stared at her for a moment, inscrutable behind his dark sunglasses. Finally, he pinched a piece off between his thumb and finger and ate it.

She smiled as she turned to watch the little funny cars making their way down the street before the parade began. "Hard to be cranky when there's something in your mouth that tastes that good."

"I'm not cranky." He spoke softly, maybe because they were surrounded by people now.

"Hah." She fed another long strand of spun sugar into her mouth. "You obviously woke up on the wrong side of the bed this morning, but you really need to get over it. I apologized. There's nothing more I can do."

He grunted in response.

She sighed and watched as the parade began. The Nocturne Falls High School marching band and cheerleaders led the way with two majorettes carrying a banner that read Panic Parade 2015. The school's colors were orange and black—because, what else?—and the band was playing Monster Mash.

She couldn't help but grin at the silliness of it all when the band was followed by the local gardening group who were all dressed as Tippi Hedren from the movie The Birds. They sauntered by with their stuffed fowl clinging to their vintage suits and pillbox hats, tossing packs of flower seeds to the crowd.

The next float was an enormous spider on wheels pulled along by the flies tangled in its web. She leaned in toward Hugh, whose shoulder she was already touching thanks to the press of the crowd. "This is a riot."

His answer was another grunt.

She stuffed bite after bite of cotton candy into

her mouth, her patience wearing thin. She'd apologized. She was being nice. What else could she do? She wasn't psychic. If he wasn't going to tell her what was wrong, how on earth was she supposed to know?

Anger made the cotton candy disappear at an alarming rate. A few more floats went by, including a Jaws-themed one complete with bloody beach-goers, and suddenly all she was holding was a paper stick. She folded it up, stuck it back in the cellophane and balled it up in her hand.

Maybe it was the sugar talking, but she'd had enough of Hugh's grump. She stared at him, ignoring the seven-person snake trailing past like a Chinese dragon. "Can you just tell me what's wrong so we can fix and move on?"

"Nothing's wrong."

She rolled her eyes and gave him her best look of absolute skepticism. "What a relief! I was starting to think you not talking to me was because I'd done something. Glad to know this whole cold shoulder thing is over."

His nostrils flared once, then he went back to stony silence.

She glared at him, her anger genuinely piqued. "Are you kidding me?"

Finally he leaned in, his voice softer and a little kinder. "Delaney, enough. This is not the place.

Everything is fine. We'll discuss it more when we get home."

Considering that was the most he'd said to her all day, she'd take it. "Okay."

What there was to discuss, she had no idea, but clearly something else must have happened. Something serious by the tone of his voice. Why it required him to be so cold, she couldn't imagine, but hopefully it would all make sense after they talked.

That didn't mean her heart didn't ache at the thought that something serious had gone amiss between them. She'd fallen in love with this man. To think their fledgling relationship was hitting a bumpy road already hurt almost as much as the thought that she might have given her heart away too soon.

Again.

Maybe she just had terrible taste in men. Russell was a perfect example. She'd fallen for him and then into his bed, only to find out a few weeks later that she was just a piece on the side to him.

But Hugh wasn't a cheater. That much she felt sure of. So what had gone wrong? The only thing she could come up with was...blood. Her blood. She'd pushed him too much on the subject in the lab, trying to force the issue. She glanced at Hugh. Had she upset him more than she'd realized with all that? She didn't know how all this vampire stuff worked.

Was he so upset about it that he'd suddenly changed his mind about her?

No. She couldn't believe Hugh was that fickle. He'd been sweet and caring and he'd protected her from Rastinelli's men, even warning her about staying close today. Something else had to be going on.

Whatever it was, thinking about it only made the ache in her chest widen. She slipped her hand into his, needing to touch him, to connect and know that the man she'd fallen in love with was still the same man standing beside her.

His fingers tightened around hers, then he tensed and shook her hand away.

"Hugh," she whispered, hating the sound of the tears caught at the back of her throat.

He spoke without looking at her. "Enough."

The rejection cut through her like a knife.

She couldn't be here right now. Couldn't face another betrayal. Without another thought, she turned and took off into the crowd.

He was a fool. And a coward. The woman he loved was standing beside him, trying to reach him, to make things right even though she didn't know what had gone wrong and he was shutting her down.

As far as his plan to turn her away went, it was a spectacular success if the pain in his heart was any indicator.

He couldn't do this. He loved her too much. Needed her more than anything else he could think of. Maybe…he could just love her for the rest of her natural life and then find a way to deal with the grief of being alone again when that time came. It was better than not having her at all. He turned toward her. "Delaney—"

She was gone.

He growled a curse and twisted, scanning the packed crowd for any sign of her. Nothing. Panic tripped over his skin in electric bursts. Where the hell had she gone?

"Delaney!"

But her name was lost in the noise from the parade and the crowd. He shoved through the crush, ignored the protests of the people he pushed aside, and headed toward the shops. Maybe she'd gone inside one of them.

He scanned each one as he strode by. Nothing. He tried calling her phone. It rang once and then disconnected. He called again. It went straight to voice mail. Had she turned her phone off to avoid him?

Two blocks ahead, Sheriff Merrow's squad car sat crosswise, blocking off one of the intersections from Main Street. Merrow leaned against the car, his eyes on the crowd. Maybe he'd seen her.

Hugh took off at a run, careful to keep his speed to human levels since he was in public view. "Merrow."

The sheriff straightened. "Ellingham. What's going on?

Hugh came to a stop. "Delaney's gone. We were watching the parade and I turned to speak to her and she was gone. I've searched the last two blocks, looked in the stores, nothing."

"Someone grab her?"

"No. I would have noticed that."

Merrow shoved his hat back. "She left on her own?"

Hugh frowned. "We had a disagreement. But she couldn't have been gone more than a few seconds before I realized she'd left."

"You think Rastinelli got a new crew in town that fast?"

"I don't know. I just know she's gone."

Merrow squeezed the button on the walkie-talkie pinned to his shoulder. "Be advised we have a 10-57, Caucasian female, medium build, brown hair, wearing—" He looked at Hugh.

"A blue T-shirt and jeans."

Merrow added that information. "Give me her 20 when found. Do not detain." He released the button. "If you two were having a spat, she probably went back to the house. She know how to find her way from town?"

Hugh nodded. "We've walked it."

"Get in your car, drive the route, then call me when you get home and tell me if she's there. I hear anything I'll call you."

"All right." The sheriff had a point. Delaney had probably just gone home. He thought about phoning Stanhill, but she wouldn't have made it back yet. He gave Merrow a nod, then took a side street to avoid the crowd and raced back to where he'd parked.

He maneuvered the Jag out of the spot and drove toward home, following the route they'd walked. Hopeful he'd see her.

But that hope was gone by the time he pulled into his driveway. He stormed into the house. "Stanhill? Bloody hell, where are you?"

The rook yelled back at him from far end of the house. "In my room. What do you need?"

Hugh stood just outside the living room. "Is Delaney here?"

"No." Stanhill came around the corner to stand on the other side of the room. "Why isn't she with you?"

"She was. We got separated."

Stanhill frowned. "Is that so?"

"She got mad at me and disappeared. Happy?"

"Of course not. But I told you so." He rushed forward. "Where do you think she is?"

"No bloody clue. I already let Merrow know." Hugh could feel his heart racing, the panic building, the anger at his own stupidity churning his insides like a washing machine.

A car screeched into the drive and even in the middle of the day, the flashing blue and red lights spilled through the front windows and washed the foyer. He turned to see Merrow jump out of the car and head to the front door.

Hugh met him there, throwing the door wide. "What is it?"

"Did Delaney drink anything today?"

"Alcoholic? No. Why?"

"One of the deputies was with Nick Hardwin when I called the 10-57 in so Nick helped search the crowd."

"And?"

"The gargoyle spotted her with two largish men. She looked like she was being supported by them. Possibly under the influence of something. They helped her into a black SUV and took off before Hardwin could follow. He got a partial plate, though."

"He can bloody fly, damn it. Why didn't he take to the air?"

Merrow's eyes narrowed. "Because we have rules about that sort of thing. Rules your grandmother put into place."

"Rules that should be broken when a life is at

stake." Hugh swore again. "Where were they headed?"

"North most likely. Into the mountains past the park. There are hundreds of cabins and hideaways up there. They could be anywhere."

That area started directly behind Hugh's backyard. It was one of the reasons he'd built here, to have that buffer of forest between him and the rest of the town. Hugh's hands tightened into fists, his body tensing with the anticipation of what was to come. "Mobilize everyone you can think of. We need to search the area."

21

Delaney woke with her head hanging down and her body strapped to a hard wooden chair. She tugged at her hands, but they were bound behind her with zip ties. Her ankles were secured the same way to the legs of the chair.

Duct tape covered her mouth. She lifted her head a few inches and pain radiated from her shoulder. She remembered being stabbed with a needle. That explained how they'd knocked her out and dragged her off the street.

Crap on a cracker, she'd been abducted. Panic shot through her, making her gulp air but there was no air to be had, not with duct tape sealing her mouth. She had to calm down.

Approximately 400 cacao beans make one pound of chocolate.

People who feel depressed eat about 55% more chocolate than non-depressed people.

July 20th was National Lollipop Day.

Her breathing was back to normal, and although she was still scared out of her mind, she knew she needed to do whatever she could to keep herself alive long enough to be rescued. That meant clues.

The room had stairs leading upstairs, and judging by the lack of windows, she guessed it was a basement of a cabin. Oaky paneling covered the walls, and varnished lengths of light, knotted wood that looked like branches stripped of bark made up the stair handrail. Where was she? The smell of mildew and coffee didn't give her much insight.

Footsteps and muted voices sounded from upstairs. Maybe from the two men who had grabbed her. Thinking about them made her shiver in fear. Not a good direction for her mind to wander in.

She went back to assessing the room. It was a typical basement—big-screen TV, worn plaid couch from an era best forgotten, an old recliner and a few knickknacks. An open door across from her led into a small bathroom.

She tried inching the chair forward and almost fell over. She growled in frustration. Above her, a door opened and a light over the stairs flicked on. "Hey. She's awake."

At the sound of the Brooklyn accent, she went still. These had to be more of Rastinelli's crew. Crap. She was in all kinds of trouble.

Panic made her breathe harder, which caused

her to suck in against the duct tape. It made a faint whistling sound. *Calm down.*

Why had she walked away from Hugh? She knew why. He'd been giving her the cold shoulder and her fear of confrontation had made her leave. In retrospect, facing off with Hugh would have been a much better decision.

She could have at least told him off like she had her father at his wedding. Heavy, plodding footsteps started down the stairs. Now she'd probably never get that chance.

She turned her head to see who was coming. One of the guys from the street. At least it looked like one of the guys. It had all happened so fast.

He stood in front of her, his black Adidas track suit and gold chain with the Italian horn not that familiar after all. A get up like that she would have remembered. He jerked his head at her, one hand resting on his protruding gut. A gold ring with the Masons symbol set onto a red stone was wedged onto his fat sausage of a pinky. "Hello there. You're Delaney, right?"

She grunted at him, her fear giving way to anger. What did he expect her to do with duct tape over her mouth? Sing him an aria?

"Oh yeah." He reached down and ripped the duct tape off.

She said a very unladylike word, followed by, "Ow."

"Yeah, sorry about that, but you know." He shrugged.

"No, I don't know." He looked like a guy who'd be named something like Fat Eddie or Tommy Two Fingers. Except he had all his fingers. Fat Eddie it was. She glared at him. "Why did you kidnap me?"

"Kidnap? Whoa, that's a loaded word there, girly. We's just wanted to talk to you. That's all."

"We who? You and that other goon that dragged me off the street?" She glared at him. "People are already looking for me. Dangerous people."

He laughed. "Sweetheart, I'm about as dangerous as they get. I don't think your little friends are gonna be much of a threat."

"You're dangerous, are you? And why's that?"

His jovial nature went icy in a split second. "Because my boss and your boss are the same man, but I do a very different kinda job for him, if you get my drift."

She got it all right. "You mean you kill people."

He jerked back like he was shocked by her plain language. "You got a mouth on you, you know that?"

"Am I wrong?"

He slapped the duct tape back over her mouth, but she grimaced, giving herself some wiggle room behind the tape. He stomped back upstairs.

More muted tones. Some not as muted. Then more footsteps.

She poked at the tape with her tongue and managed to separate it from her skin enough so she could breathe better. How was she going to get out of here alive?

She tried to think, but her head was still thick with the drug they'd given her. She also wasn't exactly boned up on the latest survival training. Did Hugh have an idea about what had happened to her? He'd probably think she'd just stormed off.

If he'd even noticed she was gone. He must have, right? She had no idea what time it was, no idea how long she'd been here and no real hope for getting out.

She was going to have to figure this out herself. A ping of sadness echoed through her, followed by a sharp stab of fear. They were probably going to kill her. Like, any *second*. That sent a burst of angry motivation through her. She wasn't going down without a fight.

Footsteps on the stairs again. She craned her neck, ignoring the bruise from where she'd been jabbed. Fat Eddie again.

He walked up to her, tore the duct tape off again, then plopped down on the couch. "My compatriots and I need to know what you know. If you know what I mean."

"Speak English, not Brooklynese." She bit her tongue to keep from calling him a name that would only make him want to kill her sooner.

He leaned forward, causing the zipper on the jacket of his track suit to panic. The gleam in his eyes made her think of a great white checking out a baby seal. "What did you see that night at the restaurant?"

"Which night?"

He frowned. "The last night youse was there."

"I saw a bartender pouring weak drinks. I saw a woman stuff one of the oregano shakers in her purse. I even saw a kid grind half a fried cheese stick into the carpeting. It's a crazy world, the restaurant biz."

He stood, hiking up his track pants. "You think you're funny?"

"Sometimes, yes." She was being a smartass, and she didn't care. If she was going to die, she was going on her terms. Not that she wanted to go at all.

He walked over to her, glowering. "It doesn't matter. The boss says the word and you're done. You get what I'm saying?"

So they were going to kill her regardless. "Melting chocolate led to the invention of the microwave."

He screwed up his face. "What?"

"Nothing." *Breathe.* She had to come up with a reason for them not to kill her. A way to buy some time. *Think think think.* "If anything happens to me—"

"What?" he sneered. "Your boyfriend is gonna come looking for you?"

Maybe. Probably not. "I have an email scheduled to send if I don't log into my laptop every twenty-four hours."

"So?"

"That email is set to go to the police, the FBI, Facebook and a whole bunch of media."

"And I should care about this why?"

"Because attached to that email is the video I took that night in the restaurant along with a message that says if the email's been received, I've been murdered by Anthony Rastinelli." Sure, Sheriff Merrow already had that video, but Fat Eddie didn't need to know that.

He laughed. "Sure, kid. You got a video."

"Get my phone. I'll show you."

He thought for a second, then shook a finger at her. "If you're lying to me…" But he marched upstairs, coming back down a few minutes later with her phone.

"Okay," he said. "How do I get in?"

"Connect the dots in an L shape starting at the top corner."

He squinted at the screen, his fat fingers tracing the pattern. It took him three tries. "Here." He showed her it was unlocked. "Now what?"

"Gallery. Then videos. It's the first one."

He watched it while she listened and mentally replayed the scene in her head. When it was over, he stared at the screen for a second, then his fingers started tapping away like he was playing Angry Birds.

"There. I deleted it."

She narrowed her eyes. "Really? You think that's all you had to do? I already downloaded it to my computer, you numb nut. You think I wouldn't make a copy? Multiple copies?" She blew out an exasperated breath.

Fat Eddie's expression flattened. "You little piece of —"

He backhanded her, splitting her lip and filling her mouth with the taste of blood. Pain radiated through her face. She spit the blood out. "You feel manly hitting a woman tied to a chair? Punk. You're going down so hard when my friends get here." *If* they got there. Before she was dead.

He leaned in, his face so close to hers she could smell his garlicky breath. "Where's the laptop?"

"19 Hitchcock Lane." Maybe if she sent them to Hugh's, he'd figure out what happened and come after her. It could be her only chance.

Fat Eddie pointed one of his sausage fingers at her. "If you're lying about this, I'm gonna kill you myself."

Hugh stripped the pillow case off Delaney's pillow. He paused and gave Captain a scratch on the head. "I'm going to find her, don't worry."

He was talking to a cat. That's how insane Delaney's disappearance had made him. Shaking his head, Hugh marched downstairs to where Stanhill, Merrow, his deputies and a few others had gathered, including Nick the gargoyle and Merrow's fire chief brother, Titus.

Julian and Sebastian met him as he hit the landing. "I didn't expect to see you two here."

Sebastian's appraising gaze held less judgment than Hugh would have expected. "You love her?"

"I do."

"Then we're here to help."

Julian nodded, oddly serious. "We understand she might be in real danger."

"Yes." Hugh explained about Rastinelli and the confrontation with his men outside of Howlers.

"Mafia? They still exist?" Julian rubbed his hands together. "This might actually be fun.

Sebastian pointed to the pillow case. "Merrow going to track her?"

"All the shifters are." Hugh nodded. "And that needs to happen now." He left his brothers behind and went to Merrow, handing him the pillow case. "This will have her scent."

He sniffed it and grimaced. "Is she a shifter?"

"No, she's human." Hugh frowned. "Why?"

Merrow sniffed the linen again. "I smell cat."

"That's Captain. He sleeps with her."

"That explains it." Merrow nodded. "I can find her. Provided they're in one of those cabins."

"And if they're not?"

"I've already put a BOLO out on the black SUV with the partial plate Nick was able to get."

"Good. Let's go." Hugh was leaving on his own if things didn't get underway in the next sixty seconds. Because if Rastinelli's men had her...there was no telling what was happening to Delaney right now. If they hurt her, he would kill them.

Hell, he was going to kill them if they left one little bruise on her.

Merrow held his hand up. "We're going in three teams. Hugh, Stanhill and I will be the first. We'll handle the east side." Merrow tossed the pillow case to Titus, who'd left the fire station to help. "Titus, you've got a radio? "

Titus nodded and held the two-way up. "Right here."

"Good. You take Julian and Sebastian and go west. Give the pillow case to Alex and Nick after you've locked on to her scent."

Titus passed the pillow case to Merrow's deputy Alex Cruz, a panther shifter. He took a good whiff, then passed it to Nick. Both men nodded. They were ready to go.

Merrow pointed to Nick, who was standing by Merrow's other deputy, Jenna Blythe, a Valkyrie.

"You, Jenna and Alex go straight north. Alex will lead as tracker."

Alex nodded. "We'll find her."

Merrow hooked his hands on his gun belt. "If we haven't accomplished that by dark, Nick, you go airborne. Search that way."

"You got it." Nick shot a questioning glance at Hugh.

Hugh shook his head, already knowing what the man was thinking. "I'll handle my grandmother if it comes to that. Which it won't. Night flights are permissible by any flying supernatural so long as they happen after twilight." They were already going to have two wolves and a black panther running through the woods. Having a gargoyle in the air after dark was the least of their worries. He looked at Merrow. "Can we go already?"

Merrow nodded. "Let's shift and move out."

Fifteen minutes later, Hugh and Stanhill were deep into the woods following Merrow in wolf form as he rustled through the undergrowth searching for Delaney's scent.

Fifteen minutes after that, Merrow came to a stop beside the stream where Hugh had stopped Delaney from running off the night she'd found out he was a vampire. Merrow lifted his big wolf head and whuffed at Hugh.

"It's nothing," Hugh said. "She and I were here. Out for a walk a few nights back."

Merrow went back to sniffing the ground and pawing through leaves.

Hugh carried Merrow's walkie-talkie and gun belt, but the weight of that was nothing compared to the burden of worry pressing on his nerves. They were stretched thin. Ready to snap at the first opportunity. Which seemed like it might never come. All because he'd been a jerk and shut Delaney out. He had a habit of putting the women he loved in danger. But he could not let Delaney suffer the same fate as Juliette. "We're getting nowhere," he snapped.

"Patience," Stanhill muttered.

"When her life could be in danger? How the hell am I supposed to be patient?"

Before Stanhill could respond, the walkie-talkie crackled with an incoming call. "Sheriff, this is Jenna. Alex picked something up along Carraway Lane, near the old Miller house. We're doing a wide sweep and—"

Merrow flashed back into human form, his pelt turning into his uniform once again, and grabbed the radio. "We're on our way. Locate Delaney but stand down until we get there."

He took his gun belt back from Hugh and strapped it around his waist. "Faster to drive."

"Back to the house then." Hugh didn't need to be told twice. He broke into a run, dodging branches and jumping fallen trees. He made it back to the house a minute before Stanhill and Merrow and met them on the back porch, car keys in hand. "I assume you're going in quiet, no sirens."

Merrow nodded. "We don't want to tip our hand."

"Good."

"You and Stanhill follow in your car. Mine will be too full of mobsters on the way back." Merrow unhooked his keys from his belt and a few minutes later, Hugh and Stanhill were tearing up the mountain road toward Carraway Lane behind the sheriff.

Hugh followed the patrol car into a driveway, unsure of where the sheriff was headed. Carraway was the next road, not more than a quarter of a mile away. Merrow parked and got out, so Hugh and Stanhill did the same.

Stanhill looked at Hugh. "We must be going on foot from here."

"Makes sense." Hugh looked around. The trees were covered in green and despite the warm day, the scent of woodsmoke wafted through the air. Tourists who rented the cabins up here liked to use the fireplaces no matter what the season. Made it harder to pick up other scents but hopefully that wouldn't be an issue for the shifters.

Merrow was speaking into his radio as they approached him. "We're here. We'll meet you in five minutes." He let the button go and glanced at

Hugh. "Nick, Jenna and Alex have pinpointed the house. There are men stationed at the front and back, and they think at least two more inside. Maybe three."

Four or five didn't matter. He could take them all if he had to. Any sign of Delaney?"

"No, but both Alex and Nick confirm her scent there is strong." Merrow hesitated. "You should stay here."

Hugh stared at the man. "You know that's not going to happen."

Merrow sighed. "Ellingham, Alex and Nick also confirmed the scent of blood."

A chill zipped down Hugh's spine. *Blood.* Images, none of them good, spun through his head. "If they've hurt her—"

"They'll be dealt with. Legally. I don't want to arrest you today, you understand what I'm saying?"

Hugh stepped into the sheriff's personal space, let his fangs slide down and spoke with slow deliberation. "If they have hurt her, I will do what needs to be done."

Merrow's radio went off. "Sheriff, one of the men is leaving in a black Chevy Tahoe."

Hugh jabbed a finger at Merrow. "If you don't want to arrest me today, maybe you should go after him instead."

"I don't have a choice," Merrow shot back. "No

one else has a car but you and me, and I'm sure as hell not sending you." He yanked the door to the squad car open. "Go rescue Delaney. Just keep it *legal*."

A black SUV rumbled past them. Merrow jumped into his car and went after it.

Hugh narrowed his eyes at Stanhill. "I'm not that concerned about legal."

Stanhill shook his head. "That's for bleedin' sure."

Hugh stared into the trees. The scents of the other supernaturals danced at the edge of his sensory perimeters. Then another stronger, more familiar smell broke through.

Blood. Delaney's blood.

With a growl, he started forward, racing along the scent lines of the other supernaturals. Stanhill followed. They joined the gargoyle and the two deputies near a small hollow in the mountain side just as Julian, Sebastian and Titus jogged toward them from the other side of the ridge.

"Hank went after the one that left since he had the squad car." Hugh nodded at Nick. "Where's the house?"

"Other side of this rise."

"Any better idea of how many are inside?"

"Since that one left, we think there's only three. One at each exit front and back, and one inside."

"With Delaney," Hugh added.

Nick nodded.

"Julian and Sebastian have the rest of you beat for speed, so they can take out the guards. As soon as they do that, Nick, you get to the electric box and cut power to the house. Then Stanhill and I will go in and deal with whoever's left in there. And I'll find Delaney."

Alex held out his hands. "What about Jenna and I?"

Hugh's mouth bent into a wry smile. "I wouldn't want you to have to arrest any of us for doing something your boss might not approve of. You two stay here. Maybe Merrow will come back."

Jenna leaned against a tree and shrugged. "Less paperwork. I'm cool."

Hugh gave the rest of them a nod. "Here we go."

Fat Eddie jerked Delaney's chin up, his thick fingers bruising her skin.

She yanked at the zip ties restraining her hands, causing them to cut deeper into her skin. Her desire to shove him away was greater than the pain.

He laughed at her struggles. "When my boy gets to that house and finds that computer, you'd better give me the password on the first go or things are gonna get ugly."

"Uglier, you mean," she managed. "I'm already looking at your face."

He shoved her chin away and balled his hand into a fist, threatening her with it. "It's like you want me to hit you."

She glared at him. "I swear to God, you have no idea how much trouble you're going to be in."

He snorted. "Is this another story about how your big bad boyfriend is gonna tear my throat out?"

"Yes," she hissed. Please let Hugh be home. Please let him figure out what was going on. Please, *please* let him rescue her. "He'll probably do it literally. He's a pretty scary guy. Do you have any bladder issues? Because you might pee yourself when you see him."

"You're getting on my last good nerve, you know that?" Fat Eddie leaned in. "I don't usually whack women on account of them being women and all, but I'm kinda looking forward to this."

"So that's a yes on the incontinence?"

He snarled, spilling an odorous wash of garlicky breath over her. "Shut. Up."

She grimaced, anger making her mouth smart even as she trembled with fear. "In a strange way, I almost welcome death." He looked surprised. She shrugged as best she could while bound. "At least I wouldn't have to smell your breath anymore."

That earned her another crack across the face. She blinked at the pain, the stars in her eyes the only thing she could see. Holy crap. He'd hit her so hard, she'd lost her vision.

As her cheek throbbed, Fat Eddie cursed and yelled upstairs. "Who turned the friggin' lights out?"

Good to know she wasn't blind.

A cacophony of footsteps, muffled screams, loud thumps and the soft whistle of fast-moving air followed in the darkness. Someone snapped the zip ties, releasing her wrists. Then a hand brushed her cheek and she yelped. Her heart hammered in her chest. This was it. Fat Eddie was either about to kill her or going to drag her to a new location. She swung wildly, trying to fight. "Don't touch me!"

A hand caught her wrist. "Delaney, it's me. Hugh."

She sucked in a breath that filled her entire body with relief so strong she could taste it. Way better than chocolate. "You found me."

A voice from upstairs asked, "All right for lights again?"

"Yes," Hugh answered. He snapped the zip ties off her ankles.

The lights flickered back on. Hugh was kneeling in front of her, the broken zip ties in his hand. Fat Eddie sprawled on the floor, unmoving. Unbreathing, too, by the looks of him.

"Thank you," she whispered. The words still came out like a half sob. A bead of cold sweat trickled down her spine. Going from certain death to being rescued in a few short seconds had a way of whipsawing the nervous system.

Hugh wiped her tears away. There was anger in his softly glowing eyes. "You're bruised. He's lucky I didn't see that first." A muscle in his jaw tightened. "No one's ever going to hurt you again."

"Rastinelli's still out there."

"Merrow will make sure he's dealt with, or I'll

take a trip to New York and handle it myself."

Stanhill came halfway down the stairs and smiled at her, but his gaze lingered on her face with great concern. "You all right, miss?"

"I am now." She smiled, feeling tears streak her face and not caring. "Thank you." She looked at Hugh. "Thank you, both. He was going to kill me."

She slumped forward and rolled her shoulders to relieve the pins and needles from being strapped into the same position for so long. "Are you still mad at me for what I did in the lab?"

He reached up and massaged her upper arms and shoulders, sending the most heavenly sensations through her. "I was never mad at you. I was mad at myself."

Eyes heavy-lidded from his tender caresses and the relief of being safe, she forced herself to pay attention. "For what?"

"For being a coward."

She laughed. "You? You're not even close to being a coward."

He stared at her, reaching out to lightly stroke her cheek. The skin was tender where she'd been hit. "I was so afraid of losing you to a possibility that I refused to let myself love you anymore. After what happened in the lab, I thought the only way to save you was to run you off."

"So you were cold to me on purpose?"

He nodded. "I've never done anything so hard

and so awful to another person in my entire life. Forgive me."

"You saved my life. I think we're even."

"Thank you." He kissed her mouth tenderly, but as he pulled away, his eyes went luminescent with anger. "I am so sorry he hurt you. It's a good thing I couldn't see the bruises he put on you with the lights out, otherwise I would have killed him."

She looked over Hugh's shoulder at the fallen mobster. "Are you sure you didn't? He looks pretty dead to me."

"No, only unconscious. I didn't want his murder on my hands. I don't want anything else keeping us apart. Ever." He stood and helped her to her feet. "I love you, Delaney James. Be my wife. For eternity."

She blinked at him, feeling a little speechless. "I…"

"If you were a vampire, those men wouldn't have been a match for you. I cannot stand the thought of you being unable to protect yourself."

"Are you saying you're willing to turn me even after what happened to Juliette?"

"Yes. Maybe." He sighed. "I am saying I will research the turning until I am absolutely certain that what happened to Juliette will *not* happen to you. The thought of that haunts me to the point of madness, but losing out on an eternity with you because of my own inaction is far worse." He kissed her, then leaned his forehead against hers. "Save me from myself. Please say yes."

She put her hand on his chest and smiled, the joy inside her erasing the last shred of fear the mobsters had caused. "Yes, Hugh. I'll be your vampire bride."

With a guttural growl of joy, he scooped her into his arms and started up the steps.

She threw her arms around his shoulders. "I can walk, you know."

"I don't care."

Hugh had no intention of putting Delaney down, even when Deputy Blythe had to turn sideways to get past them on her way down to secure the other Mafioso. When they got to the top of the steps, Sheriff Merrow had returned.

Merrow barely raised an eyebrow at Delaney being in Hugh's arms. "Injuries?"

"None beyond the bruising to her face and wrists."

Merrow nodded. "Still ought to see the medics. I'll need a statement too."

She poked at Hugh's shoulder and whispered, "I'm not giving my statement to the sheriff with you holding me like a baby."

"Whatever you say, sweetheart." He put her

down, and she went to talk to Merrow. Hugh was delirious with happiness, both from finding her relatively unhurt and from her agreeing to marry him. And to think he'd started the day determined to scare her off.

The part about turning her into a vampire—about the consequences of that—still held a paralyzing amount of fear, but he would conquer it with research. It was what he knew. It was the only recourse he had.

Stanhill came to stand beside him. "From the looks of you, I'd say you've given up on your daft plan to run her off."

Hugh nodded, unable to take his eyes off her. "I asked her to marry me."

Stanhill's disbelief was evident from the jerk of his head. "You did? What did she say?"

Hugh frowned at him. "She said yes, you muppet."

Stanhill laughed and clapped him on the back. "Good for you, old man. About bloody time."

Then he sobered, his voice lowering to conspiratorial levels. "Does this mean you're going to turn her?"

Hugh took a long pause before answering. "Yes. Eventually. But not before I can test some things out, try a few experiments to see if—"

"I've been talking to Corette about this and—"

"You told her about Juliette?" Hugh stared at his

rook. Never had the man been so loose-lipped.

"Don't get your knickers in a twist. She actually has an idea."

Hugh waited. "And?"

"Do you know Willa Iscove?"

Hugh frowned at him. "Of course I know her. My brothers and I set her up with her shop and apartment to convince her to stay in town. She's the one who designed the official Nocturne Falls pumpkin charm."

Stanhill frowned right back. "You and your brothers did all that?"

"Yes. I don't tell you everything, you know." Willa was young for someone with such talents, but the fae were a different than most supernaturals. They tended to keep to themselves.

"Apparently." A small light came on in Stanhill's gaze. "You brought her in to try to duplicate the amulets, didn't you?"

"No comment. Is there a point to this?"

Stanhill shook his head. "I'm not sure. You already know Willa can work magic into her jewelry."

"I do."

"So why not ask her for help with turning Delaney? It's fae magic, not witchcraft. I know how you feel about that."

"Because if it takes powerful witchcraft to keep us from frying, how is fae magic going to make any difference keeping Delaney alive?"

"You could at least go talk to her."

Hugh thought about it. As much as he hated mixing in outside help—anyone was liable to become an enemy at some point and use whatever information they'd gained against him—this was too important a chance to pass up without further investigation. "You didn't already talk to Willa about this did you?"

Stanhill made a face. "Not me."

"Corette?"

Stanhill stared at the ceiling.

Hugh gave him a hard look. "You didn't say anything about the amulets to her, did you?"

That snapped his attention back. "No. You know I wouldn't. Speaking of the amulets, why don't you ask Alice about help with the turning?"

Hugh snorted derisively. "And give Didi one more thing to lord over me? And Delaney? No, Alice has done enough for us."

"Then go see Willa."

"I will." He realized how brusque he must sound. "Thank you, Stanhill. It was a good suggestion." He didn't think much would come of it, but anything was worth a try.

"You're welcome, your lordship." Stanhill snickered. "I do hope it works out. For Delaney's sake. And yours. You both deserve to be happy."

"Thank you."

"One thing..." Stanhill raised his brows slightly. "I know you brought Willa here, but Corette says her services aren't cheap."

Hugh almost laughed. "You know money's not an issue."

Stanhill shook his head. "I'm not talking dollars."

"Then what?"

"I don't know. Corette just said to tell you to expect to pay dearly."

"Understood. Listen, let's keep this between us right now. I don't want to get Delaney's hopes up in case this doesn't pan out."

Stanhill nodded. "Agreed. She's been through enough."

Hugh looked over at her sitting beside Merrow at the kitchen table. The bruises on her face were darkening, and her lip had swollen like she'd been stung. She looked delicate, but fierce. She'd been so calm, despite what she'd been through. Impressive. This woman who'd stolen his heart was a warrior.

If Willa could help Delaney, there was no price he wouldn't pay.

With Captain trailing her, Delaney stumbled into the kitchen earlier than she'd expected to be awake considering the day she'd had yesterday. Her face hurt, but the swelling on her lip had gone down. A good thing, considering the kitchen smelled like bacon and something else delicious. Her mouth watered. The last thing she'd eaten was cotton candy.

Stanhill was in his usual spot at the table, paper in hand.

"Morning."

He put the paper down. "Morning, miss. I didn't even hear you come down. How did you sleep? How are you feeling?" He got to his feet. "Coffee? Breakfast? I've got bacon and Quiche Florentine, if you're interested."

"Um, good, okay and yes to coffee and breakfast. I'm starving." She sat at the table and let him wait on her.

Captain wound around Stanhill's feet, meowing.

"And good morning to you, Captain. Kippers then?"

"No people food." Delaney shot Stanhill a look.

He frowned back at her. "How can you say no to that face?"

"With great restraint. He's too tubby." Her smile turned into a painful yawn. She'd been so exhausted last night that she'd let Hugh carry her up to bed and had fallen asleep within minutes. Spending the night in Hugh's bed, as tempting as that might be, had been out of the question. "Hugh still sleeping?"

"No, he just left on an errand. Not sure when he'll be back." Stanhill put a cup of coffee in front of her, then set to work fixing her a plate.

Hugh's absence was perfect timing. "Do you think you could take me to see Elenora?"

Stanhill's brows jumped. "You want to visit her? Voluntarily?" He *accidentally* dropped a piece of bacon on the floor. Captain went full piranha, devouring it in seconds.

Delaney overlooked the incident, choosing to answer instead. "I have some unfinished business with her."

"Do tell." He presented her with a plate of quiche and bacon, then scooped Captain up and sat with him on his lap at the table.

"Actually, why don't you go with me? It might be good to have a witness on my side."

Stanhill's eyes widened. "Is that so? What on earth are you planning?"

"You'll see." She took a bite of the quiche. It was custardy and delicious with the flakiest pastry she'd ever tasted. And she knew about pastry. "And when we get home, you're going to show me exactly how you made this crust."

Hugh walked into Illusions and realized he should have called ahead. The crowds brought in by the parade were still in town and, apparently, shopping. He caught Willa's attention as soon as she was free. He'd seen her at some of his grandmother's fundraisers, but hadn't had any real conversations with her since he and his brothers had convinced her to stay in Nocturne Falls. Hard to believe someone so young was already a master of their craft. "Miss Iscove?"

She smiled, and her startling aqua eyes sparked with interest. If her eyes weren't enough to announce she was fae, her pointed ears were. Hugh wondered what was more of a customer draw, the beautiful jewelry creations in the shop or the shop's owner. "Mr. Ellingham." She stuck out her hand. "How are you?"

"I'm well enough."

"What brings you by?"

"I have a situation I'm hoping you can help me with."

Willa tucked a strand of honey-blond hair behind one ear as she nodded. "Be happy to. Let's go in my office and talk. Come around the far end of the counter and follow me back." She waved at the woman working behind the other side of the counter. "Ramona, watch the floor, please."

He did as she asked. She waited at the office door for him to go in, then shut it behind her. "Please have a seat."

He took the one chair available, leaving the desk chair for her. She settled into it. "What can I do for you?"

"I know it's been a while since we've spoken. I hope everything is going well?"

"It is. I think the last time we talked was at the Black and Orange Ball."

He smiled politely. "I'm sad to say I don't remember that conversation."

She shrugged. "Don't worry about it. It was thirty seconds of small talk. One conversation out of probably a hundred you had that night. Your brother, on the other hand, he had better remember talking to me."

Please let her not have slept with Julian and want to hold that against him. He asked hopefully, "You mean Sebastian?"

"No, Julian."

Damn it. "I'm sorry if he offended you in any way. I can assure you, my brother and I are two very different people."

She gave him a strange look. "He didn't offend me." Her face suddenly brightened. "Oh, you think he and I slept together and then he never called, huh?" She laughed. "Nothing like that. I made him a charm."

Relief made Hugh chatty. "Really? What was it?"

She squinted for a second. "He never asked me to keep it secret, so I guess I can tell you. You are family after all. I made him a charm that makes him extra charming. His apologies included."

Hugh laughed. "I've always wondered how he gets away with his womanizing."

"With help, that's how." She shook her head, smiling. "I assume you're here for a charm too?"

"Yes, but it's not for me."

She pursed her lips. "I won't do work that harms anyone else, so this can only be for good."

"It is, I swear."

"All right then. As you know, my gifts lie in metal and stone work. Using one or both of those talents, I can create a piece of jewelry for you that will aid in accomplishing a specific goal. What did you have in mind?"

Everything about Willa seemed genuine. Not that he'd doubted her, but this was Delaney's life in the balance. It didn't hurt that the charm Willa had made for Julian was working, well, like a charm. Hugh relaxed a little. "I need an engagement ring that will keep the wearer safe from harm."

Willa made an understanding sound. "I see. What sort of harm are we talking? General protection? That's a pretty easy construct."

"More than that. Life or death."

Willa's lips parted in a soft breath. "Oh. That's something else entirely." She pulled out a notebook, flipped it open and grabbed a pen. "I'm going to need specifics. This is much more serious than what I usually do."

"How specific?"

"The more details you give me, the more complex and specific I can weave the magic that goes into the piece. You want this ring to be as successful as it can be, don't you?"

"Of course."

"Then tell me everything."

He hesitated, trying to think of where to start and what details would be important.

Willa tipped her head. "I promise everything you tell me will be confidential. And I've made many pieces for delicate situations. There's very little I haven't heard."

Her assurances were nice, but he'd already been prepared to tell her whatever was necessary. "My first wife did not survive the process of being turned."

"Into a vampire?"

He nodded.

Willa scribbled something in her notebook. "Go on."

"There is another woman—"

Willa grinned, her eyes on her notebook. "There always is."

Hugh ignored the comment. "I want to marry her, and she wants to be turned, but…" He shook his head. "I fear history will repeat itself."

"So you want the ring to do more than protect her. You want the ring to ensure this turning goes smoothly." She jotted a few more things in her notebook. "That's good. That gives me something to work with."

"Can you do it then?"

"I'll tell you what I tell all my custom clients. My end will be a hundred percent."

He frowned. "What does that mean?"

"That means there are always factors I can't control." She gave him an apologetic shrug. "Fae magic is born of the earth, and the truth is, if you were human and asking me for a fertility bracelet or a pendant to bring you love, I could guarantee it. But when it comes to other supernaturals, fae magic can't always control the situation. I can guide what happens. Beyond that, there are no certainties. It's part of the reason I was never able to create anything that would allow your kind to walk in the sun. Whatever gift your family has that allows that is beyond me."

Frustration tightened his jaw. "How is that any different than how the situation would turn out without your magic?"

"She's human, right?"

"Yes."

"Then it ups your odds greatly. If that isn't enough, then maybe there's no point in continuing this conversation."

"No. I'm sorry." He combed his fingers through his hair. "I want your help. Any additional protection is welcome."

She reached across the space between them and put her hand on his arm. The reassuring gesture gave him hope. "I understand how frightening a situation this must be for you. I promise you I will give this ring my full focus."

"Thank you." And now on to the rest of it. "Not to be crass, but I know you're not doing this for free, nor would I expect you to. What is this going to cost?"

"There will be the cost of the materials, the diamond—assuming you want a diamond?"

He nodded. "Something large but not ostentatious. As perfect a stone as you can find."

"Two carats?"

"Three." He wanted Delaney to know he meant business. This was forever.

Her pen rolled across the page as she made a note. "Hmm. I have an idea. Give me a sec."

She opened her laptop, angling it so he could see the screen but she could reach the keyboard. With a few key strokes, she called up a program and started designing a ring right in front of him. "I'm thinking cushion cut. I have a great supplier who will overnight me anything I want and he's got beautiful goods."

"Excellent."

She tapped away. "I'll set it with a halo of smaller diamonds, round brilliants, then do a split shank paved with round sapphires." She looked at him. "Great stone for protection and strength."

"Perfect." He studied the design she'd produced. "It's beautiful. Classic but different."

"I'm going to set a few stones on the inside of the band. Moonstones, peridot, a little turquoise, maybe. They won't be felt when the ring is on, but for our purposes, they'll add another layer of protection."

"Absolutely. Whatever you think it'll take."

"All right then." She pulled out a calculator and did a few sums that resulted in her making a little noise in her throat. "It's going to be a *very* nice ring."

"I understand. How much does very nice cost?"

"Based on the quality of the stones and the amount I'll need...about fifty to sixty thousand."

"That's fine." He would have paid twice that. Triple, even. "And that's all you need from me?"

She put the calculator down. "No. In order for me to charge the magic and make it directly relatable to you, I need something very dear to you."

"Which is?"

She shook her head. "I don't know. That's up to you. It doesn't need to have actual value, but it must be valuable to you. Giving it to me should feel like a sacrifice."

"Will I get this thing back?"

"No, I'm sorry. The creation of the magic will use it up. Whatever you give me will be gone for good."

An odd sensation trickled through him. A sense of inevitability. Stanhill had said there would be a cost beyond dollars, but it wasn't just that. It was as if Hugh had lived his whole life knowing a moment like this would come one day.

"I understand." Without hesitation, he knew what he would give her. "I'll have a package delivered to you this afternoon. How long after you get that can you have the ring ready?"

"Two weeks, maybe three."

"No. Too long. You said you could have the stones overnight."

"I can, but I have other projects sitting on my bench—"

"I'll pay you an extra ten thousand to ignore them. How long then?"

She thought for a moment. "If I put all my other projects aside, a week."

"Still too long."

She made a face. "I can work while I'm here, but I still have to wait on customers and run the shop. I only have two other employees besides myself."

"I'll find you a third. I'll even pay their wages if that's what it takes."

She stared at him hard. "You're desperate to turn her, huh?"

"Not at all." He'd rather ignore that part altogether. "What I am desperate for is to give her that ring. To make this engagement official. To show her how serious I am."

Willa smiled. "For love, I can have the ring in three, maybe four days."

He nodded. "Done. I assume you accept cash?"

"I do. Prefer it, actually."

"Then I'll send the money along with the item you requested."

"Half is fine upfront."

"I'll send it all. I don't want that to be an issue."

"All righty then." She grinned as she stood. "My very next task will be ordering the stones."

"Call if you have any issues. I'll arrange for the temporary help to start tomorrow then."

She held out her hand. "Pleasure doing business with you, Mr. Ellingham."

"Call me Hugh, please." He shook her hand.

"I'll be in touch, Hugh."

"Very good." He left the shop and walked back to where he'd parked. He tipped his face into the sun, enjoying the warmth one last time. Stanhill had been right about the cost, but an eternity with Delaney was priceless.

His fingers went to the amulet around his neck.

She was all the sun he needed.

Delaney had to knock only once before Alice Bishop came to answer the door.

The woman shifted her gaze from Delaney to Stanhill. "I'm sorry, Elenora didn't tell me you were coming."

"That's because it's a surprise visit," Delaney answered.

"Is everything all right?"

"No. That's why I need to talk to her. Can you let us in please?"

"Yes, of course." Alice moved out of the way. "She's in the drawing room. I'll just go get her and—"

Delaney looked at Stanhill. "Do you know where that is?"

"Yes."

"Good. Lead the way."

Alice sputtered. "You can't just barge in—"

But Stanhill was already moving, his eyes sparkling with mischievous joy. Delaney followed, leaving Alice to scamper after them.

The witch wasn't up on her cardio, judging by the panting. "You...can't..."

"Already there, Alice." Stanhill turned a corner, yanked a set of double doors open and bowed to Delaney. "After you, miss."

A small wave of self-doubt struck Delaney as she walked into the gorgeous room. She shoved it away. This wasn't about her, it was about Hugh. About their life together.

Elenora sat near a window, reading. She put her book down and peered at Delaney. "Good afternoon."

"Hi. Sorry about the short notice, but I saw an opportunity and took it."

Alice charged in after Delaney. "They got away from me." She shot Delaney a glare. "Very impolite."

Elenora waved a hand at Alice. "It's all right." Her attention shifted to Delaney, and for a moment, the same luminescence Delaney often glimpsed in Hugh's eyes shone in his grandmother's. "I imagine you must have something very important to discuss with me to arrive unannounced."

"I do."

"Thank you, Alice. That will be all." Elenora

tapered her gaze at Stanhill. "You may leave us also."

"He stays." Delaney lifted her chin a little, finding courage in her love for Hugh. "Alice can stay too. She should, actually, since this concerns her in a roundabout way."

Elenora frowned. "Whatever are you talking about?"

"It's about the deal you offered me if I got Hugh to ask me to marry him. He asked. I said yes."

Elenora's mouth came open in a very unbecoming gape. She closed it and smiled. "Nicely done. But our deal was for him to ask *and* for a date to be set."

"Here's the thing, that deal is off the table. There's a new deal in play."

Elenora's brows rose stiffly. "And that is?"

Delaney could see Stanhill's surprised look out of the corner of her eye. No doubt this was news to him, and probably not the kind that made him happy, but he'd understand things soon enough. "You will never again threaten to take away Hugh's amulet. Ever. Not in the next five hundred years. Not in the next thousand years. *Never.* You're not to even speak the word *amulet* to him. And Alice will not remove or destroy the magic that keeps it working. It is his, free and clear. No strings attached. Not even a thread. Are we clear?"

The woman snorted softly. "You're giving up

the candy shop in exchange for..." She shrugged.

"In exchange for you lifting your thumb off his neck."

"That's a rather crude way of putting it, don't you think?"

"No, I don't. You used that amulet to force him into entertaining a strange woman in his home all so you could end up with grandbabies to play with. I'd say that was pretty crude, wouldn't you?"

She laughed, a cultured, deliberate sound. "You are a sweet child. And your love for Hugh is admirable." She stood and walked over to stand in front of Delaney, making no effort to hide her fangs or flashing eyes. Probably an attempt at intimidation, but Delaney had just been kidnapped by mobsters. A little vampire plumage wasn't about to scare her off.

Elenora leaned in. "There's just one thing you have overlooked."

"What's that?"

"Leverage. You have none. Which means I will continue to do what I think is best for my grandson. Are we clear?"

Delaney laughed. "I may not have leverage now, but I will." She grinned at the woman. "See, Hugh and I are going to get married, and he's going to turn me into a vampire, and then someday, we're going to have babies. Lots of babies."

Delaney canted toward Elenora, leaving very

little space between them. "Babies you're going to want to see and spend time with and spoil. But if you defy my wishes on the amulet, I will do everything in my power to keep those children from you. Is that enough leverage for you?"

Elenora's victorious expression faded. "You wouldn't dare keep those grandbabies from me."

Delaney smiled, but was careful not to overdo it. She didn't want to make an enemy of the woman, just put her firmly in check. "I certainly wouldn't *want* to, but for their protection and the happiness of their father, I will do whatever necessary. And if you think I wouldn't, that's only because you don't know me well enough yet."

Several long seconds passed. Elenora swallowed but said nothing. Emotions clouded her eyes. Delaney felt a little guilt seeing Hugh's grandmother coming to grips with this harsh new reality, but this was about protecting Hugh. Just like he'd protected her.

Finally, Elenora composed herself and spoke. "I had no idea you were so ruthless. Our original deal is done. There will be no financing for the candy shop. No backing from me whatsoever. But I will abide by your wishes. You can tell Hugh I will never again bring up the amulet. Alice won't do anything to void it, either."

"But I will expect to be an active part of those grandbabies' lives." She sniffed. "When they arrive." She fussed at her blouse, smoothing the silk that was already perfectly smooth. "Which I hope is not too long from now."

Delaney smiled. "I would much rather we be friends than enemies, Mrs. Ellingham. Especially since we're going to be family for a long, long time."

Elenora picked her head up. "I would like that too. You're a far better match for Hugh than I could have ever chosen."

"Thank you. Turns out blondes really aren't his type after all."

Elenora relaxed and a genuine smile lit her face. "Please, call me Elenora. Or Didi, like the boys do."

"Thank you, Elenora." That the woman could refer to her nearly four-hundred-year-old grandsons as boys made Delaney grin. "So you were a duchess, huh? What was that like?"

"My dear, I am *still* a duchess. And when you marry Hugh, you'll become a Lady, although obviously we don't use those titles anymore. Shame, that. Ah, well." She lifted her hand as though signaling the start of something and began walking toward the door. "Now, about this wedding…"

Hugh stood safely within the shadows of the house and stared out the French doors into the garden. The sun had begun to set, painting everything in broad strokes of gold and orange. A subtle melancholy lingered in his bones, but it would pass just as it had centuries ago when he'd said goodbye to the sun the first time.

Merrow had taken the amulet and the cash to Willa, at first balking at being Hugh's messenger until Hugh had explained just how much money he was sending her and the significance of the amulet. What was the point of keeping the secret now? The amulet would be destroyed in the creation of Delaney's ring, and the sheriff certainly wasn't going to use the knowledge against Julian or Sebastian. Not with his loyalty to the town.

Elenora's days of manipulating him were over.

Hugh smiled, at peace with his decision, despite the magnitude of it. Using the amulet in the production of Delaney's ring was full circle in a way. The very thing that had forced him into allowing Delaney into his life would be the very thing that might keep her in it.

He'd know three days after giving her the ring.

Three days to get the ring, three days to turn her. It was sobering to think he might have less than a week left with the woman he loved.

The kitchen door opened, and Delaney's and Stanhill's voices carried into the living room. Their laughter was infectious. He smiled and went to see what all the hubbub was about. He leaned against the kitchen door jamb. "What have you two been up to?"

Delaney grinned and threw her arms around him. "Just taking care of some family business."

He kissed her. "I have no idea what that means."

"She set Didi straight is what she did." Stanhill preened like a proud hen.

Hugh cocked a brow. This was all very interesting. "I still have no idea what that means." He shifted his attention back to Delaney. "What did you do?"

Stanhill answered before Delaney had a chance to. "She threatened her proper, that's what she did."

"She who? Who got threatened? Delaney, you answer. Stanhill, pipe down."

Delaney laughed. "I just explained to your grandmother that things were progressing between us in such a way that…if she ever wanted to see her grandbabies, she'd never use the amulet to force you to do anything again." She shrugged one shoulder. "That's all."

Hugh let her go and sank into one of the kitchen chairs. *Grandbabies*. He tried to smile. "You're an amazing woman. Courageous to take on a granddame like Didi."

She frowned at him. "Why does it sound like there's a but coming?"

He didn't want to tell her she'd put herself out there for nothing, but she'd find out about the amulet soon enough. "I love you." He shook his head. "But the amulet's gone."

"Gone?" She sat across from him and grabbed his hands. "What do you mean?"

He glanced at Stanhill before answering. "I gave it up for a very good cause."

Stanhill came to stand by them. "You went to see Willa?"

Hugh nodded. "You were right about the cost."

Delaney's face scrunched up in question. "Now I have no idea what we're talking about."

Hugh wanted the ring to be a surprise, so he chose his words carefully. "There is someone in town who has the potential to make turning you safer. We won't know until we actually do it, but she promises to at least increase the odds of things going in our favor. And a part of her magic required me to sacrifice something valuable to me. I chose to give her the amulet."

"No," Delaney cried. "You need that."

"I *need* you. I can live without the sun. Vampires all over the world manage." He took her face in his hands and kissed away her frown. "I would do anything for you, Delaney. Especially if it means I'll have you with me for eternity."

"No, Hugh, it's too much for you to give up. You can't."

"I can and I have. No more argument."

She kissed him back, a little teary-eyed. "I don't like it, but I just got done telling your grandmother to stop forcing her will on you. I can't very well do that to you myself now, can I?"

He smiled. "You can always try."

She laughed. "Since we'll be keeping the same hours pretty soon, I'm not even going to bother. Speaking of, how long before we…attempt the turning?"

"The magic will be available to us in three days. We'll start the process of turning you that night, which is a three evening process, so three days after that and we'll know."

"Do we have to wait for the magic to start? If we start tonight, then the night we get the magic could be *the* night. Number three."

Her eagerness was endearing, but three days left with her? He swallowed and nodded reluctantly. "Yes, we could also do that."

"I'd like that. The sooner we can start our life together, the better. Plus, I have a lot to learn about being a vampire." She stood. "If you'll excuse me, I'd better go check on Captain. Then I'm going to bake something. Or make some truffles. Or something. It's been too long."

"The kitchen is yours," Stanhill said.

"Good. I'll be back down in a few minutes." She put her hand on Hugh's shoulder. "Thank you."

He squeezed her hand. "Always. And thank you for standing up to Didi. That was brave."

She gave him a wink. "It was also a little fun."

She left and Stanhill took her chair. "Are you thinking of getting her a wedding present?"

Hugh nodded. "Of course. I just don't know what yet."

Stanhill glanced toward the upstairs, affection shining in his eyes. "Based on what I heard today, I have a very good idea."

Delaney made a simple flourless chocolate cake, a tribute more to the ingredients on hand than anything else. Stanhill had made her promise to save him a slice before he left for an evening out with Corette.

Hugh was in his lab, working on what, Delaney wasn't sure. She stared at the cooling cake, her mind going in a thousand different directions. She'd have to stock up on supplies before she was no longer able to leave the house during daylight hours. Or rely on Stanhill, who seemed to be a fairly adept shopper based on what was already in the house.

Three days. The reality of that ticking clock focused her thoughts. In three days, she'd be a vampire. If things went well.

If they didn't, she'd be dead.

But she had to believe that everything would be

fine, because giving in to the fear of what if wasn't going to help. Hugh had lived with that fear for centuries. It wouldn't do for her to be the one to suddenly back out after he'd finally come around.

"You all right?"

She jumped, her heart thumping. Hugh stood in the basement doorway. "You scared me. You're so quiet!"

"Sorry." He closed the door.

"Will I be that quiet too?"

He nodded and came to sit beside her. "Yes. And faster and stronger. Your senses will sharpen unbelievably. The first week or so will be the biggest adjustment, but it will be enjoyable. You'll feel like you're experiencing the world for the first time."

"Does the sharpening of senses include the taste buds?"

He smiled. "Yes. It's one of the reasons the house is stocked with the best groceries money can buy."

"I've noticed. I appreciated the Belgian baking chocolate I found in the cupboard. That's all gone, by the way."

He tipped his head toward the cake. "If that's what you turned it into, it sounds like a fair trade."

"The cake needs to cool, and I still need to make whipped cream to top it, so keep your hands to yourself."

A serious light filled his eyes. "If you don't want to start this process tonight, we can wait as long as it takes for you to feel ready."

"I'm not stalling." Not much anyway. "I just needed to bake something. Helps me think. Anyway, I'm committed to this. To you." She smiled. "To us."

He took her hand. "I could just turn you into a rook, you know. You'd have almost all the benefits of being a vampire—"

"Except there'd be no chance for babies, would there?"

He hesitated. "How do you know that?"

"Your grandmother."

He sighed. "She's relentless."

"Hugh, I want children. I always have. If you don't—"

"It's not that. It's just..." He didn't finish, his words replaced by a look of pain.

"What aren't you telling me?"

"Nothing." He smiled thinly. "With Stanhill out, we have the house to ourselves." He kissed the inside of her wrist. "We could do *anything*."

"Anything, hmm?"

His mouth trailed toward her elbow, tickling her with pleasure. "Whatever your heart desires."

"If there's a chance I might die in three days, I—"

"Don't say that." He let go of her hand and pushed to his feet. He paced stiffly toward the other side of the kitchen. "Maybe I can't do this after all. I can't lose you, Delaney. I can't."

She got up and went after him. "You're not going to. I thought you were okay with this. You said you were getting magical help from this woman in town. It's all going to be fine, you'll see."

He turned and leaned against the counter, his hands on the granite as he faced her. "You don't understand. Death follows me." His mouth twisted with pain, and his gaze held a longing that made her heart ache.

She stood in front of him, hands on his arms. "What are you talking about? Hugh, please tell me. We said no secrets."

He was quiet for a few long moments, and she let him be. He dropped his gaze when he finally spoke. "Within the first year we were married, Juliette got pregnant. She miscarried, but got pregnant again rather quickly." Hugh shook his head at the memory, his words edged with pain. "The second child was stillborn."

"I'm so sorry." No wonder he'd been struggling with this decision so much. He thought death was all he had to offer her. "But what's past is past."

"And I want to leave it there. But…" He raised his head, eyes glazed in darkness. "Death is my legacy. Why should a little fae magic change that?" He broke free of her embrace and walked a few steps away. "I cannot do this."

"Hugh, you're blaming yourself for what happened, but Juliette had as much of a part in it as you did. I'm sorry if it hurts you to hear this, but those deaths could have had everything to do with Juliette and nothing to do with you."

He just shook his head. "I helped make those children. And I'm the reason she turned."

She grabbed his arm. "Enough. I am not going to let another woman and the chance of what *might* happen stand between me and an eternity of happiness with you."

"Delaney—"

"No, Hugh. It's decided. We're not discussing it anymore. You're turning me into a vampire, and we're getting married and living a happy, sun-free life. Do you hear me?"

His expression went from pained to curious. "You're not frightened by what I've told you? Not scared that you could be the next to succumb to whatever curse is attached to me?"

"There's no curse attached to you. But yes, I'm scared. I'm human. I didn't even know vampires existed until a week ago, and now I'm about to become one. Who *wouldn't* be scared? But I'm not going to let that fear make decisions for me."

His mouth bent into something close to a smile. "You never fail to amaze me." He wrapped her in his arms and kissed her. "You never fail to make me fall deeper in love with you. You're right. We cannot let fear dictate how we live."

"Exactly."

The wicked sparkle she'd come to love danced in his eyes. "In fact, I could bite you right now."

She grabbed his hand and pulled him toward the steps. "Sounds like a plan. Right after you take me to bed."

Thirty passionate minutes later, Delaney lay curled beside him, a sheen of sweat cooling on her skin. Moonlight spilled through the sheers, setting her aglow. The sated look on her face only made her more gorgeous than ever. Her eyes were heavy-lidded with bliss, and a lazy grin curved her mouth. A mouth he'd kissed thoroughly.

He could *not* get enough of her. Already, the desire to have her again curled through him, bringing his body back to life with the pleasurable tightness of need.

"You're not falling asleep, are you, my love?" He traced a finger from the hollow of her throat down between her breasts to the dip of her navel.

"No." She laughed and swatted at his hand. "Stop that, you're tickling me."

"Really? Ticklish there? I'm making a mental note of that."

She reached up to stroke his cheek. "Behave or no cake."

He splayed his hand on her stomach. "I've earned that cake. Don't think you're taking it away from me now."

Her thumb brushed the corner of his mouth. "Show me your fangs," she whispered.

He obliged her, knowing his eyes reflected the glow of his kind as well.

"You're too handsome to be real." She smiled shyly, a curious thing given what they'd just done. Her voice was soft and dreamy. "I never knew I was the kind of girl who went in for the whole vampire thing until I had one of my very own."

He turned his face into her hand and kissed the inside of her wrist. "I hope you know I'm going to spoil you senseless. And I don't want to hear a single complaint. Jewels, clothes, trips, whatever you want."

"All I want is you. And maybe a new cat condo for Captain."

"We'll put one in every room."

She stared at him then took a long breath. "I'm ready."

He knew what she meant, had been waiting for her to say something, but he still didn't feel prepared.

"Tell me what's going to happen?" Her smile brightened. "I'm not scared, I just want to know. And we've never really had this talk."

For good reason. He'd never thought things would actually get this far. But they had and there was no going back. "After I bite you—"

"It won't hurt much, right? It's okay if it does, I just want to know."

"You'll feel a pinch, maybe. Nothing more."

"Okay." She nodded. "Go on."

"After that, I'll bite my own wrist so that you can have a drop or two of my blood. That's all that's necessary. You'll fall asleep pretty quickly after that. You'll feel normal after the first bite. After the second, you'll feel the changes. We'll repeat the process three nights in a row, and after the third night, you'll either be turned or…"

"I'll be turned. There is no *or*."

"Right. There is no or." But if there was, it would be the end of both of them. "You can stop at any time before the third night."

"I'm not going to change my mind."

"My love for you won't be any different if you do."

"Good to know. And as tempted as I am to have cake, I have no desire to leave this bed." She pulled her hair out of the way and tipped her chin up. "Go ahead. Do it."

He bent his head to her collarbone and feathered kisses across the creamy expanse of her body, making his way leisurely up to her throat to nip softly at her earlobe.

A soft moan pearled on her lips.

He laced one arm behind her head, cradling her, while the other explored the tempting planes of her body.

She purred with pleasure, aching to whisper into his ear. "When I said do it, I meant bite me, not—"

"Shh. Just relax and enjoy."

He could feel her smile against his skin.

"Yes, your lordship."

He smirked at her impudence and scraped his fangs over her skin, causing her to suck in a breath. The warmth and scent of her drove him wild, urging him to take her roughly. To mark her as his. He restrained himself, unwilling to hurt her for his own pleasure.

He clung to the last thread of control and continued worshipping her until the rhythm of her breathing changed and she'd gone boneless with sensation in his arms.

Then, in an act that both excited him and scared him, he sank his fangs into her neck.

She cried out, a muted exclamation of pain and pleasure, her hands clutching at him as he drank from her.

The taste of her seared his soul, erasing all trepidation. But even in that moment, he understood the feeling of omnipotence was temporary. He was intoxicated by her. The feeling would pass and he would once again fear for her life.

But now? All he wanted to do was drink her in and claim her as his own. Her pulse throbbed in his veins. Their hearts beat in rhythm. They were, for a few unending seconds, one being.

He released her, closing the two small punctures he'd opened with the press of his tongue. Then he put his fangs to his own wrist and tore the skin, reckless with the abandon of the moment. As red beaded on his skin, he held his wrist to her lips.

"Drink," he urged.

She did as he commanded, her hands coming up weakly to grip his wrist. As soon as she'd had a taste, he shook her hands off. "Now rest, my darling."

"Hugh," she muttered, her eyes fluttering closed.

"Yes?" The wound on his wrist was halfway closed. He tucked her into the bed covers.

"I love you."

"I love you too."

But she was already asleep.

26

"I don't feel any different." Delaney stuck her arm into the sun streaming through the library window. Hugh was up on the rolling ladder, looking for a book on one of the top shelves. She'd followed him in, hoping to hang out with him. He'd been avoiding her since she'd woken up.

He glanced down at her and smiled, thin-lipped. "I told you one bite won't do anything to you. Tomorrow you'll feel different."

"Tomorrow I'll technically be a rook, right?"

"Right." He went back to skimming the shelf.

She leaned against the window. "You should climb ladders more often."

"Why is that?" he asked distractedly.

"Because your butt looks amazing from this angle."

His hand stopped mid-reach, and he twisted to look at her. His eyes gleamed with vampire light.

"Are you trying to spend the rest of the day in bed?"

A tingle of pleasure shot through her, taking her breath away for a moment. She bit her lip. If she did die on the third night, at least she'd go happy. "Maybe."

He stared at her for a moment. Then jumped off the ladder, landing as lightly as Captain would have. Actually, Captain wished he could land that lightly. Hugh strode toward her, stopping just at the edge of the sunbeam she'd been playing with. "If I take you to bed now, you won't leave it again until tomorrow."

His voice held a dangerous growl that raised goose bumps on her skin. "Is that so?"

"Yes. I'm not trying to scare you or seduce you, just telling you the truth. When a vampire drinks from a mortal he loves, it…does something to him. Something he can't ignore."

"That's why you didn't want to drink from me in the lab. So what does it do?"

He sighed. "It turns the vampire wild with blood lust and physical desire. There wouldn't be enough of you to satisfy me. I would exhaust you and still not be sated. Or drain you dry." He turned away from her. "I'm fighting it right now."

"And that's why you've been avoiding me today."

He nodded. "I'd rather be with you every waking moment, but my control won't fully return until you've completed the change."

Hugh had already left her worn out after last night, and she thought she'd done the same for him. Hearing this, she tried to imagine what it would be like to feel as though she couldn't get enough of him. A shiver ran through her, as pleasurable as it was frightening.

He stepped away from her. "You're going to need your strength for the next two nights. I don't want to do anything that might lessen our odds of success. I'm going to my brother's for the rest of the day. It's for the best."

"How can you? It's daylight, and you have no amulet."

His face fell. "I'd forgotten that." He smiled a little sadly. "That's going to take some getting used to. To the lab then. And I'm locking the door."

"Don't leave. I'll behave. I swear." The last thing she wanted was to be away from him. Or to be the reason he left.

He laughed, the sound making her feel better. "My darling. If you wore a burlap sack, it wouldn't diminish my attraction to you. This burden is mine to bear."

Could he make her fall in love with him any harder? "Will I be too close if I'm in the kitchen? I was thinking I'd have Stanhill take me to the store to get ingredients for royal icing and sugar cookies." She had her antique star cookie cutters. They'd be perfect. "I want to make some for the woman who's helping us with the magic."

"No, that would be fine."

"I'll probably take Captain out to the garden for a while too."

Hugh nodded. "Enjoy the sun while you can?"

"Exactly."

"Good plan. I'll see you this evening then." With a nod, he left.

She almost stopped him to ask for a kiss, then thought better of it. She didn't want him to have to say no.

Stanhill was an eager companion, gladly taking her to the store and even keeping her company in the kitchen while she worked. She wondered if he was hanging close to act as a buffer in case Hugh changed his mind about staying away. Or maybe Stanhill knew she needed the company to keep her mind off the two nights that lay ahead.

"It'll be all right, miss."

"What's that?" She pulled herself out of her thoughts.

Stanhill was icing the last of the stars, outlining them in royal icing like she'd showed him. "You hadn't said anything in a little bit. I thought maybe you were thinking about…what could happen."

"I was. A little." She shrugged and smiled, then shook it off and went to inspect his work. "Not bad for your first time. Nice straight lines, good evenness." She patted his shoulder. "I might have to hire you. I'm going to have a shop of my own someday, you know."

"Like the shop Didi promised you?"

She nodded. "That never would have worked out anyway."

"Why's that?"

She made a face. "Um, because she would have used that shop as leverage to bend me to her whims. Can you imagine? No, thank you."

He laughed. "You're a smart cookie. No pun intended."

She grinned. "Does Hugh like tiramisu?"

"He does." Stanhill waggled his brows. "I don't hate it either."

"Good. I'll make that tomorrow." Her tiramisu took time, and she'd have another day to spend away from Hugh tomorrow, so why not? She'd rather spend the day with Hugh, but since that wasn't an option, tiramisu it was. "We'll take another run to the store after I get up, then. Okay?"

He nodded. "Excellent plan." An enormous smile came over his face. "You'll be a rook tomorrow, just like me."

"That's right." And only one more night away from the rest of her life.

Or the end of it.

The day seemed like it would never end, made worse by the fact that Hugh could hear Delaney and Stanhill one floor above him, laughing and having fun. He shouldn't miss her like this when they were in the same house together, but that was part of the turning.

He'd felt like this with Juliette too.

Correction, he'd felt *some* of this with Juliette. The longing for Delaney was almost crippling. He'd spent the entire day in his lab and accomplished nothing. Well, he'd reread every book that dealt with turning a mortal into a vampire and found nothing new. After that, he'd broken a test tube, ruining his most current working formula and then left another beaker on the flame too long, turning a new batch of formula to syrup.

He would be useless until this was over.

Fortunately, he could feel the sun set. That was something the amulet had suppressed—that inherent sense of the sun's rise and fall. It had still been there, but muted as if turned to the lowest setting.

Now it was like a switch had been flipped off. The subtle itch that rode his skin while the sun was up disappeared, replaced by the calm of evening. After Delaney fell sleep this evening, he would go out. Visit Sebastian and see how the plans he'd set into motion were coming.

Anything to put some room between him and his bride-to-be.

He cleaned up the mess he'd made and went upstairs.

Stanhill stood at the sink washing cookie sheets, and Delaney was by the table, folding a thick piece of waxed white cardboard into the shape of a box. Wire racks held dozens of iced and sugared stars, and the kitchen smelled of vanilla.

"How was your day?"

She looked up and smiled, and his entire being relaxed. "Hi there. It was great. Stanhill and I made sugar cookies. I'm boxing them up now so you can take them to the lady who's helping us. How was your day?"

Horrible. Lonely. "Fine."

"Good. Did you get a lot done?"

Not a thing. "Enough."

"That's good. Let me just box these up, and we can...do what we're going to do." With a wink, she went back to her work. She taped the sides of the box, then started carefully arranging the cookies into it, putting a sheet of wax paper between each layer.

"Stanhill, I need you here tonight." He didn't want Delaney alone in the house, not when she'd be incapacitated by the second bite.

The rook looked at him and nodded. "I'll be here."

"Thank you." He returned his attention to Delaney. He wanted to hold her and kiss her and prepare her the way he had last night, but that would take him down a very dangerous path. "I'll be upstairs when you're ready."

An uncertain look crossed her face, but she just nodded and said, "Okay."

Leaving her behind in the kitchen was like trying to break free of the earth's gravitational pull. As soon as he was in his room, he paced, going from the fireplace to the dressing room door and back again.

After what seemed like years, he sensed her presence outside his door, a sure sign that their bond had already begun to form. She knocked a second later.

"Come in."

She entered, tentative but smiling. "I'm guessing you're acting a little weird because of what you said earlier about not wanting to wear me out? I'm basically taking this as a big compliment."

He laughed. "That's a good attitude. Yes, believe me, I am struggling. I want nothing more than to be with you." He sighed. "I got nothing done today. Unless you consider ruining everything I touched an accomplishment."

"I'm sorry."

He waved it off. "It will pass soon enough, but right now, being around you without being able to touch you is torture. Stanhill will be here tonight so that you won't be alone while you're sleeping. I'm going to my brother's after we're done. And I won't be back until after the sun sets tomorrow."

He studied her face for signs of disappointment, finding them immediately in the downturn of her mouth and the sadness in her eyes. "Please don't be sad. It's for the best."

She nodded. "I know."

"You'll sleep even longer after this next bite, and you'll have Stanhill with you all day, and then, before you know it…" He forced himself to smile. "We'll have the rest of eternity to be together."

Her smile looked just as contrived as his felt. "I can't wait. Literally. Let's do this."

He held out his hand to her. "Lingering over you as I would like cannot be part of the process tonight. This will be fast and less pleasant than last night, for both our sakes."

"That's okay." She took his hand, the warmth of her seeping into him like a drug.

The touch of her caused a shudder of pleasure to ripple through him. Somehow, he managed to lead her to the bed and let her go. "You should undress and get under the covers. I won't be able to help you with that tonight."

"Okay." She stripped down to her bra and knickers, then crawled under the covers.

Her pulse had kicked up, giving him pause. "We don't have to do this if you don't want to."

"I want to." She smiled at him again, and this time, it reached her eyes. "I'm ready."

He nodded and bent his head to her throat. He inhaled her perfume and teetered on the verge of giving in to a very different set of desires. With a final burst of control, he bared his fangs and bit her as gently as he could manage.

She gasped, her cry this time containing only pain. She grabbed his arm and squeezed but made no effort to pull away.

He drank quickly, releasing her just as fast. The ache in his soul for more was instantaneous. He ignored it to bite through his own flesh. He fed her a few drops of his blood as he'd done the night before, this time with as little contact as possible.

A minute passed. Her pulse slowed and she succumbed to sleep.

He headed for the door, stopping when he reached it to take a long look at her. So peaceful. So beautiful.

She would never be human again. If he didn't bite her again tomorrow night, she could still be his companion. Still live at his side, as a rook, for centuries to come.

All he would have to do is stay away on the third night. He snorted softly. If only it were that easy. He knew her well enough to know she'd never forgive him for that. If she didn't just hunt him down. Instead, he would return to her and bite her again, completing the turning.

And taking the greatest risk he'd ever taken. The thought unsettled him. Made him wish he could know the future.

"Sleep well, my darling."

One of them should.

Delaney woke with a start. Bolt upright. Wide awake.

That never happened.

She blinked twice to make sure she wasn't dreaming. The world around her was...not the same one she'd last seen. Colors were brilliant. The air seemed crystalline. Like her vision had suddenly become some new version of high-definition. "Stanhill!"

Her voice echoed in her ears, and she cringed at how loud she sounded.

"Downstairs, miss. Be right up."

She looked around. He sounded close enough to be in the room with her. She pulled on Hugh's robe to cover the bra and panties she'd fallen asleep in, went to the door and peeked out.

Stanhill was coming down the hall.

"Were you downstairs when you answered me?"

He nodded.

"Holy fudgeballs, this is weird. Good weird. But weird." The wood grain on the door was so sharp she could count every line.

He grinned. "Good afternoon, rook."

"Afternoon? What time is it?"

"After four. Sun'll be down in a few hours."

"What? I didn't want to sleep that long. I wanted to make tiramisu."

"It's the change. Takes it out of you. The third night, you shouldn't sleep nearly as long. You're halfway there now."

"Everything is so bright and colorful, and sounds are crystal clear. I could have sworn you were right next to me when you answered me." She wrapped her arms around her torso. And went very still when she felt what was beneath her arms.

She glanced down at her body. "Are you kidding me?"

"What's wrong?"

"Nothing. I feel skinny. Skinny-ish." She yanked the robe open for a better look. "Oh, that is *not* the waistline I went to bed with."

Stanhill made a grunting sound. When she looked at him, he was staring at the ceiling. She pulled her robe shut while he spoke. "It's the change, miss. Impacts the metabolism as well. It sharpens everything. Of course, tomorrow will be even greater."

"I need a mirror." She ran back into the room, stopped and ran back out, amazed at how fast she could move. "Also, I'm starving. Like I want to eat everything. What have we got?"

"In anticipation, I picked up a few steaks this morning, plus I've got some jacket potatoes in the oven—"

"Do we have sour cream and butter? And bacon bits? Oh! Cheese. I need cheese."

He nodded. "All of that. Also, made some stuffed mushrooms and chilled some steamed jumbo shrimp. Will that do?"

"For round one, yes." She ran to the bathroom mirror. And stared. "Wow."

The body she now inhabited didn't look like it had any issues with those last fifteen pounds. She was still curvy, but things had tightened up a bit. There was even a little visible muscle tone, which was amazing.

Her hair, which had always been on the wavy edge of frizzy, fell in soft, luscious waves. The color seemed more dark honey than boring brown.

She leaned in. The standard green of her eyes had taken on a sparkling clearness she'd never seen before.

Even her skin, which had always been decent, seemed to radiate with health. She looked at Stanhill, who stood by the bedroom door. "This is flat-out amazing. I mean, I always thought I was cute before, but now I'm actually pretty."

"You're beautiful, miss. You always have been. The change magnifies what was already there."

She smiled, feeling a little heat in her face at his compliments. "Thanks, Stanhill."

He pointed downstairs. "I'll go fix you that steak while you get dressed."

"I'll be down as soon as I can."

He turned to go and then stopped. "I took the liberty of feeding Captain this morning as well. I hope that was all right."

"Thank you. That was nice of—what did you feed him?"

Stanhill suddenly seemed very interested in the cuff of his shirt. "Nothing much. There was a little crabmeat left over from the mushrooms, so…"

"You keep that up, and he's not going to eat his kibble." She shook her head as Stanhill left. No wonder Captain hadn't been asleep on the bed next to her when she'd woken up. He was probably passed out in some hideaway, sleeping off the catch of the day.

She cranked on the shower. Hugh would be back from his brother's soon. Which meant the last step in her transformation was only a matter of hours away. Anticipation tripped along her skin, the kind of feeling she used to get right before a big test in school.

Except this time, the consequences of failing were fatal.

She jumped into the shower. "That isn't going to happen."

Hugh had it all worked out. The extra magic would protect her. She'd be fine. Dwelling on it wasn't going to do her any good anyway, and knowing Hugh, he'd be worried enough for the both of them.

Determined to put on a happy, confident face, she showered and got dressed, then went downstairs to see what Stanhill had fixed for her.

The meal he'd laid out was enough to feed two, but she ate it all and still felt like she had room in her stomach.

She pressed a hand to her belly as he took her plate. His brows lifted. "Everything all right?"

"I can't believe I ate all that."

"Your body needs the energy. And like I said, your metabolism burns at a much higher rate now. It will be almost impossible to gain weight as a rook or vampire."

She shook her head. "Kind of a dream come true for someone who likes sweets as much as I do. Speaking of, where's that chocolate cake I made?"

"Coming right up." He fixed her a large slice with whipped cream.

She made a sound of pleasure after the first bite. "I hope it's not bad manners to think your own food is so delicious, but seriously, that's what chocolate cake should taste like."

He cut a piece for himself and joined her at the table. "You're very talented with sweets."

She shrugged. "You know what they say, if you find something you enjoy doing, it's not really work. I love creating all those wonderful things. Not to make it sound all lofty and important, but it kind of feels like art to me."

"I'd agree. What you do with sugar and eggs and chocolate? Definitely worthy of being admired."

"Actually, what I like best about it is making people happy. My mom was a baker. She made cakes, never had a shop, just did it out of our house. Until she got sick."

"What happened? If you don't mind me asking."

"Cancer." She told him about her dad and how'd he left and remarried, and how she'd told him off at the wedding.

Stanhill scowled. "Sounds like the right bastard deserved it. Good for you."

"It wasn't my finest hour, but he did sort of deserve it. He really let us down." She poked at the cake with her fork. "Did you have family that you had to leave behind when Hugh made you a rook?"

"My family was all in service at different

households. My mum and dad were taken by the plague. My older sister was in France. She was a ladies' maid and traveling with the family she served." He stared at his plate. "I saw her once after I was turned. Tried to explain what happened, but she didn't want anything to do with me."

He smiled weakly. "That was centuries ago. Water under the bridge, as it were."

"Is it hard?"

"What's that, love?"

"Outliving your friends?"

He nodded, then stopped. "It was at first. But since we've been here, not so much. That's why there are so many supernatural folk here. Like kind and all that. Most of 'em tend to have much longer lifespans than your average human. Makes things easier."

"That's good."

"It is."

She pushed her plate away. "I'm going out to the garden. Enjoy the last bit of sun while I can. Do you have any idea where Captain is? I thought I might take him out there with me."

"Last I saw he was headed into the living room. I put his new cat bed in there."

She stared at Stanhill. "You bought him a cat bed?"

"Three, actually. There's one in the library and one in Hugh's sitting room."

She laughed. "I'm glad you like him so much. Makes me feel good."

"He's a sweet creature."

With a smile, she wandered into the living room and found Captain curled up in his new bed, which looked to be burgundy velvet with gold trim. "Fit for a prince," she muttered.

She scooped him up and sniffed his toasty head, all warm from sleep. "Let's go get some fresh air, Cappy."

Sunlight and gentle breezes spilled through the garden. Flowers were in fragrant bloom, and the soft buzz of insects sounded like a chorus. To her amped-up senses, it was a wonderland. She put Captain down to roam. He immediately began stalking something in the tall, feathery grasses that bordered a small pond in the back.

She sat on the steps that led down to a serpentine section of pavers. Her last glimpse of the sun. Sure, she'd see it through the windows as long as she was safely tucked in the shadows, but this was the last time she'd feel it on her face. The last time she'd sit beneath its rays and soak up its warmth.

A price to pay, but not such a large one that it changed her mind. Life with Hugh offered so much more.

Orange and coral streaked the sky, and little by little the light disappeared. Captain had settled into a patch of flowers, wide awake as he watched a bug crawl through the dirt. The door opened behind her.

She didn't have to look to know it was Hugh. She turned and smiled. "I knew it was you without even looking. I realize the odds were low that it was anyone else, but it was like...I could sense you."

He nodded. "It's the bond between us forming. It will strengthen even more tomorrow."

"That's pretty cool."

He sat beside her, closed his eyes and inhaled. "I missed you."

"I missed you too."

"How was your day as a rook?"

"Sadly, I slept most of it. Then I spent the rest of it eating."

He laughed. "Sounds about right." He dug into his pocket, pulled out a little blue velvet box and held it out to her. "I have something for you."

She took it. "What is it?"

"You'd already know if you'd opened it." He kissed her temple. "It's the magic I promised you."

She snapped the lid back and gasped. "Oh, it's magic all right. Oh my."

"Does that mean you like it?"

"It's stunning. And outrageous in the best possible way. This can't be my...is this my engagement ring?"

He nodded, took the ring from the box and shifted to face her, putting one knee on the ground. "Delaney James, will you do me the great honor of becoming my wife?"

She clapped a hand over her mouth. This was so real she couldn't breathe. Tears filled her eyes, blurring the diamonds and sapphires into one big glittering mass. "Yes," she managed. "Yes."

"Don't cry, sweetheart." He slipped the ring on her finger.

"You crazy, ridiculous man. It's so big and sparkly, and that diamond is enormous. Enormous. It's too much. No, it's not. Actually, it's perfect, but I feel a little guilty liking a ring that's this over-the-top so much. It must have cost a freaking fortune. I love it. I love *you*. Thank you. Holy rock candy, it's enormous."

"I love the way you ramble when you're nervous." He laughed as she stared at her hand. "I'm very happy you like it."

"Who wouldn't like this? You weren't kidding about spoiling me."

"And it's only the beginning." He sat beside her. "The ring was made by a fae jeweler and has been imbued with all sorts of protection spells."

She looked at the ring with fresh eyes. It didn't feel like it had any magic in it, but maybe she was still too human to tell. "So this is going to get me through the transition?"

He nodded. "Yes."

He sounded confident. Mostly. She lifted her chin, wanting to give him some of her own certainty. Because she believed. How could the universe not want them to be together? They were perfect for each other. "Well, then. I'm ready when you are."

Hugh had vowed never to attempt the turning again, and yet here he was, about to do just that. Delaney lay on his bed, her smile eager. Her ring sparkling with the magic Willa had crafted into it.

Enough magic that he'd felt it when he'd first touched the ring. That alone should have quelled the last of his reservations, but it wasn't until he saw the look of determination on Delaney's face that he finally stopped questioning whether or not they should continue.

"Everything okay?"

He nodded. "I was just thinking."

"You're going to give me the speech about how I can still back out of this, aren't you? Because while being a rook is pretty cool, I want to be your equal." She winked at him. "Also, your baby mama, but that's for later."

"You are a strange and wonderful creature,

Delaney." He took her hand. "I wasn't going to try to talk you out of the final step."

"Then what was the serious look on your face about?"

"I was thinking that I have no more reservations. It's clear now that Juliette's body betrayed her. Her inability to survive the change had nothing to do with me. You've taken to it exceedingly well. On her second day, Juliette was pale and weak and barely rose from her bed. You, however, have a glow about you. The change has somehow made you even more beautiful."

Delaney smiled shyly. "I was pretty surprised by that myself."

"My only concern is how many men I'm going to have to scare off once your turning is complete."

She laughed. "Now you're just being silly."

"Trust me." He kissed her knuckles. "And now, with the added protection of the magic in the ring, my fear is gone."

She pulled him down to her. "Then do it. Bite me and let's get this new life started."

His fangs pierced his gums, his desire for that new life just as strong. "As you wish."

In minutes, he'd completed the final step, and as the wounds on his wrist healed, he kissed her lips. "Sleep well, my love."

She smiled, her lids heavy already with the

drowsiness brought on by the turning. "See you on the other side, baby."

Baby. She'd never called him that before. No one had, that he could recall. The word was sweet and silly and caused a fierce surge of protectiveness to rise up in him.

He stayed at her side as she drifted off. Watched as the color drained from her and she went ashen. As startling as that was, he knew it was part of the process. Both his brothers and Juliette had done the same.

In four or five hours, the turning would be complete. He pulled a chair near the bed and settled in, his only desire now to be at her side and be the first face she saw upon waking in her new life.

At the second hour, Stanhill stuck his head in. "Can I get you anything? Coffee? Brandy? Blood?"

"Brandy. I fed at Sebastian's."

Stanhill returned with the drink. He refilled it on the third hour. Hugh drank, reveling in the thoughts of the things he would show Delaney, how he would spoil her with experiences and find new joy in life through her eyes.

At the fourth hour, Hugh's anticipation lived on his skin. The tiniest sound brought him to full alert. He searched her face and body for signs of life, but she still lay like the dead. No pulse. No breath. All part of the turning. He knew that. But knowing didn't help.

Captain sauntered in and sat by Hugh's chair. Hugh scratched the animal's head until he left again.

Hour five came and went, bringing nothing but a return of the fear Hugh thought behind him. He paced the room. Stopped twice to check that her ring hadn't somehow slipped off.

Finally, he sat beside her and clutched her hand. Her cold, lifeless hand.

Stanhill hovered at the door. "Every turning is different."

Hugh said nothing. This turning seemed very much like the last one he'd been a part of.

Hour six dawned, and the sun's imminent rise announced itself with the delicate irritation of his skin. It was nothing compared to the ache in his soul. He couldn't bring himself to think the truth of what had happened, to give place to the reality that his beloved was gone, but it shadowed his thoughts, lingering like a specter at the edge of his mind.

Another half an hour, and there was no way to deny what had happened.

Again.

He went numb with pain as his reason to live slipped away.

Finally, at hour seven, he stood.

Stanhill was at his side. How long the rook had been there, Hugh had no idea. "She'll come around, you'll see."

Hugh had no words. No hope. No desire to endure this pain again. He bent and kissed his sweet Delaney one last time. "Goodbye, my angel. I am so sorry."

Then he turned and walked downstairs, vaguely aware of Stanhill's footsteps behind him, but the man didn't speak until Hugh reached the French doors.

"What do you mean to do, your lordship?"

Hugh stopped, his hand on the lever handle. "She's gone."

"I know." Stanhill's voice broke. "I am so very sorry."

"So am I." He turned the lever and stepped outside.

The sun had not yet broken the tree line, but when it did, the end would be painful but quick. He closed his eyes and pictured Delaney so that he could meet his end with her as his last thought.

Stanhill gasped.

A hand grabbed Hugh's arm and pulled him toward the house.

He spun, grief and anger driving him. "Stanhill, do not—"

"Hugh." Delaney stood before him, eyes luminous with fear. "What are you doing?"

He gaped at her for one long moment. "I thought you were..." He swept her into his arms and buried his face in her neck. "My darling." He almost choked on the words. "So much time went by, and I thought you hadn't survived."

She pulled away, holding his face in her hands. "Well, I did."

He kissed her, but she pushed at him. "Hugh!"

"What?"

"The sun?"

Stanhill yanked them back inside as the first rays hit the deck. "Is it possible for a rook to die of a heart attack? Because the two of you are going to be the death of me, I bleedin' swear."

He shut the door and glared at them.

"Nice to see you too, Stanhill," Delaney said.

He smiled. "Very happy to see you, miss. Can I get you anything?"

"How about that other steak?"

"You're going to need more than steak, but I'll let Hugh handle that while I fix you your second meal." He headed for the kitchen. Captain jumped off the living room sofa and followed him.

Hugh kissed her soundly as he eased her to her feet. "You scared me to death."

She kept her arms around his neck and stared adoringly up at him. "Almost literally, apparently." The adoration changed to scolding. "I can't believe you were going to walk into the sun like that. What if I hadn't woken up in time? Or made it down here before you—"

"But you did." His hands settled at her hips,

splaying possessively over her curves. "And technically, it's called facing the dawn."

"Sounds like a bad romance novel." She made a face, showing off her fledgling fangs. "One I don't ever want to read. I only like happily ever afters."

He laughed, the ache in his soul replaced by the glorious lightness of Delaney's presence. "I love you. Let's go down to the lab and get you fed." His hands slipped from her waist to cup her backside. "I have *plans* for you."

"Really? What kind of plans?"

"The kind you're going to need a lot of energy for."

Two days—actually, two *nights*—later, Delaney stood beside Hugh's car, about to take her first nervous steps toward Main Street as a vampire. Where she would mingle with humans.

What a weird thought to get used to.

What wasn't weird anymore was how sharp her senses were. Even at night, colors seemed oddly bright. She'd imagined Hugh having to live in some dark, muted world without his amulet, but the truth was vampire sight wasn't like that at all.

Things were crisp and clear and she could see for what seemed like miles. Hugh came up beside her and slid his hand into hers and squeezed. She squeezed back, finding strength in the power and size of her fiancé's hand. Her fiancé. Now *there* was a thought that never failed to leave her giddy.

"Everything all right?" he asked.

She nodded, but was already second-guessing

herself. "What if I forget and my fangs slip down? What if my eyes glow? Maybe I should wear sunglasses."

He pressed a reassuring kiss to her lips. "First of all, you've practiced, and you can control both of those things very well."

"And second?"

"Second, this is Nocturne Falls. If you forget and let your guard down, people are going to think you're pretending to be a vampire."

"Right. I just feel like I'm wearing a big blinking sign that says 'Hey, I'm a vampire!' Which wouldn't be much of a costume, but—" She took a breath. "Did you know the smell of chocolate increases theta brain waves, which trigger relaxation?"

He put his arm around her waist. "In that case, I know exactly what you need."

He guided her down Main Street in a familiar direction. "Please tell me we're going to the Hallowed Bean."

"We are, but now you've ruined the surprise."

She stuck her hand out and flashed her gorgeous ring. "*This* is a surprise. A trip to the Hallowed Bean is nice, but doesn't quite compare."

"I set a high bar for myself, is that what you're saying?"

She laughed. "Pretty much. But don't worry, I don't expect you to top this."

He made a strange, throaty chuckle but said nothing else.

They turned onto Black Cat Boulevard and walked toward the Hallowed Bean, but Hugh didn't cross the street like she'd expected him to. Instead, he stopped them across from the coffee shop and faced her. "Maybe I did set a high bar with that ring, but I'm hoping that you'll like what I'm about to show you just as much."

She stared at him curiously. There wasn't much on this side of the street except an empty storefront with paper over its windows. "What are you up to?"

He grabbed the shop's door and pulled it open. "Look for yourself."

Light spilled out. She stuck her head in. The shop was large and empty, its white walls and dark hardwood floors pretty but nondescript. A sofa covered with a drop cloth and a floor lamp were all the furniture it contained. "I still don't get it."

He nudged her inside and pulled the door closed. "This was an insurance office, but now it's all yours, Delaney."

She began to tremble as the realization of what he was saying came over her. "Do you mean…" Something stuck in her throat.

"Yes. This is your shop to fill with sweets and cookies and cakes and whatever else you want to make."

Happy tears stung her eyes. A shop of her own. "Are you serious?"

He nodded. "Stanhill told me what my grandmother promised you and how you turned it down for me. There was no way I could let you give up your dream like that."

With a soft sob, she hugged him, kissing his face and mouth with delirious abandon. "I don't even know what to say. Thank you, thank you, thank you."

He grinned and held her tight. "I want my wife to be happy."

"I am. More than I ever thought I could be. And not just because of the shop but because of you. I had no idea stealing someone's identity could be so rewarding."

"Yes, well, I don't think that's how it usually ends up." He looked around. "Do whatever you need to fix the place up and make it exactly the way you want it. What are you going to name the place?"

She was about to respond when the shop door opened, and a stern-faced man walked in, his resemblance to Hugh uncanny.

Hugh nodded at him. "Delaney, this is my brother Sebastian."

So this was Sebastian. He eyed her like she was a dangerous thing to be wary of. "Hmph. You're the one my brother's ruining his life for."

"Sebastian." Hugh's voice held a warning.

"Just a joke." But Sebastian's tone was less than convincing. "Pleasure to meet you."

"I can tell by the way you're all smiles." Delaney didn't bother to offer to shake his hand. He didn't look like he'd take her up on it anyway. She let it slide considering she knew he'd been part of the crew that had rescued her from Fat Eddie and his gang.

Hugh held a hand up. "You two need to find some common ground. You're going to be working together. Delaney, Sebastian handles the finances for the family. I've already told him you're to have our full resources at your disposal to get things started."

Sebastian nodded. "Whatever you need."

"Really? After all that 'ruining his life' business?"

Sebastian shrugged. "He's a grown man. Who am I to stop him from making his own mistakes?"

"Love the vote of confidence," she muttered in Hugh's direction.

Sebastian made a noise in his throat. "You know I can hear you, right?"

She smiled, showing off her fangs. "Yes."

She turned to Hugh. "There's just one problem."

"What's that, sweetheart?"

"How am I going to run a shop like this when I can't go out in the daylight?"

"You can always hire —"

"That reminds me," Sebastian interrupted. He pulled a thick, ivory envelope from his inside jacket pocket and handed it to Hugh. "Didi sent these for you."

Hugh opened the envelope, took out two tissue-covered bundles and unwrapped them. A matching set of amulets.

Delaney's mouth fell open in surprise.

Sebastian put his hand on the door as if to leave. "She said there are no strings attached according to the deal she and Delaney made, whatever that means."

Hugh stared at his brother. "How did she know I needed another one?"

Sebastian shrugged. "You really have to ask how Didi knows anything?" He looked at Delaney. "There's seventy-five thousand dollars in an account in your name in the Nocturne Falls Credit Union. When you need more, let me know." With that, he left.

Even with that news, Delaney still couldn't get over the amulets. "I can't believe she gave these to us. She must really want grandchildren."

Hugh handed one amulet to her, then tucked the other in his pocket before nuzzling her neck with a kiss. His arms wrapped around her and his voice was soft and breathy on her skin, spiraling a delicious shiver through her. "Then we really ought to go home and start working on that."

A laugh trilled out of her, a mix of sheer pleasure, happiness and the overwhelming desire to have Hugh as immediately as possible. "Or…"

He looked at her, brows raised in question. "Or?"

She reached over and turned the lock. "We could christen the shop."

His eyes took on the wicked glow she'd come to love. "Miss James, I like the way your mind works."

Want to be up to date on all books & release dates by Kristen Painter? Sign-up for my newsletter on my website, www.kristenpainter.com. No spam, just news (sales, freebies, and releases.)

If you loved the book and want to help the series grow, tell a friend about the book and take time to leave a review!

Other Books by Kristen Painter

URBAN FANTASY

The House of Comarré series:
Forbidden Blood
Blood Rights
Flesh and Blood
Bad Blood
Out For Blood
Last Blood

Crescent City series:
House of the Rising Sun
City of Eternal Night

PARANORMAL ROMANCE

Dark Kiss of the Reaper
Heart of Fire
All Fired Up

SIN CITY COLLECTORS

Queen of Hearts
Dead Man's Hand
Double or Nothing

Nothing is completed without an amazing team.

Many thanks to:

Cover design: Janet Holmes
Interior formatting: Author E.M.S.
Editor: Joyce Lamb
Copyedits/proofs: Dana Waganer

About the Author

Kristen Painter likes to balance her obsessions with shoes and cats by making the lives of her characters miserable and surprising her readers with interesting twists. She currently writes paranormal romance and award-winning urban fantasy. The former college English teacher can often be found all over social media where she loves to interact with readers. Visit her web site to learn more.

www.kristenpainter.com

Printed in Great Britain
by Amazon